RIO NOIR

EDITED BY TONY BELLOTTO

Translated by Clifford E. Landers

Published by Akashic Books
©2016 Akashic Books

Series concept by Tim McLoughlin and Johnny Temple
Rio map by Aaron Petrovich

Published with the support of the Ministry of Culture of Brazil/
National Library Foundation.
Obra publicada com o apoio do Ministério da Cultura do Brasil/
Fundação Biblioteca Nacional.

 MINISTÉRIO DA CULTURA
Fundação BIBLIOTECA NACIONAL

ISBN: 978-1-61775-312-1
Library of Congress Control Number: 2015954062
All rights reserved

First printing

Akashic Books
Twitter: @AkashicBooks
Facebook: AkashicBooks
E-mail: info@akashicbooks.com
Website: www.akashicbooks.com

ALSO IN THE AKASHIC NOIR SERIES

ORANGE COUNTY NOIR, edited by GARY PHILLIPS
PARIS NOIR (FRANCE), edited by AURÉLIEN MASSON
PHILADELPHIA NOIR, edited by CARLIN ROMANO
PHOENIX NOIR, edited by PATRICK MILLIKIN
PITTSBURGH NOIR, edited by KATHLEEN GEORGE
PORTLAND NOIR, edited by KEVIN SAMPSELL
PRISON NOIR, edited by JOYCE CAROL OATES
PROVIDENCE NOIR, edited by ANN HOOD
QUEENS NOIR, edited by ROBERT KNIGHTLY
RICHMOND NOIR, edited by ANDREW BLOSSOM, BRIAN CASTLEBERRY & TOM DE HAVEN
ROME NOIR (ITALY), edited by CHIARA STANGALINO & MAXIM JAKUBOWSKI
SAN DIEGO NOIR, edited by MARYELIZABETH HART
SAN FRANCISCO NOIR, edited by PETER MARAVELIS
SAN FRANCISCO NOIR 2: THE CLASSICS, edited by PETER MARAVELIS
SEATTLE NOIR, edited by CURT COLBERT
SINGAPORE NOIR, edited by CHERYL LU-LIEN TAN
STATEN ISLAND NOIR, edited by PATRICIA SMITH
STOCKHOLM NOIR (SWEDEN), edited by NATHAN LARSON & CARL-MICHAEL EDENBORG
ST. PETERSBURG NOIR (RUSSIA), edited by NATALIA SMIRNOVA & JULIA GOUMEN
TEHRAN NOIR (IRAN), edited by SALAR ABDOH
TEL AVIV NOIR (ISRAEL), edited by ETGAR KERET & ASSAF GAVRON
TORONTO NOIR (CANADA), edited by JANINE ARMIN & NATHANIEL G. MOORE
TRINIDAD NOIR (TRINIDAD & TOBAGO), edited by LISA ALLEN-AGOSTINI & JEANNE MASON
TWIN CITIES NOIR, edited by JULIE SCHAPER & STEVEN HORWITZ
USA NOIR, edited by JOHNNY TEMPLE
VENICE NOIR (ITALY), edited by MAXIM JAKUBOWSKI
WALL STREET NOIR, edited by PETER SPIEGELMAN
ZAGREB NOIR (CROATIA), edited by IVAN SRŠEN

FORTHCOMING

ACCRA NOIR (GHANA), edited by MERI NANA-AMA DANQUAH
ADDIS ABABA NOIR (ETHIOPIA), edited by MAAZA MENGISTE
ATLANTA NOIR, edited by TAYARI JONES
BAGHDAD NOIR (IRAQ), edited by SAMUEL SHIMON
BOGOTÁ NOIR (COLOMBIA), edited by ANDREA MONTEJO
BRUSSELS NOIR (BELGIUM), edited by MICHEL DUFRANNE
BUENOS AIRES NOIR (ARGENTINA), edited by ERNESTO MALLO
JERUSALEM NOIR, edited by DROR MISHANI
LAGOS NOIR (NIGERIA), edited by CHRIS ABANI
MARRAKECH NOIR (MOROCCO), edited by YASSIN ADNAN
MISSISSIPPI NOIR, edited by TOM FRANKLIN
MONTREAL NOIR (CANADA), edited by JOHN McFETRIDGE & JACQUES FILIPPI
NEW HAVEN NOIR, edited by AMY BLOOM
OAKLAND NOIR, edited by JERRY THOMPSON & EDDIE MULLER
SAN JUAN NOIR (PUERTO RICO), edited by MAYRA SANTOS-FEBRES
SÃO PAULO NOIR (BRAZIL), edited by TONY BELLOTTO
ST. LOUIS NOIR, edited by SCOTT PHILLIPS
TRINIDAD NOIR: THE CLASSICS (TRINIDAD & TOBAGO), edited by EARL LOVELACE & ROBERT ANTONI

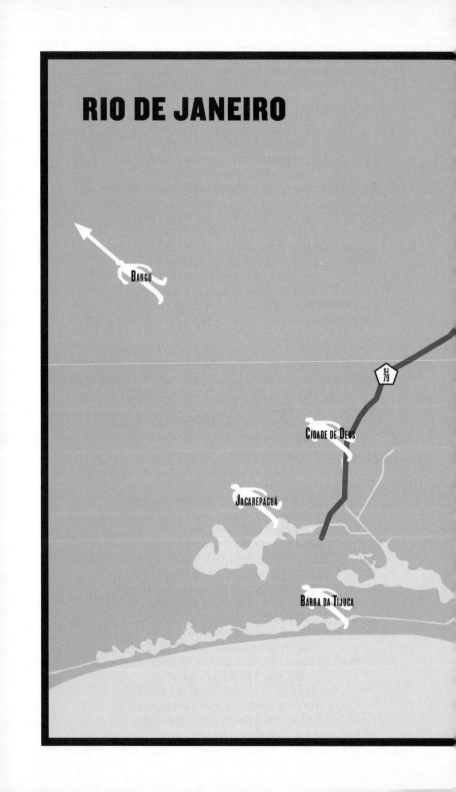

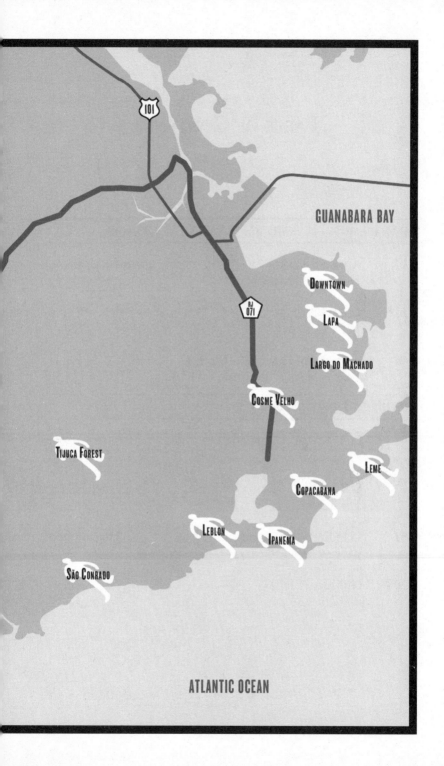

TABLE OF CONTENTS

PART III: MURMURING FOUNTAINS

PART IV: RIO BABYLON

INTRODUCTION
Deciphering an Enigma

The images of Rio de Janeiro are well known: high rises aligned along white sandy beaches, a blue sea, freshwater lakes, and luxuriant forests that stretch through winding mountains of stone; Sugar Loaf linked to the ground by cable cars in hypnotic shuttle; hang gliders crossing the sky in flights without destination; the open arms of Christ the Redeemer blessing a happy, cordial, mixed-race people ever ready to dance a samba or offer a welcoming smile to the tourists who move about in the streets admiring beautiful women shimmying nude atop floats in Carnival parades . . . *Opa!*

This is not a tourist guide. The city revealed in this book is a different Rio.

Even though famous landscapes are present in the pages of *Rio Noir*, what is exposed here is a world of shadows, blood, intrigue, violence, hideouts, and mystery (and also of humor, of course, as is necessary with any undertaking involving Cariocas).

Long ago, Rio ceased to be an idyllic city of tourist enchantment, and crime scenes of savage drug traffickers, violent cops, and corrupt politicians document that fact with disturbing regularity in newscasts worldwide. Nowadays, the image of the city of beautiful beaches, sensual women, lively gay people, and likable swindlers is inexorably tied to shootouts and bloody disputes between criminal factions. The divided city, fractured into a cosmopolitan middle class and a populace residing in neglected poverty-ridden communities, has become the poster child for a country of enormous social inequality and disquieting violence.

All of which holds great excitement as raw material for crime fiction!

This conclusion is paradoxical and somewhat disturbing, I admit, but is there any city more paradoxical than Rio de Janeiro?

The capital of Brazil from 1773 to 1960—and of the entire Portuguese Empire during the Napoleonic Wars—the international symbol of the nation, the principal tourist destination of the southern hemisphere, host city of the 2016 Olympics, characterized by the highest indices of violence and poverty, Rio is much more than the city seen on postcards, in socioeconomic statistics, and shocking newspaper reports.

The city is above all an enigma in search of being deciphered.

I may sound off base in stating that no one is better suited to decipher enigmas than writers of crime stories. Among other functions, noir fiction allows exploration of the social aspects, the human strengths and weaknesses that make up the daily life of any great city.

In an effort to decipher this enigma, I invited Luiz Alfredo Garcia-Roza, MV Bill, Luiz Eduardo Soares, Guilherme Fiuza, Arthur Dapieve, Victoria Saramago, Arnaldo Bloch, Adriana Lisboa, Alexandre Fraga dos Santos, Marcelo Ferroni, Flávio Carneiro, Raphael Montes, and Luis Fernando Verissimo to join me in the creation of the anthology you are leafing through (not, I warn, without some risk of getting blood on your hands).

Choosing these authors was like climbing Sugar Loaf for the simple pleasure, after having stealthily scaled the sheer vertical rock, of gazing upon a limitless horizon. In this work, writers of both sexes skillfully move between fiction of different genres, journalism, humor, horror, philosophy, public safety, psychoanalysis, rock, rap, social and political activism, and law. Even those who had never written noir fiction were moved to tell stories that, in distinct forms and twists, present a puzzle that dares to test the limits of the genre. Whether we have succeeded in deciphering an enigma with the dramas of our procurers, card readers, colonels, cops, traffickers, socialites, slum dwellers, embezzlers, tourists, brokers, detectives, journalists, politicians, assassins, editors, outlaws, travelers, coup plotters, writers, lovers, and everyday citizens, I don't know. But we have surely added a large shadow to the sunny landscape of this wonderful city.

Tony Bellotto
March 2016

PART I

PURGATORY OF BEAUTY & CHAOS

THE HANGED MAN

BY Adriana Lisboa

Largo do Machado

Nowadays I almost never come to Largo do Machado. The gymnastics equipment I see when I leave the subway, for example, I'm not familiar with, and I think it was put here in the square some years back. I remember having read something about it in the paper. Today, under the fine, cold rain, it appears no one is motivated to exercise. The concrete tables where I used to see old men playing checkers and cards are also unoccupied. The pigeons look for shelter wherever they can. There in the distance, haughty and sad, the church watches.

The traffic moves around the square, a sluggish flow of buses and cars, but the square itself seems strangely uninhabited beyond the irregular stream of people entering or leaving the subway station, their umbrellas challenging one another.

I miss the gypsies. In the period when I lived here they used to hang out in the square offering to read your palm or divine your future in their cards. At the time, they irritated me. Today I feel they would provide me a certain comfort, as proof that my past didn't totally unravel.

I very rarely come by here. Currently we live in Recreio and our life is there, my work and my wife's, the children's school. Before that, there was the long stay in Belo Horizonte. But in the 1980s I lived near here in a two-room apartment on Rua Bento Lisboa. Those weren't easy times, and I was right to take the job in Belo Horizonte.

I think about going by my old building to see what has changed in the decades since—in this city some things have begun changing with such treacherous speed that I sometimes can't keep up with it. But I don't, because of the rain. Distracted, I step in a puddle, soaking my foot. Shit.

Remembering the gypsies takes me back to my girlfriend in those days, Simone, who was interested in tarot. I always considered that kind of thing utter foolishness, but even so there was a homey comfort in seeing her take out the deck from its old box, shuffle the cards, place some on the table—turning them this way and that. There were some curious images. From time to time she would raise her eyes from the cards and observe me obliquely. But whatever the cards told her about me, it was without my approval.

Simone claimed to have gypsy ancestors. I don't know if she actually did. She was a bit crazy, to tell the truth. "Ask your cousins to stop bothering people in Largo do Machado," I once told my alleged gypsy.

"They're not my cousins," she replied.

Ours was an unhappy story. We didn't part on good terms. I take my share of responsibility, but Simone was excessively dramatic. Everything was serious, everything was yes or no, black or white, she recognized no in-between. I learned, years later, of her death in an automobile accident. It apparently happened shortly after our breakup. She was so young. I don't usually revisit that topic, it pains me, but returning to Largo do Machado (we used to go to the Portuguese wine cellar, and we would have *sfihas* and tabouli at the Arab's in the Condor Gallery; sometimes Simone would buy Indian skirts at the Meu Cantinho boutique) knots something in my heart.

The rain gets heavier. My wet sock bothers me. I wait until I make it to the building where I have to take the documents.

I could handle the matter of the documents another way, but I'm up for promotion at the end of the year and until then have to suck up to the boss. I sit on a bench in the reception area, take off the shoe and sock, wring out the sock, and put it back on. My foot is still wet, but at least now it doesn't sink into a puddle of water with each step. The building's doorman watches me.

I spend more time with the client than I had planned. I know that now, in the late afternoon, especially with the rain, the subway will be hell. I decide to kill time around here, maybe get something to eat, have a beer. The idea of getting home later isn't all bad. I can't recall just when I became a slave to routine, but I swear it was involuntary. I think about how odd that is. How we become fossilized in the apathy of that production line. And still have to suck up to the boss.

I call my wife to say that I'll be home a little late, that I decided to wait for rush hour to end because I'm in Largo do Machado and it's raining, she knows how it is. They shouldn't wait for me to have dinner.

I think about checking to see if anything worthwhile is playing at the São Luiz Cinema (when I lived here there was also a movie theater in the Condor gallery, which later became an evangelical church and today I have no idea what it is). I walk under the marquees of the buildings and pass a young boy handing out leaflets. *I buy gold,* or something similar, I imagine, but when I take one of the papers the coincidence surprises me: *Tarot readings. Guidance in love, spiritual issues, answers to your most pressing concerns.*

I smile. It looks as if the gypsies who used to wander around the square have also moved up in life and now some have their own private offices. I read the address, which is in the old Condor Gallery building, 29 Largo do Machado.

I stop at the entrance, in front of the gallery. What the hell, I'm not doing anything, isn't one lie as good as another, whether it's going to the movies or getting a tarot reading? And who knows, maybe it's a way of paying homage, however belatedly, to Simone. Who was kind of crazy but wasn't a bad person and didn't deserve to have her life cut short so tragically. I decide to look for the place. I take the elevator to the fourth floor.

The door is opened by a beautiful, well-dressed young woman who in no way resembles the gypsies of two decades ago, and I automatically smooth my hair and adjust my collar. I explain that I'd like a reading, is she available?

"When?" she asks.

"Right now, if possible," I reply. "I live pretty far away, in Recreio, but on the street here I saw a leaflet with your address and was interested."

"I'm with a client at the moment," she says.

"I can wait."

It's true, I can wait, but more than that, suddenly it has become strangely important for this beautiful girl to read whatever there is to be read about me in the tarot cards.

"It's going to be awhile. Half an hour, forty minutes," she says.

I look around. The waiting room is tiny and windowless, but there's a pile of magazines in one corner, next to a candle and a vase with plastic flowers. An iron thing on the wall representing a sun and moon. A vague smell of incense.

"I'll stay here and read a little, if you can see me next?"

Everything seems totally professional. The phrases: *I'd like a reading. I'm with a client. If you can see me right away.* I sit in the black faux-leather armchair, pick up a magazine, begin leafing through it. I see orderly stacks of business cards: other people offering alternative therapies there in the same small space. Every Wednesday night, transcendental meditation. Right, I didn't imagine that tarot readings would pay the rent.

My reading lasts an hour. I sign a check and leave there transformed. I don't remember much of anything that was said, except for the comments about a particularly interesting card, the Hanged Man (actually, a guy dangling upside down, tied by one of his feet). According to the card reader—Renata—the Hanged Man indicates a situation of personal sacrifice of something valuable: when I leave the building, words like *destiny*, *initiation*, *indecision*, and *self-denial* are still floating in my head, like moths around a lamppost. A well-conceived plan that remains only a theory, Renata also says. Loss and helplessness would be the negative aspects of the card. On the other hand, there's also a very positive aspect, the possibility of changing one's life, of interior peace.

I leave there dreaming of changing my life and interior peace. More than that, I leave there dreaming of Renata.

My wife and I have had our crises, some of them quite serious, but awhile ago we fashioned a modus vivendi without major disturbance, for the sake of the children. We've been married for twelve years, which is the number of the Hanged Man tarot card, I think, I who always found that sort of thing utter nonsense. But suddenly, while being jostled on the subway en route to the Cantagalo Station, I'm making plans to set up another reading with Renata, to return to Largo do Machado.

I'd left the car in my sister's garage in Copacabana. I collect the car without going up to say goodbye to her. I put on music and think about Renata on the long journey from Cantagalo to the Avenue of the Americas. I'm still thinking about her when I turn onto my street, park the car in my spot in the garage, and take the elevator to my floor—still thinking about her when I open the door to the apartment.

At my second reading, two weeks later, I want to talk more about myself. I want Renata to know me. The first time, I was reticent, asked generic questions to which she gave generic answers. Now I want to pluck my soul out from under the skin and spread it out for Renata, take it, explain this, please—and you don't need to return it afterward. As far as I'm concerned, she can spread my soul on the floor and walk on it if she wishes.

This reading takes almost two hours. The World card (challenge of seeing something that must be concluded) and the Tower (imminent moment when it will be necessary to knock down old structures) appear in meaningful positions. Renata's hair is loose this time, long dark hair like that of the gypsy she is not. She is wearing large silver earrings and a T-shirt that outlines her pert, pretty breasts. She is more sexy this time, and I want to believe it's not by chance.

At the end of the reading she asks me if I'd like another cup of tea, and obviously I accept, while still debating with myself whether I should invite her to get something to eat nearby. She brings the teapot with hot water and a small box with tea bags of various kinds. Then she brings a plate with raisins. I conclude it's better to leave the invitation for the next reading, today would be hasty. In any case, we have time to chat a little.

"Well," she says, sitting down and pushing her hair behind her ears, "how did you become interested in tarot?"

"Oh, it's a long story," I answer. "I had a girlfriend, many years ago, more than twenty years—almost thirty, actually—who liked tarot. She wasn't a professional but liked to do it for herself, for her friends. I confess that I thought it sheer foolishness, I thought that in the readings the person heard what he wanted to hear. For example, if the card said, *It's necessary to knock down old structures*, the person would always manage to frame it in the context of his own life—that's what I thought."

"But you don't think that anymore?"

"You've changed my opinion about tarot," I say excitedly. "When I was here the first time I was quite skeptical, but now I'm seeing things differently."

"And why did you come the first time if you thought tarot was silly?"

"That old girlfriend of mine. We had a difficult relationship, at the end. Ugly fights, things I don't miss at all. Later I found out she died in a car accident. She was still quite young."

"Oh, that's so sad, I'm sorry."

The tarot reader's almond eyes fall on mine. She seems so sweet.

I take a raisin from the plate, put it in my mouth, and chew. Sweet. The wedding ring on my left hand bothers me.

"It's very rare for me to come to Largo do Machado," I continue. "My life these days is all in Recreio and Barra, but that afternoon, two weeks ago, I happened to be here on business and started thinking about Simone, my ex-girlfriend. When a boy handed me your leaflet I thought I should come, as a kind of homage to her. I don't know. It's as if something made the decision for me."

Renata gets up and goes to the window overlooking the square. "We never know the reason for certain decisions," she says. "It's as if they were made not by us but by some entity, something external."

I rise and go over to her. "There's something I have to tell you, Renata. Forgive me if it seems rather sudden. But I haven't been able to get you off my mind since the first time I was here."

She doesn't turn to look at me. I see her in profile and the tension is obvious in her face. The situation isn't easy, she knows I'm married, but I don't want to come across as rash, just one more guy trying to get her into bed. (I imagine there must be many, and I don't even know if she's in a committed relationship. She probably is.) I'm genuinely interested in Renata, although beyond that nothing is clear to me.

I find myself thinking again about the Hanged Man, card number 12, thinking about fate, indecision, self-denial, sacrifice, the possibility of changing one's life.

How pretty she is. I run my hand lightly over her hair, and she doesn't move away. I'm about to kiss her, but then she goes back to the table and begins putting away the deck of cards.

"I've thought a lot about you too," she says, her eyes averted. "But we have to give things time, everything's happening too quickly. I think it's best for you to leave now, and we'll agree to meet again soon. There are so many things in my personal life that I have to resolve, so many things."

"Will you call me? I'd love for you to call me," I say.

I give her my cell phone number and, on my way down, float in the elevator like a young boy. I'm coming back for a reading as soon as possible. I'd come back tomorrow if I could. I'd come back in half an hour.

Self-denial, sacrifice, indecision. That night I make love to my wife thinking furiously about Renata. Rather, I don't make love at all, I try to identify love in the act but after twelve years our love has become a digression. Marriage Inc., for the sake of the children. Exactly when is it that we sign on the dotted line? Or is it that we don't necessarily sign, that the agreement is by default, one more decision something else makes for us?

My situation is the most common in the world, and I know it. I'm a man in his fifties who's fed up with life and his family, dying to experience something different. But I ask myself, is it possible my wife is fed up too? She must be. Impossible for her not to be.

I think about the tarot cards again when I awaken—*imminent moment when it will be necessary to knock down old structures*, said the Tower card. It all makes sense. I need to see Renata right away.

Three days later she calls me in the afternoon and asks if I have a minute. I close the door to my office.

"Of course, we can talk."

"I've been thinking about the two of us. I think we need to see each other again," she says.

I imagine Renata in my arms. I want to get to know her, find out everything about her, but we can begin like that, with her in my arms. I remember the T-shirt clinging to her body. I think about my hands touching her breasts, lingering there. Over the shirt, under the shirt, and the rest, calmly. I imagine the cloth grazing her nipples. Afterward we can decide what comes next.

"Can you come next week?" she asks.

"Of course," I answer. "Of course I can."

"On Tuesday I have clients until seven. Come right after that, we'll have time. Is that possible?"

I make up an excuse at home and arrive at Largo do Machado almost an hour early on the appointed day. It's hard to calculate the time it takes to travel around Rio de Janeiro, even more so when you have to cross the entire city. And I can't afford to be late.

Unlike my last two visits, today's weather is good. Largo do Machado is back to normal. The game tables are all occupied, a dozen people take turns on the exercise equipment, others sit on the edge of the dry fountain. Hordes of pigeons on the Portuguese mosaic stones. I don't remember who once told me that the name *Largo do Machado* came from a butcher shop with a large ax, or *machado*, on its façade that used to be there, at the beginning of the nineteenth century. I remember that a street kid once assaulted Simone with a piece of broken glass as she was leaving the ATM beside the supermarket.

I kill time by walking around the square, think once again about visiting my old building only to once again decide against doing so: my past holds no appeal. Especially today. I prefer to stop for a few moments and watch a young man play the saxophone. You didn't see that when I lived here. Largo do Machado is much more together than in my time, even with the beggar sleeping by the fountain. In certain parts of Rio you're used to beggars sleeping in the street, and what can you do? I buy flowers for Renata at one of the kiosks.

I wait until a bit past seven and go up.

"How good that you came," she says when she opens the door.

"It was great that you called," I answer.

I hand her the flowers and embrace her, smell her perfume, but I know I have to proceed slowly. I sense that it must be that way with Renata.

Today there's no tarot deck between us. By now, however, I have begun to think of the cards as accomplices. I'm ready to change my life. I could be an adolescent with a backpack, clutching a one-way ticket to somewhere.

Renata offers me the usual tea, bringing the teapot with hot water and the small box with tea bags for me to select. We sit at the table, the tarot silent in its packaging—the deck is wrapped in a silk cloth inside a wooden box, just like before.

I put my hand on Renata's. She doesn't draw away. She begins talking about her life, her gentle voice in harmony with her gentle eyes. She speaks of her work, then finally of her heart. She has someone, as I imagined, a boyfriend, of some years, but things aren't going well between them. From the moment I came in for the initial reading, she says, she felt a special connection between us.

"But I was involved with a married man before and suffered greatly," she warns.

Let's go to bed first and then think about the rest, I feel like suggesting. We're in Rio de Janeiro in the twenty-first century, we need to test-drive relationships before thinking about anything else, don't we? Instead, I say I've been married for twelve years and it's not a happy marriage. There's almost no sex between me and my wife anymore. So often, people stay together only because of the children, I add. I feel like an idiot saying this, but she nods in agreement.

"It was like that with the other man I was involved with. I liked him a lot. Except that in the end he wanted to stay married. Most of them do."

Another classic story, I think. I decide I'm going to rid myself of the classics once and for all, and it's going to be now.

"I have to be very careful with men," Renata says in a slightly more confrontational tone.

I smile. What an adorable girl. "No need to be careful with me," I say.

"You're married. It's the same story."

"Marriage isn't forever. Who knows what tomorrow will bring?"

"Tell me about your wife."

"I would rather talk about you."

"No, no, tell me about her. What she does in life, for example."

"She's a beautician. She has a small salon in Recreio."

"She must be pretty. Beauticians know how to take care of themselves."

"She's not ugly, but in any case that's not important."

"I think I'm very naïve around men," she says. "I get involved too quickly and end up disappointed just as quickly."

"But you can trust me. It's different. I'm truly interested in you, I'm not like that other guy."

She smiles and covers our hands with her other hand. I pat it. I caress her wrist. I feel her bones, the texture of her delicate skin.

"My mother," she says. "My mother was also naïve with men. With you, for example, she was an idiot."

I jolt back at that odd statement.

"She died because of you," Renata says. "But you didn't know, of course. She was pregnant when you disappeared."

"Your mother was pregnant?"

"Yes, my mother, Simone, who liked to do tarot readings—isn't that what you told me? Who died in a car accident many years ago."

I take my hand away quickly. Suddenly, everything is wrong. A well-conceived plan that remains a theory. "I don't know if I understand."

"No? I'll explain," she says. "My mother was pregnant when you went away without even leaving a phone number."

"Our relationship was on the rocks, I wasn't—"

"But that's not something you do. You knew she might be pregnant."

Renata opens the tarot box, unwraps the deck, then carefully folds the purple silk cloth. She shuffles the cards, takes one out, and places it on the table.

"The Fool," she says. "The card with no number."

"If she was pregnant like you say, was she pregnant . . . with you?"

"She died in a car accident, that's what they say. The truth is she crashed on purpose. Because of you. And she died, but I didn't. She was pregnant when she had the accident. The accident she caused to kill us both. Exactly twenty-eight years ago."

There's nowhere for me to look, so I stare at the card of the Fool on the table.

"I was raised by my aunt, who tried every way possible to get in contact with you, unsuccessfully. You had disappeared."

"Simone was a very complicated person. I had tried to break up with her before, and it was always a drama, she would show up at my building, stalk me, and—"

"You knew she might be pregnant."

I remain silent. Words have fled in disarray. What Renata says is true: Simone's sister did call me once, as soon as she and I separated. She said Simone might be pregnant. The test still had to be done, but it was possible. At that moment, in desperation, I considered sticking with Simone for good. A child with her! That was when I accepted the job in Belo Horizonte. Years later, I was told that Simone had died in an accident, but I never found out the details, nor did I want to know. First came the shock, then I confess to feeling a certain relief. There must not have been a child at all, or I'd have known about it. Wouldn't I? We always end up finding out about those things sooner or late, right? Sooner or later.

"The Fool has no number," Renata says after my long silence. "Sometimes they attribute the number zero to him.

Zero is the number that alters no addition. In multiplication it transforms everything into itself. It absorbs the other numbers. Look, in the deck I use, the Fool is unwittingly walking toward a cliff. But it's a good card. I like the Fool a lot. See how he's carrying a flower in his left hand? That means he appreciates beauty. And his carefree walk is as happy as a child comfortable in the world. Notice that he also carries a staff, which can represent self-denial and wisdom. The Fool always operates outside of social norms and will usually say and do whatever comes into his head."

She slides her finger along the edges of the card. Her nails are nicely manicured.

I think about the number 12 card, the Hanged Man, in an uncomfortable position, dangling upside down by one foot. A burst of noise comes from outside, and through the window I see pigeons taking flight. Suddenly a wave of intense nausea hits me, and only then, looking at my empty cup and Renata's, still full to the brim, do I understand the severity of my mistake. I dash to the door, which is unlocked, and from there to the elevator, which takes a long time to arrive. When the doors open, it's empty.

I press the button for the ground floor. Stabbing pains shoot through my stomach. I need someone to take me to the nearest emergency room. I stagger through the gallery, and when I make it to the sidewalk I see a boy distributing handbills: *I buy gold, immediate payment.* People look at me. Then Largo do Machado goes dark, and I see nothing more, not the pigeons, not the old men, not the flower kiosks, not the gypsies—but they left a long time ago.

TONED COUGARS

BY TONY BELLOTTO

Leme

1.

It was Ronald Biggs who popularized the legend of Rio as the preferred destination for gringo fugitives. It's like the photo printed on the calendar hanging on the wall of the Black Cat: the smiling thief at the beach, a caipirinha in his hand, surrounded by mulatto women, signing autographs for tourists. Right. But when you screw up in Rio, where do you run to?

2.

Toned cougars are my favorite target. Married ones, of course. Married toned cougars, MTCs for short, are the goal. Separated toned cougars, or STCs, latch onto you and won't let go. STCs are a problem. All you have to do is look at them and they come on to you. MTCs are foxes, STCs are ticks. The hard part is that when you approach them you have no way of knowing at first if the toned cougar is married or separated. Fox or tick, that is the question. Later you end up getting the hang of it. Today I can separate the wheat from the chaff. Toned widows (TWs), I've never approached. They exist but they're hard to find. They've probably let themselves go in relief once they've lost their husbands. So I've never stung a TW. As a matter of fact, you could say I got stung by one, but that's an unpleasant subject I'd rather not go into at present.

Toned widows are spiders. Maybe when they become widows they stop going to the beach and the gym and start frequenting church, all-you-can-eat restaurants, and the van that chauffeurs old ladies to the theater. They can finally do what they always wanted, without having to worry about staying in shape for the deceased. Not all of them, unfortunately. Maybe I should have gone to church more and less to the beach. Maybe, maybe, maybe. Too late now.

3.

The beach is the natural habitat of toned cougars. And of all the beaches, Copacabana is the mother lode. Of all the mother lodes, Leme is the filet mignon. I don't know exactly what a mother lode has to do with filets, but if you want to meet a top-of-the-line toned cougar, go to Leme Beach. I didn't discover these things overnight. I developed a model, the fruit of observation and reflection. I'm a PhD, philanderer highly distinguished.

Or rather, I was.

4.

The story begins with me making a complete survey of the situation: I would kick off the day by jogging from the far end of Leblon to the hill at Leme. I would wear a tight Speedo to emphasize the size of my middle leg and trot along the sand like a wild horse. I would run from Leblon to Arpoador, turn around at Diabo Beach, make a pit stop to tone biceps and triceps, cross Garota de Ipanema Square, and continue trotting along the bike lane of Francisco Otaviano. Back on the beach, I would go from the Copacabana Fort to the end of Leme, alternating between soft and hard sand to stimulate different muscles in the thighs and calves. Arriving at the foot of the hill at Leme I would do two hundred push-ups. That gave me an incredible form: thick footballer legs, a swimmer's pecs, a gym rat's washboard abs, lung capacity like Anderson Silva, and a tan that would be the envy of Kelly Slater.

On the way, I would check out the local scene. The bourgeois women of Leblon, the gays on Farme, the gringas of Copacabana, and the super-hot cougars of Leme. Not that there aren't any hotties in Copacabana, ripped forty-year-olds in Ipanema, tourists in Leme, or gays in Leblon. At the beach there's everything everywhere. But the highest incidence, let's call it, of toned cougars is in Leme. Leme and Copacabana, but the ones in Leme are the pearl in the oyster, eleven on a scale of ten.

At the end of the day I would return through Leblon, pick up my clothes from the bro at the kiosk, and catch the 434 bus for Grajaú, where I shared an apartment with my old lady.

To tell the truth, I was tired of getting gringas drunk for a lousy handful of dollars. I was pushing forty and what I wanted was security, know what I mean? Tranquility.

5.

I'm a fan of toned cougars. I admire the way they refuse to give in to the passage of time or the force of gravity. They're tough and spare no effort to stay in shape: fitness center, aquatic exercise, personal trainer, dermatologist, nutritionist, Botox, detox, massages, liposuction, meditation, yoga, acupuncture, stretching, Pilates, and in some cases neurotherapy. It's not easy. Some do triathlons. There was one who even used Ben Wa balls to strengthen her vaginal muscles.

In time I learned to distinguish the tick from the fox. It's something you can tell by how they look at you. Ticks look at you like a puppy at the window of a butcher shop, foxes like a pharaoh in a tomb. Deep down, what they all want is a cock, but that's where discernment enters the picture. My dick, pardon the immodesty, has always been able to discern. A fundamental detail: married toned cougars don't think of leaving their husbands. The topic is out of the question, never mentioned, not even in frank conversations after a few proseccos or strong caipirinhas. Married toned cougars are only looking for an available cock, affection, attention, the illusion of being young again, flirtation, the dirty stuff, sexting, the right mood, get it?

The right mood.

And that's the basic difference between the fox and the tick: foxes want you as a lover, ticks as a husband. Exclusive.

Once you learn to separate fish from fowl, things move right along.

So, I was putting together a small nest egg. Because married toned cougars always have rich husbands. Just do the math: gym fees, massage therapy, personal trainer, regular dermatology procedures, frequent trips to the beauty parlor (nails, hair, facial massage, foot therapy, colorist), doctors, acupuncturists, etc.—in addition to what the guy pays his mistress. The husband of a married toned cougar always has a lover, of course, and that's why they start working out. Deep down they love their husbands, and because they no longer have their attention they decide to make over their appearance. Out of need. And after working their asses off, when they realize that even then they don't get the least bit of attention from their better halves, I come on the scene. Because the cougar who gets along with her husband is ugly and fat, right? Beyond help. She doesn't need to work out. Really, that's psychology, it's not me saying it. There was one who wanted to set me up in a two-room apartment, but I thought it was a bit overboard. I preferred taking the money in cash.

6.

One day, during my morning run through Leme, I met Veronique.

Veronique Delamare was a blond grandma with wrinkled skin, thin but with well-defined musculature and the legs of a woman of thirty. She was easily pushing eighty. Her hands shook a bit, but her belly was a peeled tangerine, wedge upon wedge, impressive despite the chicken flesh. Her arm muscles were still taut, without that characteristic flap that usually hangs like fish gills from older women's upper arms. And she had a pretty face in spite of the wrinkles. As soon as I laid eyes on her—and she pretended not to notice and I knew then that she was married—I saw she must have been beautiful when she was young. In the depths of those wrinkles glowed two blue eyes that, I confess, hooked me. Know when you lose your way for a second? Forget what you were doing? To complicate matters, she had a very charming French accent. But I'm a pro, and I approached her the way I always do—rational, pragmatic, asking what physical activities she participated in, saying I was a personal trainer and all that crap.

And that's how we began the affair.

7.

Veronique liked variety and would take me to different places in her imported coupe. We frequented motels in Barra, in Copacabana, on Avenida Brasil, in Grumari. And she was a good fuck, the old lady. I don't know if she practiced vaginal strengthening, I never asked, but she had pretty strong pelvic musculature and liked giving me pussy squeezes, a thing that clamped my cock when I came and sent me into outer space. She was cultured too and would laugh when I didn't understand her talk after fucking, some weird stuff about the finiteness of life and the emptiness of existence. What was empty was my balls after swashing the old lady's insides.

In late afternoon, after a primo lay in a motel in São Conrado, we were having beer in Gávea at a young people's hangout. Veronique wasn't concerned, she was up for it and didn't care if everybody realized she was a rich old woman accompanied by a ripped gigolo. I think she even took pride in it. She had a gringa's mentality, a feminist. And around the third beer she says: "My husband is fucking rich. And he's a piece of shit."

That's when the alarm went off. Talking about the hubby? Veronique was different. But I already knew that. And with all the beer I had drunk, I didn't pay any attention to the alarm bell. I said, "Aren't they all? Let's talk about sexy stuff. I love your accent."

"No. Let's talk about my husband. You can enjoy the accent at the same time."

And she went on talking about how her husband was indifferent, cold, selfish, and hermetic. *Hermetic* is a word I'd never heard.

"Someone who lives inside himself like a mollusk," explained Veronique.

And she went on jerking me around with that business about the rich, cold, selfish, hermetic Mr. Mollusk. At the time it didn't really register with me, I was sleepy and I had worked out in the morning, fucked in the afternoon, and was now pounding beer. I have a weakness for drink. So that was as far as it went, and I returned to Grajaú and went to sleep.

8.

I went on with my life, but with Veronique it was different: I couldn't manage to close out the chapter and move on to another MTC like the playbook says. My strategy was never to let an affair go past three months. It's that old business about a dead fish starting to smell the next day. Cougars last three months. Then they begin demanding more than they give. They're human, are they not?

The truth is, I was starting to like Veronique.

Crazy, I know. I'll confess, she's older than my mother. But Mom is all messed up, diabetic, with high blood pressure and borderline senile. She's even wearing adult diapers and using a walker. If she was already heading downhill when my old man died, just imagine what she's like now. But Mom is younger than Veronique, just check their IDs. And I did check Veronique's ID one day when she fell asleep after fucking. That bugged me a little. Falling in love with a woman older than my mother is troubling. And with shaky hands! I should've found a shrink while there was still time. I tried to break away, let a few days go by without calling, but I missed her. Missed her, isn't that a bitch? I had never felt that, it was like some alien squeezing my chest from inside.

There was no way out—I fell in love with Veronique. I know, passion like this is a faggy sentiment, but it happened. It took a long time for me to realize it and still longer for me to admit it. I was hooked. Happy as a clam: she gave me money and didn't demand anything in return, kept my morale high and fucked like a rabbit in heat. You don't fix something that isn't broken, my father used to say, God rest his soul.

9.

One afternoon the bill arrived.

But it didn't come in the form of a summons or an arrest warrant. Nothing like that. I already said that Veronique was intelligent, tough, and she knew how to handle me. We were in Guaratiba, at an inn, Veronique on top molding my joint like clay. I screamed as I came, feeling pain and arousal at the same time. My dick was turning red from all the compressing that Veronique was doing with her tight musculature. It was like she had crab claws instead of ovaries. I was in that dopey state after coming, looking serenely at the greenish sea through the window, when she went back to making insinuations about Mr. Mollusk.

"Now then," she said, "I've got something to propose to you."

Propose? Married toned cougars don't make proposals. They make deposits. The alarm went off for the second time. But it was already too late, though I wasn't aware of it at the moment.

"What?"

"Your financial independence."

"What kind of talk is that, Veronique? You think I'm here for the dough?" I laid the indignation on thick.

"My dear." She ran her hand along my arm like an affectionate grandmother and I noticed how shaky and fleshless it was, like the hand of a witch in an animated film. "I know you make a good bit of money taking advantage of needy old women, and I see nothing wrong with that. It's an honest agreement: you give me love and attention and in exchange I give you money. Nothing could be more fair. I know life. You're forty already, think about it: pretty soon you'll be middle-aged. And the old ladies won't want to run their hands along your tired skin, full of spots like mine." She held her hand in front of my face for me to see the spots. Then she affectionately tweaked my nose. "Life starts galloping after a certain age, and no Viagra can change that. I know you're not a personal trainer here or any goddamn place. The pittance you wring out of elderly ladies isn't going to last forever. I'm talking about real money."

I felt like hugging Veronique. But I'm a pro and kept quiet, wearing the expression of a grifter caught in the act. "What?" I asked.

"You know," she said, and squeezed the end of my nose.

10.

I took some time to decide.

Deep down I had already decided, but we fool ourselves and pretend we still haven't decided about what we know is already a done deal. Isn't that how it is? And I really was in need of dough. Not only for myself but for my mother. She was costing a bundle. Being old is hell. But I'm not the kind of soulless son who dumps his mother in some shithole asylum.

The first thing I'd have to do was buy a gun. I'm a peaceful guy and have never carried a weapon. I set up a meeting with Alferes, an ex-cop I know from drinking at the Black Cat. They say he's in a militia, but I don't know about that.

"What do you want a gun for, tiger?"

"Nothing, really. Just to scare a guy."

"Then scare him with your muscle, you're ripped. Your arm's thicker than my leg," he said, and had me hold my arm next to his leg. It was nighttime and no one else was around, but I was worried someone would see us and think I was a homo paying Alferes for a blow job. In fact, his leg was short and skinny.

"I want it to be a helluva scare. Just seeing the piece pointing at his forehead will be enough to make him shit himself."

"Then you won't need any ammunition."

"Yes, I will. If the guy sees the gun isn't loaded I'll look like an idiot."

"Be careful," said Alferes.

That *Be careful* echoed in my brain for some time, but I went ahead anyway. You can't waste a chance at financial independence when it falls in your lap. Two nights later, in Nobel Square, I bought from Alferes a police .38, black, with its serial number filed off. Plus the ammo.

The next morning I started training. Doing it felt good. It was like something in a movie, when the criminals gear up for the big heist. Scientific, know what I mean?

I went to a vacant lot in the vicinity of Água Santa and took some potshots at old oil cans to improve my aim. And in my head I kept track of the information Veronique was providing me. I felt like Jason Bourne.

11.

Mr. Mollusk, self-absorbed, full of himself, spent most of his time in the couple's penthouse on Avenida Atlântica, sitting in front of his computer and investing his dough in the world's stock markets. The cuckold made his living that way. Veronique said the money was the product of the sale of a chain of laundromats and a shoe factory that he had begrudgingly administered his entire life and got rid of some years ago. The Mollusk went out three times a week to walk along the ocean-front, accompanied by his male secretary and his chauffeur. But those walks were inconsistent. If it rained, or he woke up in a bad mood, he canceled the walk. He wasn't a man of regular habits. There was only one thing that Mr. Mollusk always did the same way. At ten o'clock in the morning of the first Tuesday of each month, rain or shine, he would go to the

São João Batista Cemetery, in Botafogo, and place flowers on his mother's tomb. The old woman had died on a Tuesday, fifteen years earlier, and ever since then the nutcase visited her once a month. One detail: there inside the cemetery he insisted on going to the gravesite by himself.

With this information in mind, I began developing Veronique's plan. She gave me a photo of the old man so I could recognize him, but even so she insisted I see the bag of bones in person. One day I loitered around a kiosk in Copa, drinking coconut water through a straw, and waited for the geezer to come by. Veronique alerted me by cell phone when he left the apartment and said he was wearing a navy-blue Adidas warm-up jacket. When the geriatric passed by, I stared at him to register his features. He was just another old guy like hundreds of others wandering around Copacabana drooling, and he didn't even notice me. The secretary and the chauffeur were with him, a dark-haired man and a black dude dressed like a nurse.

I felt ready.

On Friday before the first Tuesday of the month, Veronique and I agreed to go a few days without contact, as a precaution. That weekend, before going to sleep, I spent a few minutes looking at the photo of Mr. Mollusk that Veronique had given me. Then I prayed.

12.

It breaks my heart to see a guy putting flowers on his mother's tomb because I think of my own mother, and thinking about her brings me down. Thinking that one day she's going to die.

The sky was cloudy that day. Veronique had told me the cemetery is usually quiet on Tuesdays, and it was true. Mr. Mollusk arrived with his shuffling walk and set the flowers down. Then he kneeled, with difficulty, and began to pray.

I snuck up behind him and said, "Rest easy, you're going to meet her."

I placed the revolver against the back of his neck and fired.

I remembered to take his wallet, to make it look like a robbery, and left, moving kind of unsteadily. I didn't stop walking until I got to the beach at Botafogo. I took off my sneakers and walked to the water, feeling the cold sand on my feet. Since the day was cloudy, no one was at the beach. I never thought it would be so easy to kill someone. I took the revolver and Mollusk's wallet from my pocket and threw them out into the water. I wet my face and washed my hands, which were a bit bloody. Then I stretched out on the sand and realized that my legs were trembling a little, even when I was lying down. I turned over, did about two hundred push-ups to get rid of the trembling, and left, my body feeling as heavy as if I was carrying Sugar Loaf on my back.

13.

In the days that followed, I fell into a weird listlessness, like I had caught a bad flu. My mother asked, "What's the matter, boy?" and I said it was just the flu. She thought it was dengue but I said no, dengue didn't stand a chance with me. She had some açaí delivered; I took it and then went out so she wouldn't keep worrying. I had lots of places I could go, but I decided to return to the beach at Botafogo, don't ask me why. I caught the 434 bus to Rua Real Grandeza and walked to the beach. It was sunny and I sat on a bench, watching the sea. I peered at the sand, afraid the waves had brought back the wallet and the revolver. I didn't see anything. I had a strong desire to call Veronique, but I figured everything would be in a total uproar after the wake and the burial. By now she must be talking with the lawyers about the inheritance. At one point I even dialed her cell phone but hung up. I summoned the patience to let a week go by before calling, like we had agreed.

When I returned home, my mother told me Alferes was looking for me. I found that odd. "What did he say?" I asked.

"Nothing, just for you to meet him tonight at the Black Cat."

"I'm not in the mood for the Black Cat."

"Go," my mother said, running her hand over my hair, "the distraction will do you good."

14.

As soon as I entered the Black Cat, Alferes came up and whispered in my ear: "Meet me in the square at midnight." Sometimes I have the impression that Alferes is a bit light in the loafers. That business of him wanting to talk to me made me nervous and I decided to have a few beers. Could I have screwed something up?

At midnight I was at the square, anxious. Drinking hadn't calmed me down but it had given me the urge to piss. Alferes arrived and immediately asked, "Say, tiger, you're not involved in the death of that numbers bankroller, are you?"

"What bankroller?" I asked. I hadn't killed anybody connected with the numbers racket. I was so relieved that I decided to relieve my bladder too and started to piss behind a lamppost.

"Raposo Muller, the old numbers kingpin who was murdered."

"Of course not, Alferes. I just put a scare into a guy," I said, shaking the snake before putting it back in its nest. "Why would I want to kill some racketeer? You nuts?"

"Because no professional would accept the contract. Besides his numbers connection, he was also a colonel in the army and a torturer during the dictatorship. You watch television, don't you? Only an insane person would kill that bastard. Or some fall guy. Whoever killed him must be a long way from here. Or else he's pushing up daisies."

"You calling me a sucker?"

"No. Or a dead man. It's just that I worry about my customers."

"Okay," I said, "I'm dying to get some sleep."

Alferes had a distant look, as if he'd seen a ghost come up behind me. "I never heard of anybody being murdered in a cemetery," he said.

"Cemetery? What cemetery?"

"Who told the fool to go to the cemetery without a bodyguard?"

"What are you talking about?"

"They wasted the lunatic in São João Cemetery while he was praying at his mother's tomb. This country's gone bonkers."

I felt like shitting my pants, but I concealed it and said goodbye to Alferes. Something was very wrong.

I wasn't able to sleep that night. Early the next day, when I looked at the newspaper on my way to the bakery, I saw that the old man I had killed at the cemetery wasn't Mr. Mollusk but the retired numbers kingpin Raposo Muller. In the photo of the funeral, I saw his widow, a fat old hag I didn't know. I became dizzy and had to support myself against the newsstand to keep from falling. I called Veronique, but she didn't answer. Not then or ever again.

15.

I was remembering Ronald Biggs.

There comes a time when you have to run away somewhere. He fled to Rio. I had to flee *from* Rio. My bad luck.

But it's not all that bad here. There's that crazy president, an old pothead with the air of a hippie about him. Maybe they'll be more understanding to a HIG—highly idiotic grifter—like me. I swear that weighed heavily when it was time to decide where to go. The beaches here have their charm, although the local toned cougars can't hold a candle to the ones in Leme. The advantage is that here all the cougars are gringas, including the Brazilians. And they're the ones who support me. Sure, I've had to go back to getting women tourists drunk to survive. I'm taking a break from toned cougars. Trauma. Today I settle for ugly cougars and old bags. I lead a modest life, I earn enough to pay the rent for the small apartment where I live and the fees at the shitty asylum where I had to dump Mom, near Friburgo. In any case, today is a special day for me. I've just received a letter from France. And to think I didn't believe there was such a thing as letters anymore. I kept it to open at the beach. I'm not much of a reader, but when it happens, I like to read lying on the sand so I can quickly doze off.

My dear, pardon the confusion. I hope you're not terribly angry with me. After all, stealing from a thief is not really stealing. It took some doing to find your address. Your mother helped me, but only after a lot of convincing. It was hard to find her in that asylum/exile in the mountains. Don't worry, she revealed your whereabouts to me because I'm a respectable lady and older than her. I know you'll never forgive me, but you at least deserve an explanation. In 1972 I was a few years past thirty and shared an office with my husband Ivan, like me a psychiatrist.

We weren't guerrillas but we sympathized with enemies of the military regime and even hid political fugitives in our apartment on Lagoa. One day we were dragged from the apartment by agents of the dictatorship. We were barbarously tortured and Ivan was murdered. They probably threw his body into the sea, because it was never found. The man who tortured us and killed Ivan was Colonel Raposo Muller, that monster whom you did the favor of eliminating from human society. As soon as I was released, I came to France and tried to rebuild my life. I paid a high price. I spent decades without the courage to return to Brazil. But I never gave up on the idea of one day taking revenge on Raposo Muller. The animal, after leaving the army, became a powerful racketeer and was constantly surrounded by hired gunmen, even after he retired. It wasn't until recently that I gathered the courage and returned to Rio to exact my vengeance. But no professional assassin I contacted would agree to kill him. It would be too dangerous. Even when I said I had studied the monster's movements and discovered that he visited the cemetery by himself once a month, no one would agree to kill Raposo Muller, fearing retaliation. I know that I could have—and should have—shot the abominable torturer myself. Don't think I wouldn't have felt enormous pleasure in doing so, even if it cost me my life. And it wasn't out of fear that I didn't, but from lack of confidence in my abilities. I'm old and my hands tremble a lot, as you know. Unfortunately, you can't fire a gun with your pussy. In any case, I will always be grateful to you in the time I have left, which won't be that long.

Veronique

16.

"Hey," says a guy who came up behind me without me notic-ing. I must have dozed off. There are two of them, actually. They're wearing street clothes and they're armed, which is strange on a beach, even if the beach is in Uruguay.

THE CANNIBAL OF IPANEMA

BY ALEXANDRE FRAGA DOS SANTOS

Ipanema

The cannibal had been inactive since the end of the seventies. He had sold the old family home in Santa Clara, inhabited by memories and the spirits that haunted his mind. The voice of his grandmother, always calling him a cowardly little lieutenant, a weakling, unmanly . . . By getting rid of the mansion he had blotted out all those ghosts. With the money from the sale he had bought a two-story house with a terrace on Rua Canning, along with a Siberian husky. He named the dog Dollar. He wanted the animal to be strong, like the American currency.

Retired from the army with the rank of colonel, Leopoldo passed for a peaceful citizen of Ipanema, dividing his time between walking the dog as far as the Arpoador rocks and painting, along with sporadic visits to the establishment near his building, the Centaurus, the neighborhood's traditional bordello.

Although he considered himself more a reserve officer than a professional artist, from time to time he made a little money from the sale of his canvases in exhibitions around the city. He would spend the extra income at the Centaurus, but not in a more orthodox manner. He would always make his incursions in late afternoon and take a leisurely sauna, followed by a cold shower. He would shave, powder his armpits, and slip into the white robe provided by the bordello. He would take the elevator to the third floor, to the nightclub going full blast, with the perfume of lust in the air. He would sit down next to the bar and have the waiter bring his favorite scotch. And then the pilgrimage of the whores would begin, as it did that Friday . . .

"Can I sit here, baby?"

"Do I look like a baby?"

The whore sat down and put her forefinger on Leopoldo's lips. "You look like a naughty baby."

"You can't imagine how naughty . . ."

"Maybe what I need is some fooling around." She ran her fingers through the colonel's hair. "I can't see a gray-haired man without wanting to put out."

"I can imagine."

"You don't have to imagine. Just look."

The whore took Leopoldo's hand and stuck it under her bikini bottom. The colonel allowed his finger to probe her vulva for a few moments, evaluating the wetness.

"Now take it out. If you don't, the madam gets on my case. You see how I get?"

"Yes, you're very damp."

"Wet, drenched."

"Yes. Can you tell me your name?"

"Roberta. Can I have some of your whiskey?"

"Yes."

"Can I get your key, so we can get a little friendly?"

"Yes."

"Anything you'd like."

The hooker left Leopoldo by himself at the table. The colonel took advantage of her absence to observe his surroundings. There were better-looking whores than Roberta in the place, but the young woman had been efficient in her approach. Besides, the club was infested with gringos who, judging by the tattoos of anchors and women on their arms, and the whiteness of their skin, were from some Scandinavian ship.

Roberta came back twenty minutes later, panting. *She must have blown one of those Vikings en route*. She tried to kiss the colonel, but he refused. As if by reflex, she downed a shot of whiskey in a single gulp. Then she apologized: "The house is packed, that's why I took so long."

She took Leopoldo by the hand and led him to the suite, where Roberta got naked. She told the colonel to take off his robe.

"No."

"Why not?"

"I want to stay this way. Dressed."

"Hey, I wanna get off."

"And I want to talk."

"Are you gay?"

"I'm a colonel in the Brazilian army. I expect a modicum of respect."

"Okay then. What does the colonel want to talk about?"

Leopoldo wanted to know everything about Roberta's life: how she got started in prostitution; whether she had children; her relationship with her parents; if she dreamed of having a family.

The whore let out a sob: "I don't have anybody . . . I feel so lonely . . ."

Leopoldo paid the girl extra. In dollars . . . With the colonel, everything was in dollars. She thanked him and asked if she could kiss him.

"On the cheek, please."

Roberta kissed the colonel on his right cheek and concluded the encounter.

* * *

As Roberta was leaving the nightclub, a Passat pulled up alongside her and the driver lowered the window.

"Shall we finish what we started?"

Roberta glanced around to make sure the security guys from the club weren't watching them. She couldn't have outside dates; if she were found out, she'd be sent packing. There was no one, and she was horny and needy. Besides which, she would make some dough. Making dough was good.

"Let's go." She jumped in the car. "Which motel, colonel?"

The colonel drove a short distance and clicked the remote control for his garage. The Siberian husky had its nose against the gate. Roberta took a deep breath; whenever the door to a man's house opened, she nurtured the hope of a serious relationship, of building something for herself. And this could be her lucky night.

"I love a man in uniform."

They got out of the car. Dollar jumped onto Roberta and sniffed her from head to toe. The hooker became a bit tense.

"Does he bite?"

"Not him."

"Cute," said the whore, patting the dog.

Leopoldo opened the door and let Dollar in as well.

"Is he gonna participate?" asked Roberta.

"No. Just watch."

"Do you enjoy that?"

"You talk too much."

"You're rude."

"Go wash up."

"How much are you gonna pay?"

"Two hundred dollars."

Chic, this colonel . . . Always in dollars.

"Where's the bathroom?"

"End of the hall. Last door on the left."

The working girl went down the corridor, observing the row of paintings illuminated by bluish light. *The man must really be a pervert,* and Roberta found the thought encouraging: there were two buffalo cornering a blond woman with a thick dark tuft around her vagina; a horse corralling a black woman with a vast blond tuft around her pussy, while another horse reared on its hind legs, offering his rigid member to the woman; the mad colonel had even painted bats attacking a nun. There were also rifles and antique weapons hanging on the walls, along with family photos.

Roberta laughed to herself. The game was going to be a good one.

Leopoldo waited anxiously. As did Dollar. Together they were a devilish pair. But there was never anything left for Dollar. He was only a voyeur. The colonel was aware of the insanity of his habits, but this was better than eating neighbors for lunch or dinner. The cannibal was retired, thanks to Our Lady, his devotional saint.

Roberta came out of the bathroom naked. She encountered the colonel in dress uniform complete with a short ceremonial sword. She sat on a sofa, spread her legs, and beckoned to Leopoldo.

The colonel couldn't control himself and buried his head between Roberta's legs. The whore removed his cap and put it on. A pro, she began saying dirty words and striking the colonel in the face; he obediently accepted and continued with the cunnilingus. Dollar merely watched, his ears pricked up.

"I'm coming, I'm coming!" the whore announced.

And she came.

Then the colonel's face assumed the look of a wolf that

has just attacked its prey: flushed, colored by raging blood. His formal uniform, his medals—everything was smeared with blood.

"I'm sorry, colonel. I think I got my period."

Leopoldo shook his head from side to side, unresigned. Dollar, frightened, climbed the stairs to the second floor.

"You had no right to do that."

"Colonel, forgive me. I didn't mean to—"

"I was cured!"

"A woman has no control over these things . . ."

"Get off my sofa!"

"I'm so ashamed . . ."

"Get out! Get out of my house!"

"I'm sorry, colonel . . ."

"I don't want to do it! I don't want to do it! Get out!"

"You're humiliating me . . ."

"Get out of here! Out!!"

"Don't talk to me like that . . . you coward!!"

It was his grandmother's voice returning: *Coward! Leopoldo, you're not a man and never were . . .*

From the terrace, Dollar was howling.

"Coward! You don't talk like that to a lady!" The whore was offended by the grossness . . .

Bringing home a whore, Leopoldo?

"I don't want to do that, Grandma!"

The dog howled.

Taking insults from a tramp, Leopoldo? You sissy.

"I don't want to, I don't want to, Grandma . . ."

"Grandma my ass, you calling me old? You shitty two-bit colonel, coward, faggot . . ."

The dog howled . . .

You wimp, you were never a man . . . you weakling . . .

"You flaming fag!"

"I'm a colonel in the Brazilian army—"

Faggot, she's right, Leopoldo. Ever since you were a child . . . I always knew . . .

The dog howled.

"You queer! I want my two hundred dollars!"

Then the cannibal hurled himself onto the woman, burying his sharpened teeth in the neck of his prey while his hand covered her mouth. The victim tried to escape by striking the executioner, but the man's trained jaw had tremendous strength and soon the woman surrendered, her blows losing power and her eyes closing as she yielded to death. She emitted a few moans that could have been mistaken for pleasure. And succumbed. The cannibal alternated between the vagina and the neck, leaving the remaining parts for another time. Using the sword, he cut the body into uniform pieces and stored them in the old freezer.

He was a methodical cannibal. Military.

On the terrace, Dollar let loose another howl, sharp; then in falsetto, sounding like a chant of anguish and submission. The animal recognized the smell of blood by instinct inherited from his ancestors and knew one thing: there was a predator in the house, and it wasn't him.

The cannibal was back.

PART II

DIVIDED CITY

THE BOOTY

by Luiz Alfredo Garcia-Roza

Lapa

He was known as Rat. Short, skinny, with a head shaped like a rodent's. People found him repulsive. Not because of the clothes he wore or his personal hygiene. He always wore a suit and tie, both secondhand and rather used, but of good quality. His shoes and clothes had gone through various repairs, some by his own hand, and he kept them clean and intended to go on wearing them as long as possible. Until recently he had worn a wide-brimmed felt hat, a gift from a habitué of Cinelândia. It was a lovely hat, but Rat finally convinced himself that it made him look even smaller than he was, though it had the advantage of hiding his face, which was indeed repulsive thanks to his tiny, pointed, widely spaced teeth. This general appearance made him seek out from an early age somber and poorly lit places, not always easy in a sunny city like Rio, unless one becomes the solitary, nocturnal sort. Which is in fact what happened, not because of his repulsive appearance but because of the police.

It was when he still lived downtown, in the area stretching from Cinelândia to Lapa. During the day he circulated around Cinelândia and the narrow streets, almost alleyways, that go from the square toward Lapa. At night he frequented the bars in Lapa. In Cinelândia he managed and protected the minors who committed petty thefts on pedestrians; in Lapa he managed and protected the prostitutes, not all of them, of course, but a sufficient number to maintain his lifestyle. In both businesses he kept the accounts himself and was good at it. There was also Japa, an intelligent and crafty lawyer, despite being an incorrigible alcoholic, who resolved his run-ins with the law. Besides the two of them, there were three security men who took turns maintaining order and protection from the "Germans," as the police were called. Finally, there was a network of underage lookouts who served quite efficiently as short-range radar. Rat had never dealt with drugs and traffickers, whom he considered very violent and likely to attract the police. He also neither possessed nor used guns. He was in the habit of saying his weapons were his short stature, his sharpened teeth, and the ability to disappear almost instantly when necessary. He always thought of himself as an entrepreneur. The boys he protected were required to attend school; otherwise they couldn't be part of his team. The women had regular classes in basic English, which facilitated their contact with foreign tourists. And both the boys and the women were directed by him, when necessary, to an outpatient medical clinic that received a monthly contribution from Rat and Japa for services rendered to the underserved downtown population.

Things were going smoothly, without major internal conflict and without problems of law and order, until the day the police realized that everything was going too well with him and his lawyer partner and that they, the police, had so far not received any benefit from it.

"Procuring, inducement to commit a crime, and corruption of minors, forming a criminal band . . . Serious offenses, seeing as how the second is considered a heinous crime. Know what that means, you shitass Rat? It means you're gonna spend the rest of your life behind bars just like your brothers that serve as guinea pigs in laboratories. The difference being that you won't be treated nowhere near as good as them. The researchers that're gonna take care of you will be your cellmates, and they won't be as gentle as the scientists in research labs. Because of the nature of your crimes I can take you straight from here to jail. Forget about paying bail and going back to drinking beer. Your crime is unbailable. Rat is what they call you and what you call yourself. You're gonna envy the rats that crawl over your body while you're sleeping . . . if you ever do manage to sleep."

That was the speech given by the policeman, who judging by his physique must belong to some shock troop. He accosted Rat at night on an abandoned street in Lapa, where no one was around for him to ask for help.

"What can we do for none of that to happen?" asked Rat in a small voice.

"No 'we.' Here you're the rat and I'm the cat. I'll expect you here tomorrow, at this same time, with 50 percent of what you made last month. Pay attention, I'm not demanding this or that amount, I'm demanding a percentage, 50 percent, half the money you took in last month—which will in fact be your *last* month if you try to screw me. If you got any doubts about the possibility of me making you into a lab rat, ask your partner and lawyer, who now that I think about it oughta be called Skunk."

Rat had no intention of returning the following night to give the cop half his earnings from the month before. But neither did he plan to go on hanging around Cinelândia or Lapa. He never had the calling to be a laboratory rat. The only solution was to disappear. Taking with him half the money collected in the last month—the other half Rat put in a thick brown envelope, taped it shut, and gave it to his partner—Rat became a fugitive, at least to his way of thinking. He wasn't wanted "dead or alive" by the police in the city, but the mere existence of that gorilla and his accomplices sufficed to make him vanish like smoke.

The next day, at dawn, it was still dark when he left his felt hat on the bench where he usually sat in Floriano Square in Cinelândia. A souvenir from Rat for those who remained.

The day had brightened by the time he left the Siqueira Campos subway station in Copacabana, the only district he knew as well as the downtown area, though he had no acquaintances there. Like a rat, he knew the geography of the district, not exactly its surface and its daytime inhabitants but the underground geography and some of its nocturnal dwellers. As a precaution and from fear of the cop and his team, he started moving solely in the actual underworld of Copacabana. His small stature and his skinniness facilitated his rapid disappearance and displacement in the rainwater networks of the Copacabana subsoil. To do this he had to rid himself of the suit and shoes—all that he took in his flight—and arrange for some secondhand clothing of a municipal worker. The next step was to rent a room in a fifth-rate boardinghouse on the Tabajaras slope. In reality, not a room but half a room divided down the middle by a sheet of plywood. In each half there was space for only a single bed and, underneath it, a small chest with a padlock for storing the tenant's clothes and belongings.

The plywood dividing the room didn't reach the ceiling, only the top of the door, where it forked, allowing entrance to the two halves of the room. But for someone who spent the early part of the day at the rainwater networks, that half a room was at least a one-star hotel.

Two months went by without news of the cop and his team. Rat figured that they must not operate in the South Zone. Fortunately, he had yet to be noticed by any of them. True, during the day he wore the overalls of a city worker. And his current fear was being stopped by some municipal car and being asked for his ID. He of course had no work papers from the city. Before he could arrange an identity, which would cost some money, he needed to enlarge his crew. He had two women who took care of him and he took care of them, the same setup as Cinelândia, and he also had some boys who brought in a bit of change from objects boosted from foreign tourists, objects that he passed along to fences. Two months' rent was paid in advance, and he didn't go hungry. *That's how Rat is*, he thought. The Chinese horoscope says that the rat always does well in the labyrinths of life. He didn't know if this was exactly what it said, but it was something like that.

One night when he had taken off the municipal overalls, showered, and put on his nocturnal suit, the two girls who already worked with him brought a third. Young like them. She had the look of someone experienced enough to have written on her face and body that this was no choir girl. She was of the same height as he, which was rare, a shapely body despite some signs of having been around the block a few times, eyes that were alert, expressive, and intelligent. When she spoke to him, her voice became melodious.

"Pleased to meet you, Mr. Rat," she said when she was introduced.

"My dear, anyone called Rat can't go by *Mister* or *Doctor* or *Sir*. Call me Rat. That's what everybody calls me. And you, what's your name?"

"Rita."

"Rita! Just think, Rita and Rat. Made for each other."

Rita smiled. Standing next to each other they looked like a brother-and-sister circus act: the same height, same physical type, same hair color, only their features showed no resemblance. Rita didn't have a ratlike face.

Four more months went by—six all told since he had left Cinelândia—and Rita never left Rat's side. She was observant, alert about those she approached, and possessed an intelligence that surprised Rat daily. Without his asking, Rita began to take care of him, not only emotionally but also physically, despite not having the stature of a bodyguard, though her two friends assured him that Rita knew tactics of attack and defense should they prove necessary.

Rat wanted Rita to become acquainted with downtown. He himself was beginning to miss the square, Lapa, the friends who had stayed behind without his having had time to say goodbye. The cop no doubt continued controlling the area; it was how he made money and maintained his tough-guy reputation. Rat was certain that if he were caught, one of two things would happen: either his body would be discovered floating in the Bay of Guanabara or he would wake up locked in a cell after spending the night in a hospital. One thing he was sure of: the cop wouldn't forget him, and he had a face easy to remember. Before risking his life by showing up in Cinelândia, it was best to get in contact with Japa to find out how things were.

On Wednesday night, good weather, nice temperature, he arrived in Lapa through the busiest street, in Rita's clothes and with light makeup to hide the shadow of his beard, wearing a feminine hat with a brim, prescription glasses, and sneakers. It wasn't enough to attract attention as a woman, but the important thing was not to attract attention as a man. He called Japa from the street. The phone rang until it disconnected automatically. He went to the bar he used to frequent and asked a waiter whom he knew where he could find Japa.

The waiter paused a bit before answering: "From what I hear, in the cemetery, Rat."

"Killed?"

"That's what they say."

"Who did it?"

"All I know is they killed him. How or who it was, I don't know."

"When was it?"

"Right after you disappeared. We thought that you too—"

"Make sure they go on thinking that." He gave the waiter a generous tip and went about disappearing from the area.

To avoid any risk of bumping into the cop, he walked to the Glória station instead of catching the subway in Cinelândia, only a block from where he was.

He arrived at the boardinghouse well before he expected. He removed Rita's dress and accessories, put on the city worker overalls, and waited for Rita to return, something that depended on luck and her ability of seduction in her work on Avenida Atlântica. He had learned over time to live with that conflict-laden waiting, and he began to understand why pimps frequently beat their women. It wasn't because they didn't like them, but because they did. These thoughts ran through his mind at the same time as the memories of Japa. A supercool guy, intelligent, a friend . . . The cop must have beaten Japa badly to find out where he was. And not even Rat himself would be able to say . . . He wasn't anywhere, or rather, he was in a non-place. That son-of-a-bitch cop had killed Japa. If Rat hadn't run away, though he had alerted his friend, the cop would have had no reason to do what he did. But an outlaw's life is like that. Rat was sure the cop had decreed an end to his own life on earth. From that day on, he could be killed without further notice.

Rita arrived while Rat was sleeping. He woke up and beat her without making a sound. He didn't want to wake up whoever was sleeping on the other side of the divider. And he also didn't want to hurt her. Rita asked him not to do that anymore. "It's not necessary," she said, "I'll stay with you as long as you want."

Shitty life. He had to leave the city. He had no way of hiding indefinitely. Anyone who had seen him even once would be able to pick him out of a crowd. He had to change cities or even states. The balance he had accumulated with Japa in the savings account, which was now solely his, should be enough to start over someplace where he didn't have to hide all day and go out only at night. He wasn't a bat, he thought, despite it being said that bats and rats were related. If that were true, at least he had gotten the good part; he didn't fly, but he also wasn't blind.

The next morning, after reconciling with Rita, he decided to go out to check the status of the bank account he had with Japa. The bank was on Rua do Catete, four stations beyond Siqueira Campos. He took a shower, put on a clean pressed suit, a dress shirt and tie, got his ID and bank card. He descended the Tabajaras slope as if on his way to pick up his car parked on Siqueira Campos but instead he entered the subway station, bought a round-trip ticket, and in a few minutes arrived at the Catete stop. Depending on the balance in the account, he would leave for São Paulo or Vitória. He couldn't say why one or the other. Maybe the size of the city, the number of people in the street, the behavior of the police . . .

"Yes sir?" said a guard at the turnstile, where bank customers received tickets to see a clerk.

"I want to check the balance in my savings account."

"For that you don't need a ticket, you can check it on the ATM. Any one that's unoccupied. Over there, in that row of ATMs. Just use your card."

He took the card from his pocket, checked the password on a small piece of paper kept in his wallet, and went to the first available machine. He chose the options that he wanted, typed in the two passwords requested by the machine, and removed the printed slip with the balance. He didn't immediately understand what it said. He ordered another printout, then went to look for the clerk who was helping customers and asked the meaning of what was printed on the yellow slip of paper.

"What is it you want to know?" asked the clerk.

"I want to know my balance."

The clerk took the paper and looked at it for several seconds, then said, "Your balance is zero, sir. Your savings account was closed."

"Zero? Closed? I never closed any account. Where did my money go?"

"You had best speak with the manager. I only help customers in the use of ATMs."

It was a ground-floor apartment in the rear, with windows that looked out only on a deteriorating wall two meters beyond the living room window. The apartment door had never been painted and the doorbell hung from the hole that should have housed it. At least it worked. At the second ring, a middle-aged woman opened the door halfway and hung onto the knob with one hand.

"Good evening, my name is Rita, I'm—"

"I know who you are," said the woman in an openly unfriendly manner. "Are you here for the booty or for your man?"

"Who are you?"

"Who are you, *ma'am*? I'm Rat's partner's sister. And I'll

repeat the question: are you here looking for the booty or for Rat?"

"Do you know where he is?"

"Of course. The same place he sent my brother to."

"He's in jail?"

"No. He's dead."

Silence. The two women were still at the threshold, one inside grasping the doorknob, the other outside, arms hanging loose at her side. No sound came from inside the apartment; an indistinct noise came from the street, as if it were far away.

"Dead?"

"Or disappeared, which is the same thing."

"And the other thing you asked if I came looking for?"

"The booty? You don't know what it is? It's what's stolen from the defeated, the product of illegal work, robbery. Or do you think what Rat did was legitimate work?"

"You said your brother and he were partners."

"My brother was a lawyer. What he did was get his man out of jail or keep him from getting arrested. Rat paid my brother for his work as a lawyer. They didn't do the same thing."

"I don't know your name."

"Zilda."

"I don't know why you're talking to me like this. And I didn't know your brother or you, ma'am. I came here because Rat said, in case of a problem, to look for his partner and gave me this address. I'm not here to fight or ask anybody for anything. I just want someone to tell me what they did with Rat."

"I already told you. Probably the same thing they did to my brother. Beat him to death, then throw his body in a hole somewhere."

Rita stared at Zilda without knowing what to say. She waited for the other woman to say or do something, but she just went on gripping the doorknob with both hands. Rita turned and left in the direction of the building's entrance.

Dead. With each passing day the word took on the most varied meanings. Some days it even meant its opposite, life, but this word too lost its value, coming to mean merely "not dead." Rita's head had not been nurtured enough with ideas capable of filling the emptiness she felt since Rat had disappeared. Zilda made no distinction between Rat's death and the death of her brother. They were cheap deaths, second-class deaths, devoid of ceremony or emotion. So poor that neither of the two bore a true name. One of them called himself Rat and the other was known as Japa.

Rita didn't know what to say, and she had difficulty figuring out how to express her feelings, as if for the privileged classes there were catalogs of sentiments, one for every situation, and she had no personal or literary references to orient her at such moments. So she didn't suffer, for fear of suffering the wrong way. Rat was her only reference in situations like this.

She walked away without knowing which way to go. Rat spoke a lot about Cinelândia, just as he spoke of the activity in Lapa. Rita didn't like Lapa, or didn't like Japa's sister who lived in Lapa, and she extrapolated her displeasure to the rest of the neighborhood that she hadn't even gotten to see properly. She asked someone the shortest route to Cinelândia and followed the instructions, hopeful of finding Rat or some trace of him. She wasn't wearing her "work" clothes and her petite size and absence of makeup made her look like a young woman recently out of adolescence and curious about adult life. She'd been told this was the busiest night in Lapa and its surrounding areas. But she wasn't interested in the liveliness of the place, she wanted only to be able to move in the midst of the crowd without being noticed. That was what Rat used to do. And because of this she couldn't understand how Rat had been caught. Ever since leaving Cinelândia he was extremely careful; besides which, he knew how to disguise himself. Even with his peculiar physical type and physiognomy he managed to pass unnoticed among people he had known for a long time. How could he have been caught? While she looked for the subway entrance, Rita tried to put herself in Rat's place and think as he would if he were caught.

To her, Rat would only be caught if he was the victim of a trap resulting from a tip-off. This was her first thought. He wouldn't be caught because of distraction. And who would be capable of setting that trap? He had no real friends, he didn't even socialize, he spoke only when necessary. Few knew of his life and habits. And even fewer could set a trap for him. The first such person, Rita had thought, was Japa, because he knew Rat intimately, in addition to being his business partner and lawyer. The second was Zilda, Japa's sister and caregiver, who had known Rat as long as her brother. The third was she herself, Rita, who lived with and slept with Rat but to whom Rat was still a mystery. And, finally, the two female friends who introduced her to Rat and were protected by him and knew where he lived. Those were the five people who could have set a trap for Rat or acted as informers for the police.

The first of the five to be eliminated was she herself, unless she was insane, and if she were insane she wouldn't be able to set a trap for an intelligent and shrewd guy like Rat, besides which she wouldn't be wasting her time trying to figure out who had set the trap. Rat's two friends and protégées could be at most snitches, but even so would lose out, plus were lacking the brains to set up a betrayal scheme with the police. That left Japa and his sister, the two closest both physically and historically. But Japa also would lose out; he lived on and supported his sister on the division of the income obtained through the scheme organized and maintained through Rat's activities; furthermore, the two had been close friends since adolescence, plus the fact that Japa was rarely sober, spending most of his days and nights inebriated. That meant it had to be Zilda. Caregiver for her alcoholic brother, resentful and angry, but she too had little to gain . . . unless the booty, which she had been the only one to mention, was a significant amount of money.

Disappearance and death were the same thing, according to Zilda. And she could know of Rat's disappearance by the simple fact of him not being seen in the district, but how could she know he had died? And if there was booty or money, who had the right to it? Finally, how could Zilda say, when she answered the door, that she knew who Rita was, if Rita had only come into his life two months *after* he'd left Cinelândia?

The train arrived at the Siqueira Campos station. The slope up Tabajaras was a bit steep, but Rita was so deep in her thoughts that she began the ascent as if walking on level ground. The fact is, she had already raised a few questions for which she'd found no answers, and before completing the climb she had decided to go back to Zilda's apartment to settle her remaining questions. Among them, Rat's money being withdrawn from the bank, the booty that Zilda had asked whether she had come for. And also, how did Zilda know who she was?

The next morning she left before dawn, hoping to catch Zilda still sleeping.

She had already lost Rat. She had nothing left to lose.

THE RETURN

BY MV BILL

Cidade de Deus

B y walkie-talkie Bolha passed the order along to his
managers: "Look alive there! It's one bundle for Sergeant Gonçalves's squad, two for Corporal Tenório,
and the fireworks only if you don't recognize the vehicle,
understand?"

He found it funny for the people down below to refer to
a raid as something positive. In the favela it was different. A
raid had never saved anybody's life. A police raid only sank
the guy even deeper. And sinking wasn't in Bolha's plans.
He'd gotten into trafficking through the front door, at the age
of fourteen, as successor to his older brother after seeing him
fall, never to rise again, his rifle clutched to his chest.

Since the time he was a kid, the older traffickers had
watched him carefully, as if seeing some potential in him.
They appreciated his fervor in kite battles and his ability with
guns. Years later, by then manager of a drug cartel, he was cruel
to adversaries and very good at bookkeeping. At eighteen,
he was already setting out to conquer other areas, always of
course within Cidade de Deus, his community of origin.

Bolha's charisma and courage reflected positively on the
dealings of the traffickers. Because of these talents there was
no opposition when he was nominated to assume the role of
head of the Cidade de Deus drug traffic. And the community fell in line. No one would dare object because Bolha gave

large amounts of money to the church, brought the beer to funk parties, underwrote medicine for the neediest families, and was generous in handing out Christmas presents. His motto was, *Take good care of the child of today, 'cause he'll be the soldier of tomorrow*. He assumed a regal posture, a benefactor of the favela. The dependable welfare-providing that he had learned so well from the old-time traffickers.

That Friday evening, things looked promising. The packaging was proceeding at full steam. Dozens of people were engaged in the task of cleaning and weighing the drugs on scales so they would be ready for retail sale during the late-night hours.

Friday nights in Cidade de Deus were famous the world over!

And as the hours went by, the favela boiled. To the sound of funk, half-naked women, playboys from street level, and junkies mingled in the narrow passageways, high on drugs, alcohol, and a permanent state of tension as if at any moment it could all fall apart.

In the face of such success, only one thing bothered Bolha: the decision of the Special Battalion to change the troops responsible for patrolling the favela, because the new cops, led by Sergeant Gonçalves, weren't into bribery and raids were becoming more and more frequent. And with them, the bloody gunfights and the losses represented by captured weapons and drugs.

To complicate matters, sources had dried up. His contacts in the barracks had been removed, so he was no longer getting advance word of which garrison was going to strike. Without that information it was impossible to make plans.

Bolha was lucky to be able to count on Representative Saci. Not only Bolha, but the country's entire trafficking circuit. Representative Saci had connections in Colombia and acted as middleman for a supply network of weapons and drugs. He said the guns came from FARC, the rebel army, but no one knew if that shit was true.

What was true was that Representative Saci was glib. A large, smiling guy always well dressed who wore nothing but linen. They said that in childhood he'd been in a car accident and had a fake leg. Bolha had never had the courage to ask, but he'd spent hours watching the representative's leg and had never seen any difference. *That shit must just be a rumor*, he thought. *Like that story about the guns he gets from FARC.*

Bolha didn't have time to complete the communication with the drug sites before he heard the rattle of the first burst of gunfire. With a rifle resting on the windowsill, a pistol in his hand, and his pockets filled with ammunition, Bolha assumed an alert position. He observed the confrontation outside through the scope on his AR-15. In ecstasy, he watched one of his soldiers, a skinny teenager, discharge all his rifle's ammo into a military policeman. The pride he felt! One less worm in the world.

Losing no time, Bolha went up to the roof and braced himself against the water tank; framed in the crosshairs of his rifle was the head of a cop shielding himself behind a post. Fun to see the guy's head explode and stain the air red—two thousand meters in one second! Bolha remembered the words of Representative Saci when he sold him that marvel. What a beauty. Those FARC guys really know how to live.

But his joy was short-lived.

Amid the adrenaline of the moment and the elegance of the headless body writhing on the ground, Bolha saw his soldiers in flight, running toward the interior of the favela. Those still carrying weapons shot into the air at random, disoriented. The majority simply fled in panic and dropped their guns on the ground, as if trying to avoid being caught red-handed. The police came behind, collecting the treasures abandoned in the middle of the road. Considerable battle reinforcement for the predators' next invasion.

Fuck! Bolha thought. *I'm on my own in this shit!*

For some time he had known it was problematic not to have the payoff to the police on his books anymore. Suicide to go on operating in the favela without a contact inside the Battalion. And just as one thought leads to another, Bolha was surprised when he descended from the roof and, out of nowhere, found himself facing Representative Saci.

"What you doing here, congressman?"

"The civil police called me and said you needed help," replied the representative, trying to be heard above the sound of gunshots. "But I didn't know there was an operation here in Cidade de Deus. The entire police force is out there, Bolha!"

"I know that!" said Bolha, confused. He paced back and forth, not knowing what to do.

"You need reinforcements."

"Yeah. I don't know how many are still with me . . . My security men were all out there in front," explained the trafficker. "I seen lots of my men running away, terrified. I don't know nothing no more."

"How much do you have to lose now?"

"Now? Beats me. Maybe some—"

Before he could complete the calculation, the representative's body shook. His eyes widened and he raised his hands to his chest, where a huge stain was turning his shirt red.

"Shit, I've been shot, Bolha!" Saci shouted. "Get me out of here!"

The favela was now completely surrounded by police. Getting the representative out was the same as surrendering. Bolha tried to think of an escape, but it was difficult to find any trace of lucidity in his brain.

"My car . . . my car," stammered the representative. "They won't suspect my car."

Bolha had seen thousands of people die. And the enormous amount of blood spurting from the representative's chest left no doubt: he wouldn't last long. An hour at most.

The problem was that his death created a major difficulty for Bolha, not only because he was a public figure, but also because the representative was much loved in the world of trafficking. If in any way his death were to be linked to Cidade de Deus, everyone would be after Bolha's head. Even the militias, if he screwed up. Saci provided the best representation of the underworld in the government. No one would forgive Bolha for it.

"Stay calm, congressman," said Bolha, "I'm gonna get us out of the favela."

Finding strength from God knows where, Bolha lifted Saci onto his shoulders and carried him to the car, braving the crossfire. The favela was in tumult. Not a soul in the streets. Everyone huddled in some corner, fleeing the death that rampaged there.

Bolha opened the trunk, placed the representative inside, and promised to do his best to help him, though he knew that even his best would not be enough.

"Look, whatever happens—" Saci was out of breath and couldn't finish.

When someone says "whatever happens" it's because something is surely going to happen. Almost always something bad. Bolha needed to get Saci out of there as soon as possible; after all, who would be aware of his death in Cidade de Deus? Some innocent person, no doubt. For a screw-up that wasn't going anywhere, this had already gone too far.

Bolha shut the trunk, got in the car, and drove off aimlessly. By then a hospital wouldn't do any good. Bolha knew that what he carried in the trunk was now a corpse.

In the humid night, Bolha wiped his forehead to dry the sweat. He went through Barra, Recreio, and only in Grumari did he find what he was looking for: a vacant lot covered with brush. No houses nearby, no signs of civilization. The perfect spot to dump a body.

Bolha left his headlights on low and moved around to the trunk of the car. He had seen thousands of corpses in his lifetime, but the body of the representative all twisted inside there made him shudder. With great difficulty he managed to pull it by the legs and get half the cadaver out of the trunk.

Then something startling happened.

The right leg simply detached from the representative's body. Bolha fell backward with the leg in his hands, while the rest of the body lay there in the trunk.

"Ugh!" Bolha clenched his teeth and felt bile rise in his esophagus, or his stomach, one of the two. He didn't vomit because he was a badass dude. But after fifteen seconds of panic, he understood: Saci really did have an artificial leg.

Bolha examined the plastic leg he held; he had never seen one before. And, his eyes wide with surprise, he noticed there was a card stuck in the hollow of the leg. Bolha used his fingernail to remove the tape and tossed the leg into the undergrowth. It was a white magnetic card, resembling a credit card, except instead of a chip it had a bar code and the inscription H.L.S.201. Bolha lowered his head and closed his eyes. He was facing an enigma, he knew, but without the slightest idea of how to decipher it. Bolha couldn't waste any more time. He urgently needed to get rid of the representative's body and decide what to do with his own life. He couldn't go back to Cidade de Deus. Not in this condition, poor and discredited. He needed a miracle, some kind of grand idea. That was what he had to concentrate on.

So, without time for the mystery at that moment, Bolha stuck the card in his pocket and went about dumping the body. He would do what must be done. He checked the representative's pockets, took the dead man's watch, gold chain, and wallet. Four hundred and thirty-seven *reais* and some change.

As for the documents, he didn't know whether to leave them or not. Someone might come along before the police and steal them. But who would show up there in the middle of nowhere?

Uncertain, he decided to leave the representative's ID. The other documents, he opted to take with him.

He put his hands under the dead man's armpits and dragged him to a tree. He took the trouble to place the fake leg back into the linen trousers so that when the press arrived they wouldn't photograph the representative missing a leg. As vain as the man was, he would have been embarrassed. Afterward, Bolha said a prayer he made up on the spot and when he felt there was nothing more to be done, he got in the car and drove far away to take care of the second part of his mission: getting rid of Saci's automobile.

Bolha checked the time on the representative's watch, almost three a.m. He felt it was an excellent time to park the car at the beach at Recreio and contemplate the sea. He felt almost relieved after dumping the body, but he couldn't stop thinking about the card he had discovered inside the fake leg. It must have some value, some important meaning, because no one would hide anything like that on his person if it didn't.

H.L.S.201. Bolha took the card from his jeans pocket and reread the inscription, racking his brain for an explanation. All he remembered was a crime film he had seen with his older brother the one time he had ever gone to the movies. At thirty-two, Bolha hardly noticed the years passing. Pressure, fear, and rebellion occupied his mind, leaving no time for joy and amusement. Except those connected to trafficking: women, funk parties, and drugs.

When the sun began to rise, Bolha took a dip in the ocean. It had been years since he'd last gone to the beach. He had forgotten the strength of the waves and how the saltwater stung the eyes. He would have stayed there longer if the day hadn't brightened, bringing the first kiosk workers and the first society types strolling with their poodles on the sidewalk.

Bolha drove to a shopping center in Barra and abandoned the car in the parking lot. Then he stopped at a newsstand and joined the group of workers reading the headlines while waiting for the bus. "Under Heavy Fire, Police Retake Cidade de Deus" was the headline of a leading paper. Another, more provocative, said: "Drug Trade Driven Out of Cidade de Deus."

It hurt to read that.

But although the papers mentioned his name, none carried his photo. The closest was an artist's sketch so badly done that it elicited laughter from Bolha. He thought the drawing more closely resembled a well-known footballer than him. *What a farce*, he thought, with a mixture of triumph and disquiet.

But if the safety of anonymity calmed him, there was nothing encouraging about being driven from his own community in humiliation. Shit, he had done so much for Cidade de Deus, been so cautious, so careful to make sure the bloody battles took place far from the eyes of the media, and now he couldn't even return home. From boss of the drug traffic he had been reduced to a homeless nobody. All he had was 437 *reais*, the congressman's belongings, and that white magnetic card whose use he had yet to figure out.

Without guns, money, and prestige he was just like everybody else. And he no longer had a partner he could trust. With the death of Saci, everyone would be after his head. That was a fact.

Lacking any real plan, Bolha entered a store and bought some new clothes. As a safety measure he also bought a hat. He liked seeing pagoda singers on television wearing Panama hats. For a brief moment he found it cool to be a free man and able to wear whatever hat he wanted. But the mystery of the white card and *H.L.S.201* came back into his mind like restless ghosts.

That was when he spotted an Internet café and had an idea.

"How much time do you want?" asked the girl behind the counter, indifferently, engrossed in her cell phone.

"An hour," he replied.

"Three *reais*."

Bolha didn't hesitate. On the Internet he would surely make some progress. He sat erect in the chair, put on the earphones, and began his search with the same tenacity that James Bond had displayed in the film he'd seen.

First he tried *H.L.S.201*, then *201H.L.S.*, with spaces, without spaces, with periods, without periods . . . It was only when he tried *H.L.S.* by itself that things became clear.

HOTEL LAVRADIO STAR came up as the first search result.

"Of course!" Bolha said aloud. "Hotel Lavradio, room 201. That's it."

What Bolha held was the key to a hotel room—of that he had no doubt. His hands shaking at the magnitude of the discovery, he jotted down the address and left, with the card in his pocket and the unshakable idea in his head: he was going to find out what Saci had kept so hidden in his fake leg, even if it cost Bolha his own life.

Despite a traffic jam, it wasn't too difficult to get downtown. The Hotel Lavradio Star was located on a square, though on Rua Constituição, not Lavradio.

Unnoticed, Bolha entered the hotel forthrightly as if he were any other guest. He nodded at the receptionist, but she kept her eyes on the computer. The security men also ignored him, and Bolha continued confidently to the wooden staircase. He knew that any tentativeness could cost him his life—or worse, his freedom, locked up in one of those maximum-security prisons in Mato Grosso.

On the second floor, he saw that 201 was at the end of the corridor, but before heading that way he noted the locks on the other doors. He saw exactly how to insert the card to open them.

And did so.

At the end of the corridor, standing before 201, he inserted the magnetic card in the slot and a small green light came on. Bolha smiled to himself. It had never been so easy. He looked to both sides, making sure no one was around. Then, feeling his body pouring liters of adrenaline into his bloodstream, he carefully turned the doorknob.

The grandeur of what he saw dazzled his eyes.

Bolha lost his breath.

He opened and closed his eyes.

His mouth agape, he succeeded in getting a bit of air into his lungs and exclaimed to himself, *Thank you, Saint George!*

It was the representative's private arsenal. Guns, ammunition, and explosives of every kind. It was impossible to quantify at first sight, but with a quick glance he took in what the congressman kept there, in a third-rate hotel room: veritable treasures. Machine guns, shotguns, rifles, pistols, carbines, M16s, AK-47s, ParaFal 7.62mm assault rifles.

Bolha laughed.

Bolha knelt.

He guffawed with happiness.

With this arsenal, the only way Cidade de Deus wouldn't be his was if he didn't want it.

WEEKEND IN SÃO CONRADO

BY LUIZ EDUARDO SOARES

São Conrado

Nine o'clock Saturday morning, August 20, 2010. The earth shakes in São Conrado, a sophisticated district of Rio de Janeiro, where Rocinha, the largest favela in Latin America, is located. Perhaps it would be more accurate to put it the opposite way: the earth shakes around Rocinha, at whose edges cluster sophisticated buildings and elegant mansions. Burning tires force the closing of the tunnels. Panicked drivers abandon their cars on the Lagoa-Barra freeway. Fleeing gangs brandish military weapons. Helicopters fly over the international hotel and withdraw toward the ocean, regrouping for another run over the area in flames. Sunbathers seek shelter. Pedestrians drop to the ground. Traffic on the freeway, always slow, is now a kind of motionless apocalypse. Seen from the air, the community suggests a large-scale art installation, a critic's intervention in the city's routine, dramatizing the degradation of urban life.

Eight o'clock in the morning. Without knowing what awaits him, Otto Mursa tries to relax and concentrate on the green floor tiles in the small space that the condo's exercise room allows the acupuncturist to use. He stares at the more or less subtle color variations, inspects the granulated undulations, counts the dark streaks on the right side, the abundant gray on the left, adds one to the other, divides by the number of sessions already paid for, and multiplies by the cost of each one. He tries to ignore the nervous itch at the tip of his nose and contemplates his modest salary as a civil police inspector in the state of Rio de Janeiro. His health is good, but his back is a recurring martyrdom of a herniated disk and other older problems with his spine. The legacy of sports. Lying prone on the table, his face buried in the anatomical opening, his back punctured by twenty-four needles, he feels like a slaughtered animal being marinated for a barbecue.

Every week, in his white lab coat, Ecio Nakano welcomes Otto. Methodically, he repeats the same liturgy: questions, examination, and a prolonged taking of the pulse. He identifies the points with extreme precision, from head to toe, and places the needles in two movements, the pinch and the light blow that seats them deeper. The ritual is not a pleasant one, but the effects are startling. Nakano quickly leaves the room while the patient, in semidarkness, absorbs the energy of the needles, soothed by the hypnotic arpeggios of sitars, intoxicated from the wafts of incense.

Strictly speaking, Otto shouldn't be there. The condo has only authorized access to the exercise room and physiotherapy to residents. Luckily, the São Conrado apartment had gone to his girlfriend in the division of property with her ex-husband. Friday nights last into the late hours and the morning therapy makes up for the excesses. And serves as his alibi. It's enough to wander down to the playground like any other owner, a towel over his shoulder, newspaper under his arm, slippers and a blasé air, the mark of class and distinction. No one would question his presence or find odd the pochette clipped to his Bermudas or the pocket bulging with his cell phone. Accoutrements of the rich aren't kitsch, they're exotic, personality traits. The address automatically promotes Otto Mursa to a status not his own, one to which he has never aspired. Futility isn't his thing. Just the opposite: mixing with the elite makes him queasy.

Situated between the largest favela in Latin America and Barra da Tijuca, the tacky homeland of the nouveau riche, São Conrado is a valley with a few kilometers of beach, one or two rows of buildings, and a freeway that cuts the district from end to end and divides the two sides, sea and mountain. Houses and mansions ascend Tijuca Forest to the summit. At the far extreme from the vertical clamor of Rocinha stands the Gávea stone, solemn and silent. In the middle of the route, cutting across the landscape, the golf club—exclusive, aristocratic. Seen from above, one would say the district serves as its frame and adornment. The Global Golf Club isn't situated inside the neighborhood; rather, the neighborhood marks its outline.

It is 8:09. Otto is there, hovering between sleep and tension, exorcizing the bothersome expectation that his nose is going to itch, that a sneeze is inevitable, that something is going to make his survival totally irreconcilable with this ridiculous position. He imagines himself a porcupine, paralyzed by some kind of moral blackmail only intelligible to the mind of a porcupine. He goes back to staring at the green floor, the dark stripes. At 8:10, rifle fire shakes body and soul, table and floor. More than that. The reports explode close enough to make the building vibrate. The walls seem to tremble. The needles shock as if electrified. In Otto's mind, two instincts fight for command: the provoked cop and the pierced patient. Antagonistic mental forces launch him upward and downward at the same time, calling him to action and forcing him to immobility. He rises to his knees on the table and shouts for Nakano. He pulls out the accessible needles but feels others burying themselves in his flesh when he moves.

The acupuncturist turns on the light and orders him to

wait. The gunfire comes closer and closer. Now cries can be heard. Even though he's accustomed to the confrontations that have become routine in Rio de Janeiro, Otto is on the verge of losing control. The war is out of synch. Saturday mornings there are children running around everywhere. His stepdaughter Rafaela, who is seven, went out early to play. Otto takes the pistol from his pochette, slips on his Bermudas, and dashes barefooted to the stairs. As he reaches the last steps, the sound of gunfire continues, deafening. Otto is familiar with this experience: it feels like the shots are vibrating in his body and echoing inside his skull. The policeman creeps from the stairway to the reception area. Doormen and attendants have taken refuge behind anything that acts as a shield. Breathing raggedly, they remain on the floor, some minutes after the final burst of bullets. They ask one another if the criminals have left. Otto is the only one standing, his eyes sweeping the immediate surroundings, gun in hand, his carotid artery throbbing, sweat burning his eyes, his mouth dry.

The space between the buildings of the condominium is silent; men, women, and children are too frightened to yell. They don't want to draw attention. Here and there whirling dust is visible, probably heated by fragments of gunpowder. Bullet casings everywhere. The walls of the buildings are perforated, windows shattered. A few cars parked beside the entrance gate have suffered major damage. No one is wounded. A near miracle considering the number of shots. Otto finds Rafaela and two friends hugging each other on the grass, beside overturned bicycles, behind the walnut trees that separate the tennis courts and the pools. He breathes, relaxing at last. He feels like crying with them and hugs them. Slowly, his blood pressure returns to a tolerable level. He needs to reassure Francisca.

"Run home, Rafa, tell your mother everything's all right. You too." The girl hates it when she's called Rafa, because it's a man's name, she says, but this time she doesn't censure her stepfather. All her neurons are concentrated on her rebirth and jumping into her mother's arms.

Doormen and residents begin to move about, haltingly. They shout words of comfort to one another, speaking non-stop, repeating in unison what they all witnessed as if relating for the first time an unlikely story to an incredulous and amazed audience: the flight of the criminal army that crossed the condo toward Rocinha, firing their rifles behind them, indifferent to both residents and circumstances.

Nervous chatter and the sudden sound of children crying announce the end of the scene of terror, whose meaning is soon explained in the tangle of recounting. Francisca has come down in the elevator with a few neighbors and reaches out to Rafa as soon as she sees her daughter running toward her.

Little by little, heads cautiously appear in the windows of the twenty-story towers. Otto identifies himself. He recommends that everyone go back to their apartments and stay away from the windows. He instructs the condo workers to return to the inside areas and check the security camera tapes. He calls Harley: "Sorry, man, you must've been sleeping since your shift was yesterday, but this looks like a dress rehearsal for the end of the world and it doesn't smell good at all."

The cops in the area, both civil and military, have to be alerted immediately. Detective Harley Davidson da Silva is his only childhood friend who's neither in prison, dead, nor on the take.

What the doormen whisper among themselves, inhabitants of working-class districts and favelas, including Rocinha, is obvious: the police have tried to increase the "bundle"—the bribe paid by the drug traffickers to be left alone. Since the boss trafficker refused, the cops involved in the negotiation decided to do something unprecedented: "Hit head-on the packed streetcar coming back from Vidigal." The phrase, from one of the workers interrogated by Otto, meant the following: late every Saturday night, or early the next morning, the ringleaders of the Rocinha drug trade would come home after spending the evening at the dance sponsored by their partners in the Vidigal favela, situated between Leblon and São Conrado. The Rocinha traffickers customarily traveled together, in two or three vans, armed with rifles and grenades to discourage any repressive intervention; the precautions were not actually very rigorous given that the route, the date, and the approximate schedule were widely known. That morning, frustrated by the refusal to increase the size of the bribe, the police decided to scare the traffickers, without any actual intention of carrying out arrests. They didn't want to overwhelm the predictable armed resistance, because that would necessitate greater support than was available and involve risks they were unwilling to take. They had waited for the traffickers' vans at a street corner near the condo and staged an initial confrontation which they did not follow up on, content with the dispersal they'd incited. The ambush, if for real, would never have taken place on a sunny Saturday morning, in an upper-middle-class neighborhood, amid dozens of women and children. As outlined in the script of the farce, the traffickers fled and the police withdrew. It was enough; the message had been sent. If the new amount wasn't accepted, the traffickers would have problems.

Internal communication among the various doormen in the condominium and the narrative of pedestrians seeking shelter in enclosed spots paints the picture that a call from Harley Davidson da Silva confirms: police reinforcements have no way of getting there because the traffickers have shut down the tunnels connecting São Conrado and neighboring districts. They have also blocked alternative routes via Tijuca Forest and the oceanfront. By the time the first shock troops manage to break through, the traffickers' leader and his henchmen will have escaped. Everything indicates that avoiding arrest is the sole motive for his acts. The subsequent sequence of events will confirm the hypothesis. The tunnels remain blocked, police troops are slow to clear the roadway and get to São Conrado, traffic is interrupted, and drivers abandon their vehicles on the freeway.

Abandoned cars, people in flight—everything conspires to increase the climate of terror that sweeps through the district. Radio stations interrupt their regular broadcasts to announce that their reporters are unable to get to São Conrado and that the police so far have nothing to say. They interview residents by telephone. The frantic tone of the live statements does nothing to calm spirits. What Otto knows at the moment is that traffickers coming from Vidigal to Rocinha were ambushed by police and escaped, splitting up. One group, which included the leader, ran toward Rocinha, cutting through the condominium and crossing the freeway. Another group fled in the opposite direction, probably to confuse the police, making the leader's escape easier. That was the group that invaded the international hotel, located between the condo and a shopping center, and took some of the guests hostage. The sequence of events suggests that the intent was to concentrate the cops' efforts on hostage negotiations until the leader was far away, and safe. The police broke through the barricade of burning tires and had no problem obtaining the surrender of the men who invaded the hotel. They gave up without resistance, sacrificing themselves for their boss. They had accomplished their mission. The next day, the attack on a five-star hotel full of foreign tourists, in the rich and cosmopolitan heart of Rio de Janeiro, would be a worldwide headline in the media. The violent and provincial Rio was winning one more battle against the symbolic construction for the coming Olympics, the pole of business and entertainment.

Otto returns to the acupuncture room, dons his T-shirt, puts on his sandals, goes up to Francisca's apartment to make sure she and Rafa are okay, and cancels the plans for Saturday— the beach, feijoada, children's theater at the shopping center, and a frugal night of films on TV. It is impossible to guess when he will be back. Even though it's his day off, he considers it his duty to assist his colleagues in the actions still in progress at the hotel. He says this to his girlfriend. What he doesn't say is more important. He will take advantage of the meeting with the cops to gather information about that irresponsible ambush. What unit of the military police could have done that? Who was in command? The correct adjective that occurs to him is not *irresponsible*. He has no words to describe an ambush that could have resulted in the death of dozens of innocent people including children, including Rafa. He adores the little girl, *but that doesn't matter*, he thinks. The action of the police was criminal, even if the motivation had been just. The doorman didn't believe in the virtue of the motivation. Nor does he. Otto knows police institutions very well, both the military and his own, the civil. He has experienced intensely the lacerating anguish of being and not being part of a corps that degrades itself day by day, spilling into the gutter the blood that so many honorable professionals shed in the line of duty. After all, his father's heroic death could not have been in vain. If the institutions of the police and his work stop making sense, what will remain of the memory of Elton Mursa? Will Elton be remembered as a fool who believed in the illusion of the democratic rule of law? A poor naïve fool who took pride in his office, whose mandate he always had at the tip of his tongue: to guarantee the rights of citizens, by performing a public service of the utmost necessity? A deceived democrat, resigned to his humiliating salary, who refused bribes and rejected the usual patterns of police brutality? Elton was black, militantly antiracist, and Otto insisted on identifying himself as black despite his light skin inherited from his mother's side of the family. He knew, however, that his appearance was a passport for circulating freely in places frequented by the middle class and the elite of Rio de Janeiro. His father taught him from an early age how cunning and perverse Brazilian racism was.

At the hotel, he doesn't discover much. Everyone is occupied freeing the hostages and avoiding a tragedy. He learns that a young woman did in fact die in the exchange of gunfire. She was said to be part of the criminal gang. Even so, the news is no less deplorable. Just the opposite—the fact only increases the burden of guilt for whoever conceived and carried out the ambush. Two questions are in the air: why did the police act that way, and why didn't they take measures to arrest the traffickers, especially the leader, if the date, the time, and the route were common knowledge and repeated weekly? It seems obvious that the doormen's interpretation is the only reasonable one, although the authorities, playing out their melancholy role, talk about an unexpected and surprise encounter between the traffickers' vans and the military police patrol. In the first official statement the police spokesman had mentioned an ambush. The repercussion was so negative that he disappeared, taking the original explanation with him, which was quickly replaced by the fable of the accidental encounter.

The farce mixes the worst in the police force and its promiscuous relationship with politics: extreme irresponsibility toward the suffering of people and blatant corruption. All of that in contrast with the bigwigs' rhetoric that covers up police misconduct under the pretext that it is necessary to preserve the image of the institution, even if those to blame are investigated and punished, as if there were any real image to protect and as if punishment of the guilty individuals ended the moral epidemic. Contemplating the circus put together for the media, Otto's blood boils. He looks upon the sham as a personal insult.

"Harley, wake up, man, and come over here. This shit can't end like this."

His partner is more phlegmatic than Captain Nemo and as refined as David Niven in the role of ambassador of the British Empire. He is black, tall, and thin. The two friends plan to celebrate their fortieth birthday together. Their having been born on the same day meant something. The two were the target of homophobic jokes at the precinct. The relationship was symbiotic, yes, but Otto had never felt himself attracted to men, nor was he disturbed by the preferences of Harley, who knew very clearly how to keep work and love life separate.

"Otto, out of respect for you, for decades of friendship, my father's esteem for your father, the marvelous Saturday that spreads its wings over us, and last but not least in honor of a dear friend with whom I share a glorious breakfast, I'll leave out the curse words. Is that enough, or you want some more?"

Otto is the most practical of men: "You have no idea, man.

You at home or in a motel? If you're at home, turn on the TV. My cell phone will be waiting for your call. Turn on the TV."

Harley replies patiently: "You and me are assigned to Del Castilho. Our precinct doesn't have jurisdiction to act in São Conrado. Besides which, noble colleague, our precinct belongs to a district, not a specialization. Kidnapping isn't something we deal with. Neither is drug trafficking. Did you get the chief's okay? Does the Cyrano de Bergerac of the Rio suburbs, the venerable Mr. Costinha, know that the restless spirit of Inspector Otto is contemplating sticking his nose where it shouldn't go?"

Otto cuts the conversation short: "Turn on the TV. I'm waiting for you."

Two o'clock. On the Rocinha hillside peace reigns. Seen from up there, the pacific panorama would suggest that nothing happened. But the community is still shaken up. Tension fills the air, vying with the dueling kites, amid the antennae and the tangle of wires diverting unmetered electricity.

Otto and Harley are leaning against the low wall on the terrace at the home of Hamilton, a courageous Northeasterner brought up in the community. In the local vocabulary, the small platform jutting out over the abyss is called a slab and sticks out from the house like so many other ingenious add-ons, work of the labyrinthine architecture nurtured by the ingenuity of the people. There the baroque is not a style but the involuntary result of maximizing the use of space. The three men share a beer and recall the afternoons of soccer from their adolescence. Hamilton does freight work—that is, he transports whatever will fit in his old VW station wagon. He knows the favela from one end to the other. He gets along with all types of people, including the owners of the hillside, the traffickers. As is inevitable, he also knows who's who among the police, because the payment of bribes and the agreements take place in the light of day. The "bundle," the agreement between traffickers and cops, has become institutionalized as part of the collective imagination, part of Rio tradition, as honorable as the illegal and ubiquitous lottery known as the "animal game." Hamilton has found that adaptability is necessary to survive. Among his virtues, discretion is foremost. "Anybody who blabs ends up with ants coming out of his mouth, pushing up daisies, in the grave." No sin is more serious and dangerous than informing. Therefore, being an informant—X9, in the common parlance—is fatal. There is no accusation more damning. An X9 works for the police, infiltrating the suspects. Once identified, he is summarily condemned to death by the traffickers. But it's no different on the other side. If someone without backing—read poor, an inhabitant of the outskirts or a favela—denounces a policeman, he runs the risk of being executed. So prudence and the instinct of self-preservation demand obsequious silence. The rule of the favela can be summed up thus: *No one saw, heard, or knows anything about anything whatsoever.*

Harley and Otto have never gotten involved with informants. Besides being likely targets of violence, they seem drawn by a moral curse that contaminates everyone around them. When a cop pays an X9 and benefits from his information, deep down he reviles the individual serving him. In addition, he considers him unreliable, a potential double agent. Everything happens as if betrayal is an addiction, a sick and irresistible obsession. Otto and Harley prefer to keep their distance from those actors so frequently found in the police universe. Therefore, whenever they need information they contact people proven to be reliable, with whom they enjoy sufficient credibility to share what they know. Friends of that kind, especially those knowledgeable about territories in conflict, represent an extraordinary asset to investigators. Yet it's also important not to overdo it, because the feeling of being used is discomfiting. They fear losing precious sources by going too far. And they demonstrate absolute loyalty at every opportunity.

Hamilton is one of those partners. As Otto and Harley are not known in Rocinha, they see no problem in going to their friend's residence. Before asking the question that brought them to visit him, they talk about their respective families and soccer, the lingua franca among Brazilians.

After the second bottle, they are not spared their host's bitterness: "When safety in the neighborhood becomes a headline, the government's reaction is only a matter of time, and it's the favela that pays the price. Armed invasion is usually the political response to the media's complaints. And in a raid, when the walls are fragile and the weapons military-grade, no one is safe, not even inside their homes."

Otto agrees, adding, "If such an operation occurred even once in an upper-class part of the city, everybody would be out of a job: the secretary of public safety, the chief of the military police, the head of the civil police, even the governor."

The elder Mursa would repeat the same phrase at the dinner table. He didn't raise his son to be a policeman. Despite his love of the institution, he eventually yielded to skepticism. He hoped that the end of the dictatorship and the new constitution in 1988 would change the police, the mind-set, the approaches, priorities, and practices. He died frustrated, a decade later, assassinated by criminals in revenge for extralegal executions. A tragic irony. There had been no one more radical than Elton Mursa in his opposition to police brutality.

Otto inherited that skepticism and never fully overcame the desire for vengeance, whether against the murderers of his father or the fellow officers who acted like criminals and ended up provoking Elton's death.

Harley asks Hamilton if he has any idea what happened, and he relates the same account that Otto has heard from the doormen that morning. To remove any doubt, he says he heard the explanation from one of the leaders of the drug trade. The VW van was stuck in the jam and there was a delivery to be made. He saw the guy go by with a heavily armed group and asked if the lane would be clear soon. That was when he heard the story, though hurriedly and without details. The cop who jacked up the bribe and led the fake ambush was a corporal well known in Rocinha, one Vito Florada, a.k.a. Mindinho, with a record that would be the envy of the most perverse killer. He ran a militia famous for violence in a favela in the West Zone. Rocinha being virtually a sideline for Mindinho. He made a lot more money through his militia, extorting merchants. Rocinha interested him only for the contacts it provided.

They continue the conversation in order to enjoy the scenery and reduce the impression of a professional call, but they already have what they came for.

Otto's phone vibrates and he descends to a lower level to answer privately. The name *Francisca* shows on the screen.

"I can't take it anymore. I've had it. You should see Rafa. It hurts. I don't want to stay here any longer. No one can live like this. She doesn't want to go to the theater, or go out to play, she says she's not going back to school. I'm going to sell this apartment even though I know this isn't the right time to do it. Who's going to buy a place in the middle of a cross fire? Last year it was one faction against another that was trying to invade Rocinha. Shooting everywhere, we were crawling around inside our home. I'll sell for whatever they pay, Otto. I'll take what I can get and leave. I confess that if I could I'd leave Rio. That's what I wanted. But there's my job, Rafaela, I can't do just anything that comes into my head. The thing to do is look for a place that's calmer, an area with no favela, without gun battles. A decent place to live and raise my daughter."

Otto says she shouldn't make any hasty decisions, that the violent episodes are isolated events, that she and Rafa are right to feel bad, but it won't be long before things return to normal. Francisca doesn't like her boyfriend's paternal tone and thinks he underestimates her intelligence and the gravity of what happened, because he doesn't want to admit that the police have failed in Rio and that the work to which he dedicates himself no longer makes sense.

"You should be here with me if you're trying to be useful. Don't give me that idiocy that you're doing your duty and thinking about the overall good. You're thinking about yourself. For a change."

Otto returns heavier than when he descended. He isn't dazzled by the sea, the mountains, the blue sky dotted with hang gliders. He refuses another glass of beer and says goodbye to Hamilton. The two cops descend via the main artery of the community, dodging the dozens of scooters and mototaxis.

Harley notices his change of mood: "What's eating you?"

"Francisca's not okay. She wants to leave the area, sell the apartment right now, when prices are bottoming out, when everybody's doing the same thing. She's willing to get rid of the property for a pittance. At least that's what she says. I don't know if it's just drama, or blackmail for me to feel guilty and give up the job and come home. She's hysterical."

"Not without cause, Otto. You really should go home, stay with her and Rafa. Let me . . ."

Otto doesn't reply but looks at Harley the way he looks at Harley when he's deeply irritated.

They continue in silence down the hillside. Harley is convinced it's worthwhile to butt in where they're not invited, despite the risks. He shares with Otto repugnance for what is happening in both police forces, military and civil. He agrees about the need to act, even if it's the last thing they do before being demoted to desk duty or resigning.

"Either we change this shit or everything's going to hell."

"You're right, my man, those machines of death will grind us up and destroy everything we think we are until nothing's left—not memory, not desire."

They decide to carry out a clandestine investigation in parallel with the Internal Affairs investigation, in which they have no confidence. If they obtain proof, they will give it to a serious and respected journalist, Harley's former boyfriend, and the scandal of police corruption, putting children's lives at risk in the heart of touristic Rio de Janeiro, affecting the international image of the city, will lead to a transformation of some kind. Maybe not. Other scandals have exploded without producing changes. In any case, it would be a step. Probably enough for the two friends to postpone leaving the force. They like so much what they do that they can't imagine themselves in a different profession. And the dream of a police force deserving of the work is worth the trouble.

"At least as homage to the dear departed Elton," says Harley.

"At least as homage to the old man," murmurs Otto.

"Next step?"

"To get the most information possible about Mindinho."

"I know that, Otto. The question is how to go about getting the maximum possible information on Corporal Vito Florada of the Military Police on a sunny Saturday at three in the afternoon."

"Torturra."

"Who's Torturra?"

"What do you mean, *Who's Torturra?* The congressman. Torturra."

"Ângelo Torturra?"

"Is there another member of the Chamber of Deputies with that surname?"

"I can just imagine what Francisca goes through with you. You're not easy to put up with. I had no idea you were on such good terms with the congressman that you could interrupt his family's privacy on a weekend. I'd be embarrassed if I were you. However much he might have given me the okay to call him, I'd be super embarrassed."

"I'm not going to feel the slightest embarrassment."

"Why?"

"Because I'm not going to look for the guy."

"No?"

"Negative."

"Otto, didn't you just say the next step would be to go to the congressman?"

"Yes."

"Then how can you say you're not going to look for the man?"

"I'm not. *You* are."

"You're crazy, Otto. I'm not going, period."

"While you're at his house, I'll find out who's heading up the team that handled the crime scene investigation this morning. I want to find out if there's anything fishy about the story. It's too perfect. Everything fits together too well."

"You're right about that. I have the same feeling. Something's wrong when everything fits together so neatly. The challenge is to find out what's missing, what was left out that we didn't notice."

"Or what's left over, the residual, the excess. In this case, I would bet on excess, Harley. There are too many things fitting together and fitting together too easily and too quickly."

"The incident itself was excessive, Otto. You're right. I get the feeling there's something there."

"True. Excessive. Rifle fire among children and gardens in the city's international five-star hotel on a sunny Saturday, in the morning."

"Another detail, Otto. It may be nothing, I know, but hey, we're brainstorming, right? Nelson, my ex, taught me a lot about how the media works. The Sunday edition is the most important and the most read. And it goes to press the day before."

"Every edition goes to press the day before."

"The Sunday edition goes to press at noon on Saturday because it starts being distributed Saturday afternoon. Either it was one hell of a coincidence, or whoever planned the spectacle did it just right to achieve the greatest repercussion possible."

"You think it has to do with politics?"

"Doesn't seem like it. No."

"In any case, the increase in the bribe doesn't explain everything."

"It did contribute, Otto, but it certainly doesn't encompass the whole truth."

* * *

At five o'clock, Harley is sitting in the office of Ângelo Torturra's apartment, a space packed with books and documents, in the São Francisco district of Niterói, separated from Rio de Janeiro by the ocean and linked by a bridge that even today bears the name of a general-president, decades after the end of the military dictatorship.

"That's Brazil, inspector, that's our country. It treats the crimes of the dictatorship with euphemisms and kid gloves. They torture, kill, whatever, and the democratic governments, once the dictatorship falls, turn a blind eye and wink at the audience. The elites always end up understanding one another. It's the people who get fucked."

Harley thanks the congressman for his courtesy. After all, to be received on a Saturday in his home is a courtesy. Torturra praises Otto, to whom he is grateful for having helped him in some investigations conducted by the Parliamentary Committee of Inquiry, for which he had written the report. They had ended with the indictment of over two hundred militia members—active and retired police organized like local mafias.

"Any request of Otto's is my command."

Harley explains the reason for the visit. They talk about the episode that morning in São Conrado. He addresses his partner's absence: they have divided the tasks because of the need to follow the forensics team's work first-hand, and that is Otto's forte. Harley would like access to the findings of Corporal Vito Florada's investigation. He knows the materials are public and can be researched in the archives of Rio's Legislative Assembly and in the electronic data bank, but there's no time or personnel available to invest in such a large-scale effort. Harely is cut short by the congressman. Ângelo Torturra can't resist the opportunity to talk about the PCI. He of course remembers Vito, a.k.a. Mindinho. He quickly opens a file on his laptop and shares every detail of the investigation with his visitor.

Ten o'clock Saturday night. Otto and Harley evaluate what they have collected, sitting side by side on the sand of a deserted beach in the moonlight and in the metallic illumination of the São Conrado oceanfront. Nothing unusual in the forensic report. A lot of data from the visit to Torturra.

Complaining of back pains, Otto lies down, resting his head on Harley's backpack. The key seems to lie in the odd contacts of Mindinho. Intimate contacts with individuals quite distant from Rocinha and the poverty-stricken West Zone. There is something beyond traffickers and militias. Characters not identified by Torturra's investigation, which ran into legal barriers imposed by the Justice Ministry. The congressman isn't sure, but he believes that a powerful firm of attorneys acted indirectly, protecting Vito and, above all, his network of relationships. He doesn't know what that means, nor did he have any way to demonstrate the judicial relevance of expanding the investigation to include those contacts of Vito's. Because, in fact, nothing indicated that those persons had any connections to any crimes. The congressman had no choice but to suspend the investigations.

After listening in silence to Harley's account, Otto admits he is exhausted and lost. Ready to throw in the towel. He doesn't know who could be the target, what is at stake, or how to go forward. But his partner has an idea. It's Harley's turn to inject adrenaline and change the mood.

"The congressman said one thing that struck me. He went into a long exposition, interesting but interminable, and I wasn't able to follow his reasoning, there were so many names, the crimes, the ins and outs of the investigation—until he mentioned the Global Golf Club."

Otto perks up.

Harley continues: "Mindinho frequents the Global Golf Club."

"How can that be?"

Harley doesn't answer.

"Impossible. There has to be some mistake. Are you sure? Is Torturra sure? That place is a bunker for aristocrats. Know how much you pay to be a member? One million dollars. The guy pays that fortune to prove he's a millionaire, but that's not enough. The members have to approve each new candidate. A secret vote, campaign, the whole shebang. It's a monarchy, man."

"Plutocracy."

"He's not a member. He can't be. If he frequents the place it's because he has a friend there, the backing of someone very powerful. But why? A very odd friendship."

"If we could identify the friend, we'd be halfway there. Could you maybe take advantage of a bright Sunday and visit the club? If Mindinho is a regular visitor and if there's some connection between today's events and those weird contacts, he's not going to waste the Sunday. Tomorrow's going to be sunny. You could go there with Francisca and Rafa, very innocently."

"Impossible. Nobody gets in there." Otto leaps up.

Harley, startled, does the same. Standing, looking at the sea, he continues: "There's only one way. Do you remember Fábio?"

The next two hours are dedicated to planning for the following day.

* * *

Sunday, August 21, eight a.m. Harley's cell phone rings.

"Guess where I am. A cop's life has its charms. Does it or doesn't it? How wonderful. Guess."

"A cop's life, Otto, is shit. At six this morning I was in the vicinity of the bastard's mansion. Corporal Vito Florada lives in a mansion. No exaggeration. A horror, aesthetically beneath contempt. I've never seen anything so tacky. It looks like some motel on Avenida Brasil. The guy doesn't even go to the trouble of disguising his wealth. I spent hours with my ass in this junky little car I bought with my laughable salary, without a bite to eat, without coffee, and on high alert because the guy has his hired gunmen. It's true, he goes everywhere with bodyguards. If he goes to São Conrado, I doubt the cops enter the club with him. I bet they're going to follow him to the entrance and from there go to Rocinha and drink, extort traffickers, whatever."

Nine twenty. Otto's phone rings. The name *Harley* appears on the screen.

"On the way. I really think they're headed for São Conrado."

Nine thirty-five. Another call from Harley.

"Copy that. You can get ready."

"I've been ready for hours."

"You like it."

"I love it."

Nine fifty-five. Harley calls Otto again.

"Target entering the club. No problem at the reception area. They raised the barrier immediately. He's known there. He must actually frequent the place. He went in driving his own car, alone. The gunmen stayed in the backup car and went away, in the expected direction. Stolen plates on both cars. Now it's up to you."

Otto makes the long-awaited signal to Fábio. He's hardly slept at all, anticipating this moment.

"You know what to do. Once a champ, always a champ," Fábio proclaims loudly for all near the ramp to hear. It's a kind of homage to his old companion of so many cases. Otto smiles proudly, adjusts his belt, rechecks the equipment. In the past, he flew by himself or took someone. It's the first time he will be taken. Fábio makes his living guiding tourists from Pedra Bonita, at the peak of São Conrado, to the beach, with the possibility of longer flights depending on the weather and the price negotiated for the ride. He has been to Corcovado, flown over Rodrigo de Freitas Lake, the routes vary. This morning he will make a flight for the sake of friendship. Though short, the route will demand precision.

Fábio runs to the end of the ramp, pulling vigorously on the glider's structure, and hurls himself into emptiness, dragging Otto as passenger. The hang glider dips and rises, the ocean open before it, Tijuca Forest to the left, Gávea Rock to the right. (Otto would dedicate the following weeks to describing to Rafa the sensation of that leap. He would quickly give up repeating it all to Francisca and Harley, who are less tolerant of repetition.)

Obeying Otto's instructions, Fábio maintains sufficient height so that the flight over the golf course goes unnoticed. Several hang gliders are circulating in the area, and it is not difficult to blend into the landscape. The camera is efficient. Otto has studied Mindinho's features on the Internet and has no trouble locating him. Otto focuses on the group the corporal seems to interact easily with. He soon moves away with an older man. For the next fifteen minutes he converses and walks, slowly. Mindinho says goodbye. There is no possibility that the militiaman has come to the club to play golf or drink with friends. Otto records the images in high resolution, including the face of Vito Florada's principal interlocutor. With regret, Otto tells Fábio that he's ready to descend.

Harley waits for them, sipping coconut water on the patch of beach designated for landing. Fábio receives Otto's gratitude in the form of a hearty embrace and the promise of a *feijoada*. Harley photographs the leave-taking, posts it on his Instagram account, and sends it to the two friends. They help Fábio fold the glider, forming a long tube, and carry it to the small headquarters of professional flyers in the square next to the sand.

They leave the pilot, extending their effusive compliments, and sit at a kiosk at the edge of the beach that specializes in Bahian food. It's eleven thirty, early for that spicy lunch. Harley opens his laptop. At his request, a friend at the federal police sent him, half an hour earlier, a pen drive with the list of members of the golf club. A stroke of pure luck, without which there are no conquests in love, gambling, and literature: The feds had done a survey of clubs for the elite when suspicions arose about the influx into Rio of large amounts of dirty money from various sources. Nothing was found at the Global Golf Club, but the data bank was still there and it was recent. "It must be good for something," the federal investigator told Harley in confidence, wishing him success.

Otto is anxious. He takes over the keyboard and issues the command to open the folder, whose title is explicit: GGC. He selects the images file and navigates to the album of photos. He turns his camera to exhibit mode and selects the close-up of Mindinho's interlocutor. The powerful zoom permits a clear display of the calm countenance. The man is elderly but healthy, almost athletic, corpulent, tall, and nice looking. The screens on the computer and camera allow a comparison. In short order, the individual is identified. The man is a major player in the real estate sector. There are no charges sullying his record. What now?

They eat shrimp with garlic and oil along with sliced French bread. The laptop is closed on Harley's knees. Otto carefully puts away the camera, a wish-list item that Francisca made a reality for his birthday in 2009. They yield to dispiritedness. After such high expectations, the sudden deceleration is depressing. Two bipolar days, extreme highs and lows. Enthusiasm and disappointment back to back. Frights and deferred redemption. Silently, they gaze at the sea. They pay the bill and walk toward the condo. Otto finally breaks the silence.

"You were right. It was absence, not excess. What's strange is the absence of a link. I can't conceive of anything that connects the two of them."

"The connection is unlikely, Otto, it seems unbelievable, absurd, but it exists."

"Which makes any hypothesis possible and none consistent. We're back to square one."

Harley stops suddenly. He often halts abruptly when walking, when he has an idea. Otto turns around and is surprised to see his partner's happy face.

"What?"

"Remember Francisca's phone call yesterday, when we were at Rocinha? You even commented that she was hysterical."

"She *was* hysterical."

"And what did she tell you?"

"That she wanted to get out of here."

"She told you she wanted to leave São Conrado because

she couldn't stand the violence anymore, didn't she?"

"So what?"

"From what you said, she was ready to unload the apartment for whatever she could get, no matter how bad the moment to sell, because the important thing was to get away and take Rafa."

The two men share a dense, vibrant silence.

Harley points upward: "Look."

They are on the sidewalk by the beach, in the shadow of the highest tower on the coast of Rio de Janeiro, thirty-four stories in the shape of a tube, built in 1972. Planned by the celebrated Oscar Niemeyer, hanging gardens conceived by the landscape architect Burle Marx, with a convention center for 2,800 people, a theater housing 1,400, in the most coveted area in the city. The building was designated a historical site in 1998. The hotel had gone under three years earlier. After a lengthy court battle, it was transferred to an autonomous federal agency accountable to the Treasury Ministry, which was preparing to auction it off. Otto and Harley are familiar with the history and recall it whenever they pass by there, perplexed at the sight of the most valuable building in the city abandoned, its windows broken, corroded by the sea air, moldering.

No words are necessary. For several minutes they contemplate, dumbfounded, the dirty, sordid tower that thousands of bats invade at nightfall. Harley whispers, as if sharing a secret, "The whole time, it was staring us in the face."

Otto murmurs: "There's just one thing, Harley: This changes the scale of the problem. Drug traffickers and militia are child's play next to this. This is the crown jewel, but the speculators will have a field day. There's no limit. The guy's going to swallow up the entire district."

"When all is said and done, the problem really was excess, not absence. You were right: it was an excess of evidence, the magnitude of the value at stake, the dimension of the risk. What's going to become of us, my brother? Where are we going to request exile? I'm serious, Otto. Even if we say nothing, we become a danger to ourselves."

"We're going to need a lot of calm and coolheadedness."

Otto and Harley walk along the seafront, wet their feet in the cold foam, trying to stay calm. An emergency session with Ecio Nakano may be necessary.

"Don't you want to give it a try, Harley?"

RJ-171

BY GUILHERME FIUZA

Leblon

They were within one hundred meters of the top of the hill. Narguilê carried two rifles on his back that together weighed almost half as much as his body. He was panting and beginning to puff, attracting the attention of Lizard, who was marching firmly some ten paces ahead.

Lizard stopped and turned, irritated. "What's this shit, Narguilê?! You dyin'?!"

His comrade, out of breath, didn't answer. He continued to climb the hillside, almost dragging, motivated only by awareness that in the position he occupied, showing any sign of weakness was fatal. Lizard decided to wait for him. Resting his rifles on a large rock, he took something from his vest pocket. Narguilê staggered toward his colleague and was about to rest his weapons on the same stone, but Lizard stopped him.

"Don't put them down, 'cause if you do you won't be able to pick them back up. Have a bit of oxygen."

He handed him a silver straw and with the other hand lifted a piece of broken glass close to his face. Narguilê snorted the "oxygen" in a single breath and the smile of a veteran lit up his childish face. He returned the straw and set out climbing the hill in strong strides, now with the breath even to speak: "Move it, Lizard! You're too slow."

From that point upward it was totally dark and progress

was possible only with the aid of a flashlight. And the pair had powerful flashlights—from the first world, like the rifles. In front of a huge tree, which marked exactly fifty meters to the top of the hill, the two stopped again. Time for military protocol. From the other vest pocket Lizard took out a two-way radio.

"Robocop, read me?"

A quick response from the other side: "Affirmative."

"Lizard and Narguilê here, requestin' authorization to enter the security zone."

Radio: "Take it easy. Just the two of you?"

"And our Almighty Father in Our Heart."

Hearing the password, Robocop immediately cleared the ascent. Even so, when they arrived at the summit they were in the laser sights of two machine guns that only ceased to point at them when Robocop flashed over their faces the security spotlight stolen from Maracanã Stadium during renovations for the World Cup. Narguilê was puffing again, and although he tried to disguise it, the fact wouldn't go unnoticed by the men of the General Staff. A very strong mulatto with shaven head and serene expression, Robocop had laser-sharp eyesight. Nothing escaped him.

"The soldier's tired?" asked Robocop.

Lizard answered for Narguilê, knowing that his colleague couldn't speak: "The Germans showed up unexpected at the foot of the hill. Narguilê had to shoot it out with them by hisself, then he hightailed it to the grotto—"

"How come I didn't hear no shots up here?" said Robocop suspiciously.

"It was right at the time a jackhammer was breakin' up the sidewalk at McDonald's, they never stop workin' on that," ventured Lizard.

Robocop's serene expression didn't waver. "I'm reminding both of you: a tired soldier is a dead soldier."

Narguilê gulped and followed Lizard, who followed Robocop, who had issued the warning as he withdrew, without a backward glance at the pair.

Through a narrow passageway that forced the security chief to turn his powerful body sideways, the three went in single file into what looked like a bunker—descending a long stairway carved into the rock, finally a respite for Narguilê's exhausted lungs. After crossing a crude corridor that was more like a ruin, they came to an immense, luxurious room. Home theater, cinematic lighting, new overstuffed furniture, a large marble table with chairs trimmed in gold, a sliding glass wall revealing a deck with a pool from which came an intense blue glow as if there were uranium under the water.

Robocop and the two skinny soldiers stopped before the large table, almost at attention, joining three other armed young men already there. No one said a word or greeted one another with a look. In two minutes a thin, muscular man entered the room, medium height, darker than mulatto, thin nose and lips, large greenish eyes. He nodded and everyone sat down around the table.

"There's two matters," the chief said softly as he sat down at the head of the table, the gold chain engraved with *Zéu*, his nom de guerre, swinging over his lilac-colored silk shirt. "The first is that the police have decided to raid. Not to plunder, to take over. There's gonna be war."

Zéu's soldiers absorbed the information impassively, among other reasons because the chief didn't like to be interrupted— by either word or gesture. The only one who moved was Lizard, placing his rifle on the table when he heard mention of war. Zéu stopped talking, got up, and walked silently around the table. Coming to a position behind Lizard, he hit him on the ear so violently that the soldier fell to the floor, taking the chair with him.

The chief returned quietly to the head of the table and sat down. "I already explained it's bad manners putting a gun on the table."

Zéu went back to the topic of the raid but was interrupted again, this time by a sudden noise outside that caused everyone to look through the glass wall. A person had jumped into the pool. The troop was startled, and the chief seemed surprised. For an instant all fingers were on triggers, until they saw the figure emerge from the dive. It was a woman, beautiful and nude from the waist up.

Each soldier felt, in a fraction of a second, that the delightful sight was a cruel punishment. You don't look at the chief's girlfriend, especially with her breasts exposed. The entire troop quickly shifted their eyes to the floor, aware that this front could be bloodier than the battle with the police.

But Zéu surprised everyone: "Take it easy, that one there you can look at. She ain't worth nothing."

The enormous relief wasn't enough for them to lift their gazes from the floor. No one wanted to take the chance. But they would see the girl up close, because she'd left the pool, wrapped a small towel around her breasts, slid the glass wall, and entered the room, still dripping. She was white, with nice skin and an affected manner—a broad from Leblon. She went straight to Zéu and planted a kiss on his mouth, adding a disconcerting comment about the armed troop: "How cool, Zéu. So this is your gang?"

The trafficker, who didn't like being called a trafficker, swallowed his hatred. It was against his principles to be rude to women. He told her to go change in his bedroom while he arranged her return. She asked the outlaw when they would see one another again.

Then Zéu became less cordial: "Who the hell knows. Set it up with your husband."

When the woman withdrew, the chief made contact by radio, saying, "Drop off the judge's wife on Delfim Moreira," and returned to the agenda of the meeting. "I'm moving on to the second matter, then we'll get back to the police raid. It's this: I ordered Roma brought up here. He should be getting here now. I'm going to interrogate him, and I want the guy in your sights, that way he won't lie as much. I think Roma is doing business on the side."

Robocop raised his hand asking permission to speak. Granted.

"Zéu, Roma's put together a band. Narguilê went to see it yesterday, 'cause he plays bass drum, but he was kept out. Roma ordered him to come back unarmed."

The chief exploded: "*Ordered?!* Who *ordered*, you shitass? Just who gives the orders in this fucking favela?"

Robocop lowered his head. "Sorry, chief. Of course Roma don't give no goddamn orders, but he likes to think he—"

He was interrupted by Zéu, who directed his feared dead-fish stare toward another soldier: "And you went back to that fucker's circus without your gun, Narguilê?"

Lizard knew his friend had returned there unarmed and had spent hours snorting cocaine and playing the drum in Roma's band. Now Narguilê was panting again beside him, in a cold sweat. Lizard tried to maneuver: "If you want us to, Zéu, we'll go there and shut him down for good."

The chief didn't buy it: "Shut up, Lizard! Answer me, Narguilê. Did you go back to that shithole unarmed?"

Narguilê answered, averting his eyes from the chief: "No,

I didn't, Zéu. I went to get some sleep, 'cause I had a cough . . ."

Zéu's dead-fish gaze turned to Robocop. "Take Narguilê out there and give him some cough syrup."

Robocop rose and told the skinny soldier to follow him. Choking back a sob, Narguilê said he was better and didn't need syrup. Zéu stood up and said that in that case he'd take him personally. Narguilê then agreed to follow Robocop, crying copiously. Less than five minutes later, the troop heard two gunshots from the roof of the bunker. Lizard lowered his head. No one said anything.

Zéu waited for the return of Robocop—who sat down with the same serene expression as always—before resuming his speech. He began with a rapid message about the summary execution of Narguilê: "A tired soldier's a dead soldier. If he's alive he'll end up in the hands of the police saying things he shouldn't. Any guy who's supposed to guard the chief and goes to play music unarmed is a goner."

On the wall behind the chief, framing his philosophy, was a painting of the medieval conqueror Genghis Khan smashing a foe with the hooves of his horse. Narguilê died because, in Zéu's dictionary, a weak ally becomes an enemy. But the trafficker was impatient and seemed to have already forgotten the murder.

"Where the fuck is Roma?"

"Easy, Zéu. I'm here."

Brought by two more of Zéu's soldiers, Roma entered the room at the exact moment the chief had uttered his name. Despite the tenseness of the situation, his expression was one of nonchalance.

"Shee, it's nice here, huh? You've really done all right, Zéu. Can I sit down?"

"No. Stay on your feet. Here's the story, Romário. I been

hearing 'bout some double-crossing going on, and you're gonna have to explain."

"Wow, such a long time since anybody uttered my real name. I must be real important now."

"Shove it up your ass, Romário."

"Shee. Now you went and spoiled it, Zéu. It started so good—"

"Are you fucking with me, goddamnit?!"

"No way. I may be crazy but I'm not suicidal."

The troop was visibly upset by Roma's arrogant presence. A strong black man with slanting eyes and a wide smile, twenty-seven years old—the same as Zéu—he had been born the day the famous footballer Romário first played for the Vasco team. His father had no doubts about what to name him, declaring that his son was also going to be a striker. But Roma grew up without any talent for football, nor did he join the ranks of traffickers. He was a different sort of guy. It was he who advanced the conversation.

"Well . . . what now, Zéu? You ordered me to climb this hill and I can't even sit down. So tell me: what's going on?"

"You know."

"No, I don't."

"Fuck, Roma! You want Robocop and Lizard to beat the shit outta you?"

"No thank you."

"You been takin' a lot of liberties, man. Out with it: what's this shit about you cozyin' up to the pigs and hangin' with some guy from Leblon? My spies said you been talkin' to the cops."

"Not to cops. To the chief of police."

Roma's reply paralyzed Zéu. The statement was so serious that it seemed as if the outlaw couldn't process it. Knowing he was with an intelligent guy, Zéu stared at him—with a gaze more of curiosity than of a dead fish—as if waiting for Roma to decode the nonsense. Then Roma continued.

"Shit, Zéu. You know I'm no rat. If there's a guy on this hill who's never betrayed you, it's me. The police kidnap one of your soldiers and charge you ransom. The ones who get busted are the ones who can't take you anymore, their heads are fucked up. What I'm doing is recruiting those guys to play in my band, and I made an agreement with the police: they leave them alone, they can't kidnap or question them. Know why?"

Zéu remained silent.

"Because the governor likes my project. He says it's a *sociocultural action*. I don't give a shit what he calls it. What I do know is that the police are respecting 'my' ex-traffickers. By the way, I want to tell you that Narguilê guy, one of your soldiers, is loony, nuts. He's one helluva musician, and I'm grabbing him. You can relax, the Man isn't going to touch him—"

"Narguilê is history," Zéu interrupts.

Now it's Roma who's speechless. He looks at Robocop, who averts his eyes, then at the chief again. "I can't believe you did that, Zéu."

The outlaw becomes irritated: "You got your methods, I got mine. Don't fuck with me!"

Roma starts to answer but Zéu talks over him: "Here's the thing: the police, your buddies, have a plan to raid the favela. Not just to roust us out and get in the papers. They wanna occupy the hill."

"I know."

Robocop stares at Zéu in fury, revolted by the level of information Roma has about the police.

Zéu feels the same way but tries to stay cool: "Great, you

know. Then you oughta know too there's gonna be war. And starting right now nobody in the community can talk to the police—not merchants, not mototaxis, or the owner of a band, or NGOs, no-fucking-body. You know the way our operation works here—when the shit hits the fan the pigs are gonna flay you and you'll tell 'em everything."

Now it's Roma who avoids everyone's eyes. He speaks looking at the floor, his voice muffled. "I can't promise you that. I can't just stop talking to the chief of police."

Robocop loses his cool: "Let's burn this guy right now, Zéu! The fucker's a snitch! He's sellin' you out! Let's waste this asshole right here and now, before he fucks everything up!"

This time Zéu doesn't look at Robocop, despite the soldier's exasperation, which the chief tolerates only because his adrenaline has also gone through the roof. His dead-fish gaze foretells the order in a low voice: "Kill him."

The room service attendant went to check with the kitchen on whether the bottle of Dom Pérignon had been sent to room 901. When he learned it had been, he confirmed this with the guest on the telephone. But she replied at the top of her lungs that the attendant was an idiot. After a moment, the man understood that she wasn't complaining about the bottle that had already been sent up but the other one, which hadn't yet arrived—more precisely, the third one, ordered a little less than two hours after the first.

"I'm the one who's drinking and *you* lose track? Shit," ridiculed the guest.

When the waiter arrived at 901 with the new bottle, no one came to the door. The employee heard female cries coming from inside the room. He thought about calling the manager. Then he heard giggles among the shouts and did an about-face.

Tall and slim at forty-three, with slightly exaggerated fake breasts and lips, but elegant even so, Laura Guimarães Furtado was a hurricane. Often mentioned on gossip sites, the Rio socialite overshadowed many a TV actress. A well-known newspaper editor even said he regretted the demise of the society page because of Laura. "Her adventures alone kept Zózimo's column going," murmured the old editor, citing the father of Rio society column–writing in the seventies and eighties. Now Laura Furtado was unconscious on the floor of a suite in the Sheraton.

Upon being put back on the bed, she opened her eyes and spoke, still in the arms of her younger lover: "Oh, you're still here?"

The consort was a bit confused. "Yes . . . wasn't I supposed to be?"

"Uh-huh. I don't know. I blacked out, and you had just screwed me . . . Most of them go away when that happens."

Her lover replied rather awkwardly, "It's that I still got a thing to discuss with you."

"A *thing*? How sweet . . . Let's ask about that bottle of champagne that's missing, and you tell me about your thing."

"It's serious, Dona Laura."

Laura had an attack of nervous laughter. "*Dona Laura*? You want me to jump from the ninth floor now or after we have a toast?"

"Excuse me—Laura. That comes from my family there in the favela. We usually call a married woman *Dona*."

"Oh, how nice of you to remind me I'm married. By the way, mind if I make a quick phone call to my husband?"

"It's about him that I wanted to talk to you."

Laura was taken aback. "Oh no! Three is too many. And my husband doesn't go for that. He'd kill me!"

"It's nothing like that! I already told you the thing is serious. Isn't your husband close to the governor?"

"My husband tells the governor what to do."

Laura saw her partner's eyes flash—as much or more than when she undressed for him. She even felt jealous of her husband with the lover, which was a crazy inversion of the situation. The young man then asked her to arrange an audience for him with the governor.

Irritated, the socialite cut him short: "Impossible! Who are you, boy, to be received by the governor?!"

The youth from the favela was obstinate and said that the governor knew him. Naturally, Laura Furtado didn't believe him.

"You people from the hillside are funny. You come down here to the streets and just because you're sexy you start to think you own the place, as if Leblon were the outskirts of Greater Rocinha. Back up, kid."

The young man found "Greater Rocinha" amusing and picked up on the game: "You people here on the outskirts are very prejudiced . . . Why can't the governor know me?"

"In the first place, I said you people think that *Leblon* is the outskirts. This here is São Conrado."

"Oh . . . Leblon, São Conrado . . . it's all the same. It's all Greater Rocinha," he retorted with a sly smile.

The spirited charm of the dark, muscular youth melted Laura's defenses, and she laughed and pulled him on top of her. Their tongues intertwined, but the able negotiator moved away and played his trump card.

"Hold on. First we have to decide the matter of the governor."

Laura was furious at this blackmail: "Governor my ass! Take a look at yourself, you nobody! If you go to the governor's palace you'll probably leave the place in handcuffs!"

The youth didn't take offense; he knew what he wanted. He remained serene and tried to convince the socialite that the governor really did know who he was and admired his sociocultural work with the band he had formed with a group of ex-traffickers—the RJ-171, whose name referred to the statute of the Brazilian penal code dealing with fraud. Laura was a fan of the band and had met her lover several months back at a show he had given for wealthy people on Delfim Moreira Avenue. Even so, she remained unmoved.

"It won't work, Roma. If I ask my husband to take you to the governor, he'll suspect something."

Romário felt it was time to play the ace up his sleeve: "What if I get you a meeting with Zéu?"

The feared chief of Rocinha was the terror of cougars from Rio's South Zone. With the exacerbation of the confrontation with the police, however, a visit to Zéu's bunker atop the hill could turn into a ghost-train, and the trafficker himself had begun avoiding that type of operation. But Laura knew that Roma was familiar with the geopolitics of the favela and would be able to take her safely to a tryst with the outlaw.

What the socialite didn't know was what Romário had promised Zéu in exchange for his life. That was how he had escaped being shot. He knew the chief of the hillside was crazy about Laura, despite knowing her only through Google and YouTube. A second before Robocop was about to pull the trigger, Roma had sworn to the chief that, if he didn't kill him, the coveted socialite would be his.

Zéu was going to kill Romário more from depravity than as a tactic. Roma had offended the New Order (zero contact with the police), but the boss of the hill didn't actually believe the leader of the RJ-171 band had been informing the enemy. And when he promised him Laura Furtado, Robocop had been told to lower his weapon immediately. Roma had managed what was almost a miracle in Zéu's territory: negotiation. The trafficker was aware that Romário knew Laura and had even seen photos of the two together after a show. He didn't imagine just how closely they knew each other—if he had, he might have shot him simply from jealousy.

The outlaw accepted the agreement. The moment Laura Guimarães Furtado was naked in his bed, Roma's life would be saved. But if the promise wasn't kept, it was curtains. Except that, in this case, Robocop would be authorized to exercise his favorite hobby: killing slowly.

In the suite at the Sheraton, the hyperactive socialite felt suddenly ecstatic. The offer to meet with Zéu made her eyes shine more than at any other time with Roma. And there had never been a lover happier to be in second place. The glow in Laura's eyes foretold the success of Romário's masterly ploy: to save his skin, and to reach the governor. But she was stubborn.

"Why do you want to meet the governor so badly?"

Using his final reserves of sangfroid, the maestro of the band said, "Because I want power."

Laura guffawed. "Power?! You want power?! You don't know what power is, my dear! You just came down from the favela yesterday with your little 171 band and already want a front-row seat?!"

Romário continued unruffled: "The 171 is my band and it's only a parody of crime. But the crimes of your husband's firm are no parody."

Laura was about to reply, offended, but this time Roma didn't let her speak.

"You don't need to defend the family honor. Here between four walls we know the story. I want money and power, but I have a plan for the city. And the governor's going to submit to me."

"Okay. So go there and ring the governor's doorbell, because I'm not going to usher into the palace some nobody who attacks my husband and then wants his help."

"Fine. From what I see, you don't really care about meeting Zéu . . ."

It was the last bluff Romário had left. If Laura knew he was marked to die and she was his salvation, she would trade one thing for the other, and goodbye to an audience with the governor. But Laura didn't want to miss out on the tryst with the trafficker, so her lust spoke up: "Okay, sweetheart. I'll put your name on the governor's list. But first you have to set up my meeting with the sultan of love." Roma assented.

Laura asked for the check. The third bottle of Dom Pérignon had arrived and would be charged to her bill, without having been opened. The socialite didn't even notice. She took a wad of money from her purse—the proper way to pay for misbehavior—and asked her partner to handle the checkout. She would go directly down to the garage. He would exit the Sheraton on foot (with a bottle of champagne in his hand).

As he was walking down Avenida Niemeyer toward Leblon, a police car stopped beside him. A light-brown-skinned man, almost mulatto, coming out of the Sheraton on foot carrying a bottle of Dom Pérignon was by definition suspicious. The questioning was about to begin, but Roma forestalled it.

"Look, I was going to drink this with the governor. But I think you're thirstier than he is," Roma said, sticking the bottle in the patrol car and walking away without looking back.

The policemen didn't refuse the present. The diplomat of Greater Rocinha knew the people of his territory.

Now all that remained was to conquer the palace and escape the death sentence.

The two blows to Lizard's face resounded so loudly that Zéu heard them from inside his bedroom, with the air-conditioning on. He came out and found Robocop in the game room wearing his usual frozen expression and Lizard looking panicky.

"Why're you smackin' the soldier around, Robocop?"

"Caught the son of a bitch talkin' to the police, Zéu. That means summary execution, don't it?"

Zéu scratched his head, still a bit sleepy. "Yeah. I mean— let's interrogate him first. Lemme have my goddamn coffee. You bring me problems at this hour of the morning and I can't think straight."

At that moment a shapely mulatta emerged from the chief's bedroom, stretching and still in a nightgown. Noticing the tension, she said, "Ah, Robocop . . . let Lizard go. This habit you guys have of going after people . . ."

Zéu wasn't pleased: "Shut up, Adelaide! I've told you not to stick your nose in military affairs."

Lizard ran to Adelaide, kissing her hand and swearing innocence. Zéu threw him onto the pool table.

"Get your hands off her, you traitor! You wanna die slow?!"

The chief sat down at the living room table facing the pool, drank coffee with scrambled eggs, scanned the news on his iPad, lit a Marlboro, and summoned Robocop. During the interrogation, Lizard said he had only spoken with a military police corporal because the cop had accosted him at the entrance to a McDonald's.

"The guy wanted to sell me information, Zéu. I told him

I don't talk to police, but that was when Robocop showed up and grabbed me by the neck—"

"Liar!" interrupted Robocop. "Lizard was talkin' to that Corporal Saraiva, who charges us a toll to bring cargo up the hill. Lizard's in cahoots with the German, Zéu! Let's put this fucker under the ground right now!"

Lizard begged them not to kill him, seeing Robocop with his finger already on the trigger.

Zéu had one last question: "Okay. You're sayin' Corporal Saraiva wanted to sell information. Then I wanna buy that information."

Lizard was confused. "You're gonna buy information from the police, Zéu?"

"The punk's makin' it up!" snapped Robocop.

"If he's making it up I'll know right away. How much does the German want for the information?"

"He said he wants a pretty virgin here on the hill," murmured Lizard.

"Then it's settled. How old's your kid sister, Lizard?"

"No, Zéu, for the love of God—"

"Fuck the love of God! How old is the bitch?! Has she screwed anybody?"

Lizard stared at the floor. "Twelve. She's still a virgin."

"Great. Robocop, tomorrow night bring the girl, the cop, and Lizard to the bedroom over Jacaré's bar. Let me know when they're all there. Now call that piece-of-shit Romário. And you, Lizard, you know if you run away from the favela your family dies and I'll hunt you down wherever the hell you go."

After two tries, Robocop informed the chief that Roma's cellular was turned off. He took a blow to the face stronger than those he had dealt to Lizard—Zéu had to stand on tiptoe to strike the giant's face.

"How many times have I told you I don't wanna know about the things you *don't* do, you stupid robot? Find Roma and put him on the line with me."

Robocop would have avoided the humiliating punch if he had simply told the chief what he wanted to know: he had spoken earlier with Romário, who had said that the socialite Laura Furtado had confirmed for Friday, two days from then, at four p.m. in Zéu's bunker.

Upon receiving this information, the trafficker turned into a pussycat. He told Robocop he was "fuckin' great," and he was invited to watch the Flamengo game that night at Zéu's home theater. The henchman accepted with a smile, his cheek still red from the blow.

Corporal Saraiva arrived in plainclothes and smelling of cologne for the encounter with the virgin and the trafficker in Jacaré's bar. Robocop sent him upstairs, where Lizard and his prepubescent sister Keitte awaited. Soon afterward, Zéu arrived, looking sideways at Lizard, who was there as a prisoner—suspected of treason and perhaps of ambush.

The chief didn't greet the policeman and immediately asked what the information was that he wanted to sell.

"Take it easy, Zéu. Nothing to be gained from haste," replied the corporal theatrically. "First I want the girl."

Keitte was an Indian, with the same large prominent mouth that had earned her brother the nickname of Lizard, with the subtle difference that he was hideous and she was pretty. She was frightened, but it was her brother who was crying.

"You're gonna have the girl. Robocop, take her to Jacaré's bedroom, lock it, and give the corporal the key," Zéu ordered.

The giant took the hand of the girl, who began weeping softly but offered no resistance.

With a wide grin, Corporal Saraiva took the key that guarded his prize. He stuck it in the pocket of his tight pants, over which jutted his swollen belly, and cleared his throat: "Okay, now we can start the conversation . . . Here's the deal, comrade: I know the day and time the favela's going to be raided."

Zéu glanced at Lizard in recognition of his innocence. Robocop gazed at the floor. The trafficker stared at Corporal Saraiva, indicating for him to go on.

The policeman continued, solemnly: "Prepare yourself, emperor. The police are going to raid the day after tomorrow, Friday, at midnight." And he addressed Lizard, smiling and pointing to the bedroom: "Don't let my little girl go the dance Friday, cool? It might be dangerous . . ."

Zéu shifted his dead-fish gaze to Robocop and said without raising his voice: "Kill this pig."

Corporal Saraiva quickly drew his pistol but was unable to use it. The giant's rifle had already blown his head off.

Turning on his heels and heading toward the stairs to leave, Zéu commented, "You've been practicing, eh, Robocop? That one there doesn't even know he's dead . . . Lizard, take your sister home."

At the exit to the Guanabara Palace, a police car stopped the man who was leaving the governor's residence on foot. Romário recognized the same pair who had approached him so curtly as he was leaving the Sheraton. This time, however, they were brimming with politeness.

"The governor told us to take you wherever you want to go."

Romário kept walking. "Thanks, friends, but where I'm going is too dangerous for you."

* * *

Lounging on a plastic mattress floating in the crystalline waters of the pool, Zéu had the afternoon sun in his eyes and didn't even see Roma arriving. He only noticed when he heard his panting voice.

"Goddamn, Zéu. With all that money you could install a cable car on this shithole, couldn't you? Next time we're going to talk by telephone, 'cause climbing all this way isn't good for my heart, you hear?"

The trafficker continued to float, without moving a muscle. "The raid's tomorrow at midnight."

Roma gulped. He removed his sneakers and sat on the edge of the pool with his feet in the water. "Where's that coming from, Zéu? Nobody knows the day of the raid . . . How'd you find out?"

"A friend told me . . ."

"What friend, man?! You don't have any friends! I'm your only friend."

"It's just to remind you that if Laura Furtado isn't here tomorrow at four o'clock, you die."

"What bullshit, Zéu! You've got an irritating habit of constantly threatening people! I knew that already, goddamnit. You called me here to repeat that shit?"

"No. I called you here to say that Laura will come up but she won't go down."

"Are you crazy?! The woman's the wife of Fernando Furtado, the biggest entrepreneur in the state. They'll send the army, the navy, and the air force in here!"

"No, they won't. The bitch is gonna be my shield. Two hours before the raid, you're gonna call your friends in the government and tell 'em the bigwig's wife is up here. And that she'll only come down alive if the raid is cleared with me, the way it's always been: I put a couple of old rifles in the cops' hands, along with half a dozen bags of blow and weed for them to photograph for the papers, and that's that. You're gonna tell them that if the raid is for real like they're sayin', the bitch dies."

Romário looked deep into Zéu's sunglasses. "I'm not saying a goddamn thing. I'm not calling anybody."

Robocop, who was listening in on the conversation, took a step forward with his hand on his rifle. The chief signaled for him to stand down.

Noting the gesture, Roma decided to speak: "Know where I'm coming from just now? The governor's office. RJ-171 isn't a band anymore, it's an NGO. I have authorization from the government to receive donations. And a multinational wants to bankroll me too. I've got a show scheduled in Switzerland. I have the governor's personal phone number. He received me in his home in Leblon, and he knows I grew up with you, Zéu. And that I go to your house. Know what he asked me about you? Nothing. Know what I told him about you? Nothing."

Romário splashed his suntanned face with water from the pool.

"You take good care of this water, Zéu. It's nice and clean . . . I'm going to honor my agreement with you: the woman will be here tomorrow. And after that I don't owe you anything more."

He left carrying his sneakers, and Robocop grabbed his arm. But Zéu intervened: "Let him go."

The next day, Friday, at three forty-five in the afternoon, Romário received an urgent call. It was Nareba, Narguilê's brother and an employee of RJ-171, who was taking Laura Furtado to the meeting with the trafficker. The news couldn't be worse: police security at the entrances to Rocinha was being increased, and everyone going through was being searched. There was no way the socialite could take that chance.

And Roma couldn't take the chance of not delivering Laura to Zéu. It was certain death. He could abort the plan and hope for Zéu to be killed in the raid. But he didn't want to see Zéu dead. And he also didn't want to betray the crazy woman who had opened the way to the governor. That's how Roma was—principled, as his mother said affectionately; full of tricks, as his colleagues in the favela said affectionately.

Romário told his emissary to abandon the socialite's car and go up the hill on foot. Halfway up they would catch a mototaxi. To get by the police, she would have to disguise herself as a washerwoman, wearing old clothes and carrying a bundle on her head. Roma prayed the woman would agree to the plan. She not only agreed but became even more excited. Nareba informed Robocop that Laura would be a little—or perhaps a lot—delayed.

It was late afternoon when the socialite arrived, sweaty and unkempt, at Zéu's bunker. But the sultan of love was acting as general, readying the troop's resistance to the invasion—which Laura didn't know would take place. She was cordially greeted by Robocop, who informed her that the chief would see her in half an hour. Fascinated by the gladiator's size, she asked if he could give her a massage, as the climb had been exhausting. Robocop broke into a cold sweat at the thought of what would happen to him if he did that—and sent Laura to the sauna.

When the trafficker entered his living quarters, the socialite was already on the bed, in a silk robe that emphasized her figure and a glass of champagne in her hand. Zéu stripped without saying a word. As he was about to touch her, he heard the sound of a helicopter, followed by a burst of rifle fire. The police had merely waited till nightfall to begin taking the favela.

"Goddamn shitass informant!" roared the trafficker, pulling on his pants and racing to find Robocop.

With gunfire drowning out Laura's screams, the giant burst into the room and followed the chief's orders: now with no sign of cordiality, he dragged the woman to a cubicle where he locked her in after telling her not to cry too much in order to conserve oxygen.

Despite the heavy firepower of Zéu's men, the peak of the favela was quickly encircled. The army was providing cover for the elite police battalion. In other words, this time the business was truly serious.

Zéu played his trump card: he called Roma.

"It's like this, Romário: I'm surrounded, but I got the entrepreneur's wife right here. I'll hand her over unharmed if the governor lets me get away. If you don't wanna talk to him, okay. But then the broad is gonna die with me, and I won't even be the one who kills her."

A few seconds of silence ensued, until Roma replied, "I'll call the governor."

Half an hour later, standing by Robocop's corpse, shredded by a bazooka blast, Zéu answered Roma's call.

"Zéu, I spoke to the governor. And he talked personally with Mr. Furtado, Laura's husband. The son of a bitch told the governor that he doesn't need to give anything in exchange for his wife. And that if you want to, you can keep her."

Zéu hung up without saying anything. He went to the cubicle, released the socialite, and said: "Run away through the woods behind here. If the Germans see me leavin', they'll shoot me. But maybe you can escape. If you stay here you're gonna die."

Laura Guimarães Furtado kissed the trafficker and ran toward the forest.

With the governor, Roma negotiated Zéu's surrender and saved his life. He argued it was better having him as a prisoner than dead. "There's always going to be crime, and it's better for us to be familiar with its face," philosophized Romário. The governor pretended not to understand, but he agreed.

A month later, Zéu was murdered in prison. His place in the command was taken by an evangelical preacher much more violent and dark, and the NGO RJ-171 began to suffer attacks.

The NGO headquarters soon had to leave Rocinha for Leblon.

"Okay, now we're in Greater Rocinha," stated Roma, drawing laughter from Laura Furtado, who had quickly joined RJ-171 and married a former trafficker (whose only defect, according to her, was not having more blow).

Lizard and his sister Keitte also went to work for the NGO, as juggler and dancer.

Saying he was facing death threats, Roma handed the presidency over to Nareba and went to live in Los Angeles with a female executive of the bank that sponsored him. Among other things, he discovered that Los Angeles too was part of Greater Rocinha.

PART III

Murmuring Fountains

ARGENTINE TAXI

BY ARTHUR DAPIEVE

Cosme Velho

Down below, for the moment there is nothing but filth, darkness, and cold. There is still an hour, half an hour at least, until the sun, dissipating the mist, washes away the night, bathes the buildings with light, and heats up this rock. At times the wind blows, and I can see a piece of the bridge over the bay. At times I am enveloped in the clouds that shroud the head and outspread arms of the gigantic statue at my back. The sky is silent, empty.

I have arrived before everyone else. I came in my car, which struck me as making more sense. The shift was about to end when a buddy of mine, a watchman at the monument, called. In the twilight, as the wind grew stronger, he had approached the wall, looked down expecting to see the lake, and spotted the body. A woman, blond, between thirty and forty years old. The location indicated a fall not short enough that she could escape injury nor high enough that she would be killed instantly. When I got there, my friend told me that the wind had "muffled her moans." A lovely image for a damned ugly thing. I wait for the woman to show any signs of life.

More people than one imagines climb this mountain to practice free-falling, especially in seasons other than summer, to reduce the chances that some benevolent soul will grab them and chain them to this great and cruel stone. The press doesn't publish anything so as not to give crazy people ideas and to avoid offending the church. Imagine the headline: "Adolescent Virgin Commits Suicide at the Christ Statue." Blasphemy? The work of the devil? No, a guy doesn't believe a fucking thing anymore, not even in the devil, to jump from a height of over seven hundred meters. In my profession, you either believe in everything or nothing at all. My own modus operandi would be a bullet in the brain. If the angle is right, there's no way to miss. Bye bye.

The wind taunts me, opening holes in the clouds but in the wrong places. Another piece of the bay. The hill over there. A group of soulless buildings. Even a block of the cemetery. But the body, which would be good to catch a glimpse of, doesn't materialize, remaining invisible to me. I'm no expert, but for lack of anything better I examine the wall. There's no mark to suggest that anyone had stood there before jumping. If she was wearing high heels, would she have removed them before carrying out the act? They might be there, just beyond the wall. The fog prevents me from seeing whether their shoes are there or not. Maybe they're hidden, tossed into a bush. Or else she jumped without taking off her shoes. In that case, would they have come off midair? Were they flat shoes? What kind of women wears flats? A very tall woman?

Then, as if they had tapped into my thoughts, the clouds call a truce. I stretch my neck and glimpse the body. Even at twenty, twenty-five meters I can see that, yes, she *is* very tall. Long-boned. Really large. The sight is interrupted before I can comprehend what seems wrong about her position. But I can already tell that something went very wrong. Besides, of course, all the other things that had gone wrong earlier and thrust the creature from this world. Instead of plummeting, the body evidently hit the rock, perhaps because of a gust of wind, and got caught in the low vegetation of an outcropping from the nearly vertical wall.

I continue looking down, grieving, for some ten minutes, even after the blanket of fog has closed in again. I regret leaving my sunglasses in the drawer. The low sun blinds me. I should have played dead and let my morning counterpart handle it. Shit, what would it matter? Is there still time to sneak away? No, there isn't.

Aguiar, from Forensics, a thin guy with a ridiculous mustache, appears at my side, taps me on the shoulder, and asks: "Too early or too late?"

"Too late. I should already be home, taking a shower, resting my head on a pillow. There—" I say, and make a vague gesture with my chin.

"Bad luck."

"Not as bad as the woman down there."

He looks beyond the wall. Mutters, "Can't see a damn thing. You sure it's a woman?"

Of course not. At night all cats are gray. The day didn't dawn right, with the fog. The body lies in a purgatory between yesterday and today. The woman, or whatever it may have been, didn't see the sun rise on the other side of the ocean.

"Of course. Blond, a short black dress."

"You've just described an Argentine taxi."

"Or a short brown dress, dark blue, I don't know. It's impossible to tell at this distance and in this lighting—"

"Argentine taxi!" he laughs.

"Okay, Aguiar, what's so funny? What if it's an Argentine taxi? Shit, you know that 90 percent of the women in this city dye their hair blond. Why wouldn't this one be yellow on top and black underneath? Even black women are blond these days, like Beyoncé."

"Beyonwhat?"

"A brand of hair dye," I say, dispirited.

Forensics people live in a bubble of blood that Beyoncé, Kelly Key, no hottie penetrates. That's a lie. Once in a while they find a recently deceased chick appealing, some poor thing killed in bed in an embarrassing pose, her pussy spread open, and ask each other, "Would you do her like that?" None of them would reject her. "She's English!" they say, laughing. A warped sense of humor.

"Years ago I arrived at the most disgusting crime scene I've ever witnessed," I begin, recalling more for myself than for Aguiar. "Someone had quartered a middle-aged bachelor with a large knife, the kind butchers use, and a pair of shears for cutting up poultry. Any butcher or surgeon was a priori excluded from the list of suspects. The job had been really sloppy, a shitload of blows that ignored the body's joints and practically sought out the hardest bones to sever. That kitchen on Soares Cabral . . . Jesus Christ, not a single tile that wasn't stained with blood. Or something more foul-smelling."

Aguiar emits a muffled laugh. QED.

"The dead man had soiled and pissed himself, probably when he took the first hack to the back of the neck," I continue. "There were three. And he probably didn't die until the third one, which finally separated his head from his body. Afterward, the murderer made cuts more or less at random until he tired of the game, sometimes using the shears to cut a more resistant tendon. It's likely he ate pieces of the body. Neither your team nor the morgue's could locate certain basic items like the kidneys. Nobody can live without at least one kidney, can they?"

Aguiar shook his head.

"To confirm the thesis, floating in butter in a frying pan,

browned but still intact, were the victim's dick and balls. I backed away to keep from vomiting, but your colleagues on the scene, Ramiro and the late Fontes, were having a filthy punning contest involving sausage and eggs. They sounded like they were recording the laugh track for some American TV sitcom. The next day, the editor of a tabloid topped them both. He zapped them with the headline 'Fried Food Causes Impotence.' Genius."

"Genius."

"Genius." I paused. "We never discovered who the killer was. I was sure it was a man. You needed strength to cut a femur in half with a single blow. The neighbors had never seen a woman visiting the victim, a loser named Oswaldo who'd lived there for ten years. And they hadn't seen any male visitors either, but then the guy wasn't dumb enough to make a show of the uglies he brought home, was he? If there weren't women, there had to be a man involved, sneaking up the stairs. Besides which, women like money and romance. It's queers who like dick. I concluded that anyone who hated dick that much had to be a fag. And a powerfully built fag. Am I wrong?"

Aguiar remains silent. I prolong the pause.

"Nothing was stolen as far as we could tell. No postmortem withdrawal on his bank card, no heirloom porcelain dishes in the hands of a fence. This was some three, four years ago."

Aguiar turns and leans against the wall, looking upward at the statue. At that moment, his ugliness is completely exposed. I continue gazing at the great milky emptiness below. When the blonde finally reappears, I nudge Aguiar. He agrees: definitely a woman. We contemplate the body until one of the last sheets of mist covers it, respectfully. When this happens, we remain standing there, smelling the fog. At times it's possible to hear the traffic sounds down below, which render the monument even more silent. Tourists won't be allowed to come up until the corpse is removed. The official excuse is "operational problems with the train." It always is. They would prefer that people waiting in line think maintenance is even crappier than it actually is to having them find out that somebody jumped headfirst. And glimpse the solution for whatever afflicts them: drug debts, betrayal in love, incurable disease . . . the Werther effect, I read about it in college. Death by imitation. Kind of crazy shit. It's enough for someone to demonstrate, through action, that life isn't worth living and someone else, not necessarily related to that first someone, reflects and says, *That's it, he's right, it's not worth it, I'm going to kill myself too.*

I light a cigarette and offer one to Aguiar.

He shakes his head. "That stuff'll kill you."

All I had done was come down hard without any real consequences on three shitheel potheads caught with a trifling amount of grass by cops with nothing better to do. I gave a speech about how cigarettes get you hooked, I think I even used the expression "the devil's weed," and let the kids go before they peed on my carpet. Other than that, boredom. It was shortly after midnight when the Special Ops patrol brought in the cute little couple. The guy was fat, wore glasses with dark green rims, had reddish skin, and, despite the cold of August, was soaked in sweat. He looked like an accountant wrestling with a particularly deceptive tax form, trying to make the numbers work. The other guy was much larger than him and wore red shoes with high heels—along with a blond wig, a tight black dress, and two hundred milliliters of silicone in each breast. In spite of the broad shoulders and muscular legs, he appeared feminine. After all, the concept of what's feminine has changed a lot in this city.

There was a tribe of ripped women, like girlfriends of country singers and soccer players, pumping iron and taking steroids to resemble strong men. This, in fact, would be the predictable defense of the guy in the glasses. He thought he was renting the services of a very buff woman, on the cutting edge of style, and had changed his mind when he felt that business underneath the skirt. Perfectly plausible. I thought, but didn't say, that nowadays the bulge under the skirt doesn't prove anything. The male hormones they take increase the size of the clit tremendously. There are samba school dancers who need to cut off a slice to be able to put on the cache-sexe without looking like they are on the rag or, worse, that they have a shlong. Many heterosexuals get turned on by those baby wee-wees and midfielder legs. That's why they go for a cross-dresser . . .

The citizen before me didn't understand that the question wasn't exactly that. I couldn't care less if he got off on women, men, or canned sardines. I didn't give a damn about prostitution by either sex. Fighting prostitution in this city is more or less like asking the scorpion not to sting the frog in the middle of a river. It would be going against its nature. No, the question there was quite different. Public decorum. Apparently the two had started arguing over a longstanding relationship far from the drag queen's work, which was in the Glória district. Normally it's best not to mix things. Except that the imbeciles had gone to Guinle Park, an upper-middle-class residential area just below the governor's mansion and, a worse fuck-up still, the road leading to BOPE, the Special Operations Battalion of the military police.

For whatever reason—*I don't want to take it in the ass any-*

more, I just want to screw, I want to get an operation and become a tranny, blah-blah-blah, those fag dramas—the pair started a fight and began trading blows just as a Special Operations patrol was returning from an action in one of the poor people districts in the outskirts, an action in which they had sent two more underfed but well-armed blacks to the boneyard. The soldiers in the truck were exhausted but couldn't pretend they weren't witnessing that love scene. Duty first, then rest. They banged on the side of the vehicle for the driver to stop. Before the two lovebirds realized it, they were surrounded by seven unpleasant-looking guys in black uniforms with skull patches on the shoulder. That was when the fake blonde produced a razor blade from inside her painted mouth and made an ugly gash in the accountant's right hand. Then a certain lack of control set in. The corporal leading the patrol aimed his HK at the drag queen's forehead and shouted, "Drop that shit! Drop that shit!"

By then half the neighborhood was at their windows, enjoying the circus. Antônio Sérgio Lemos de Alcântara—that was the name on his ID card—was strong, but he wasn't crazy. He dropped the razor blade and was put in a chokehold by a soldier. Another soldier applied a bandage to the hand of the accountant—Felipe Krauss Barreto, according to his ID—and the patrol brought everybody in, along with the crime weapon in a small plastic bag. When the group came into the precinct I guessed the nature of the shit, but what I said, smiling, was: "How can I help you?"

The sergeant sensed the irony, and I thought he was about to tell me to shove it up my ass, but he reconsidered, understood he was playing on my field, and related the incident in general terms, in a flat monotone. Then I listened to what the corporal and the soldiers had to say in order to release the patrol. The inspectors on duty could handle any other flesh wound from Antônio Sérgio.

Felipe's hand was bleeding a little under the bandage, and he looked at it, distressed. If his friend had AIDS, that wound was going to complicate his life. It wouldn't put an end to it, as it would have twenty years ago, before the cocktails. But it would complicate it, even if the incident never went beyond the precinct. If it did, then yes, Felipe Krauss Barreto was in for a shitload of problems. People in his office were going to look cross-eyed at him, disinfect chairs, a bunch of stupid and shitty things. Therefore it was neither startling nor even surprising when, as soon as the BOPE left, he declared he wouldn't file a complaint. The volume under the skirt had come as a surprise, the blows in the park had been unplanned, and the razor blade attack was an impulse that, God willing, would have no greater consequences than requiring five or six stitches.

"God willing," I repeated mechanically.

The silence in the room carried the implications of that observation.

"All of this is a nightmare, and the best thing is to wake up from it," said Felipe, half to himself, without taking his eyes from the bandaged hand.

The drag queen was quiet, crossing and uncrossing thick legs free of cellulite, exuding charm toward the audience, because queens always draw a crowd in the precinct, but when he heard this he couldn't hold back: "Nightmare?! Felipe Barreto, you fucker! When it's suck time—"

All Hudson had to do was squeeze the creature's clavicle lightly for him to stop roaring, moan weakly, and compose himself. The big black guy looked at me and smiled, satisfied with his physical authority. Good show. His mistake was not being able to resist a wisecrack.

"Look, boss, the doll's got an off button," he said, to guffaws from his colleagues.

But I didn't laugh. "My dear inspector, you must respect every citizen," I said in as bureaucratic a tone as possible, picking up one of the IDs from my desk. "It's no different with the citizen Antônio Sérgio Lemos de Alcântara. Or whatever name he, or she, prefers to be known by."

"Candy. Candy Spears."

It struck me that it was the first time the transvestite had spoken. Really spoken, without bellowing. A woman's voice, not that husky mewing that seemed to be the national language of poor cocksuckers. The story from the accountant—who, incidentally, wasn't an accountant but "a salesman in the field of auto parts"—became more and more consistent. Not that I cared in the least, of course, but under the influence of drugs it was possible to confuse Antônio Sérgio with a body-building woman. The guy's high, hears that voice, squeezes that thigh, he wants to fuck any which way.

"Candy Spears then," I agreed.

The pissed-off expression that Hudson made just reminded me that I didn't like his kisser all that much. That pose of his of the case-hardened cop who disdains police academy graduates. I didn't think twice before insisting on my line of reasoning. If I had thought twice, I wouldn't have insisted. What good would come from that playacting? Too bad.

"My dear Hudson," I said, "apologize to citizen Candy Spears."

Hudson wasn't the only one astonished. Paulinho, César Franco, Tião, the pseudo-accountant, and the fake blonde were too.

"Apologize to Candy Spears," I pressed, before adding,

with a gentleness that only further increased the ignominy of the scene, "please."

Hudson skewered me with his eyes and stomped off, puffing, toward the interior of the precinct. The sound of a fist punching a metal filing cabinet was heard. I felt I had fucked up, but I couldn't lose face.

"I apologize in the name of the entire precinct, my dear Candy. Just because the citizen, whether male or female, committed an infraction does not give the police the right to put him, or her, down. We must treat everyone with due respect."

Candy smiled shyly, nodding in agreement. The pseudo-accountant repeated that he didn't want to lodge a complaint against the fake blonde. I looked at the fat, sweaty face, trying to think of at least one good reason for him to register the incident. Nothing came to mind, but I wasn't going to let him off the hook so easily. I knew how to play good cop *and* bad cop at the same time.

"The blotter guards against future problems, my dear citizen. We're taking you to Forensics for a corpus delicti examination. It covers bodily harm, it doesn't have to be attempted homicide. Later you can sue Candy Spears, our friends from the BOPE will testify . . . She'll do three months in the slammer, for sure, but unfortunately in a men's prison. Besides, let's be frank, you were *both* disturbing the peace."

Felipe Krauss Barreto didn't understand, or pretended he didn't understand, my threat. I couldn't sell ice in the desert with that palaver. The phony accountant must have envisioned the scene of the fake blonde providing favors to a long line of locked-up traffickers who hadn't seen an ass in weeks. He displayed a painful expression. Ah, love.

"So, it's up to you . . ." I sighed and left this in the air.

If it was up to him, then that settled it. "Thank you very

much, detective, but I really prefer to end the matter here. I don't want to lodge any complaint. Let's agree, all of us, that this nightmare . . ." he said cautiously, looking sideways at Candy, but now she was calm, inspecting her nails. "Thank you very much for your time, your patience, and your courtesy."

He extended his right hand to me. I didn't take it. We stood there looking at the blood on his bandage. I gave him two pats on the shoulder, meaning, *Hang in there, friend*. We accompanied Felipe and Candy to the precinct door to make sure they were heading in opposite directions. We kept the false accountant for a few minutes longer, until the fake blonde disappeared from sight. As if that meant anything, but damnit, there was a ritual to observe. Paulinho, César Franco, and Tião avoided any mention of the case. It was obvious they were pissed at me too. I felt even worse, but I still wasn't convinced that I'd ever have to apologize to Hudson.

I had just gone back to my chair when two drivers, definitely sober, came in to report a fender bender—petty stuff, no one injured, but the insurance companies were going to demand an accident report. When I finished, I went outside to smoke. I was distracted, thinking about what I'd do on my day off, probably sleep and wake up just for the pleasure of going back to sleep, when Candy Spears appeared from behind the trees whose roots I was using as an ashtray. Crap, what if she was carrying another razor blade? I regretted leaving my revolver in my desk. Candy was larger than Felipe and also bigger than me. I threw the cigarette away so as to have both hands free and planted my feet in a defensive stance. She came around the flower bed, without the exaggerated female flourishes. If Antônio Sérgio had been born ten centimeters shorter and fifteen less around, maybe seventeen less between his legs, he would be a woman. Nature plays tricks on us.

"Detective," she said.

"Yes, Dona Candy?"

"I just wanted to thank you for the treatment you gave me there inside. You can imagine it's not the first time I've been in a police station, but it was the first time that I didn't feel attacked just for being . . . who I am."

I remained silent.

"Your sensitive treatment was super important for me to get out of that mega-embarrassing situation." The four hundred milliliters of silicone heaved beneath the black mesh. "Although young, you're a man of experience. You surely saw that Lipe wasn't some casual client who was disappointed when he found out I had . . . that extra something that you men are ashamed to admit you like. The two of us have had a serious relationship for seven months, see? I think he's the man of my life."

At this point my silence must have been quite eloquent, because she felt the need to reply.

"It's serious! And I think he feels the same way about me. So mentioning a men's penitentiary was a masterful stroke on your part. He must not have been able to bear the thought. I'm not a woman to tolerate all that."

Candy made a significant pause.

"He loves me, but he still doesn't have the psychological strength to come out—you know what lower-middle-class families are like. And he also doesn't have the financial fortitude to support me. So I go on having to hook to pay for a tiny place on Laranjeiras, near Rua Alice, you know it? Much better than the tenement in Lapa that, praise God, I managed to get away from. But Lipe goes crazy with jealousy about me sleeping with other men."

Candy Spears paused again. I asked myself whether she

actually was a believer or merely invoked His holy name in vain.

"Would he be bothered if I went to bed with a woman?" she wondered aloud.

I reinforced my silence. The whole thing seemed like more information than I would ever need to know. I have to admit that sometimes smoking *is* bad for one's health.

"Anyway," she continued, "I noticed a pack of cigarettes on your desk and so I waited here till you came out to smoke, just to say thank you. I don't think I can even dream of some-day repaying your kindness, but who knows? Keep my phone number and address. I don't know, maybe I can be your infor-mant. We see everything that goes on at night in the streets . . . Ciao."

Candy Spears came closer, stuck a folded piece of paper in the pocket of my jacket, kissed me gently on the cheek, and walked away, without swinging her hips much, in the direc-tion of Glória. I looked to both sides. The door to the precinct was empty, the cold light falling on the sidewalk. If anyone had witnessed that, I was fucked. I'd be mocked to death.

The cigarette is almost burning the filter, and Aguiar is nearly asleep, sitting on a step, when we hear the dragging of chains, as if the ghosts who lost their lives on this mountain were returning from hell—or on their way to hell—and had come to avenge themselves with the first survivors they met. We turn around, but it's just the firemen tasked with retrieving the body of the blonde. Soldiers drag ropes, belts, snap hooks, harnesses, a stretcher. Behind them comes a lieutenant.

"Lieutenant Vaz, at your command." He shakes our hands.

Although they're military, I'm in charge of the operation. But Aguiar takes the lead and complains about the delay. The lieutenant replies that it wouldn't have helped to come before the fog dissipated. Aguiar grumbles something that's muffled by the noise of the soldiers setting up the materials for the rappel. I bring the lieutenant up to speed on the situation, take him to the wall and point to the body, now fully exposed, at the edge of an almost cloudless sky. He asks if we plan to descend. Aguiar breaks in again and says no, that it's a matter of suicide and that our presence down there would make no difference to the case.

The lieutenant agrees and goes to join the troop, while I again contemplate the cadaver of the blond woman in the black dress. Her shoes can't be seen from this angle, though it's unlikely she ascended the mountain barefoot. Only if it was to honor a vow, but obviously there was no grace achieved there to be grateful for. Then I finally understand what bothered me from the first moment I saw her there. Not the most obvious thing, the thick legs in an impossible position even for a bone-less ballerina. It's something else, a bit more subtle. I call Aguiar, who is watching the firemen. I point to the cadaver again.

"Look, could hitting the rock leave her head twisted like that?"

"You think it's weird? Maybe the impact broke her neck and turned it a bit . . . Maybe she wears a wig that came off in the fall . . . Hard to say without examining it up close. Let's wait for them to bring her up."

I think about all the possible consequences of what Aguiar, the forensics expert, has just told me. Now he contemplates the landscape, glorious in the pristine light of winter.

"I'm going down," I say.

It takes a moment for Aguiar to digest the information. "Are you nuts, man? What for?!"

"The scene of death wasn't up here. It was down there. Or not. But we're only going to find out if we go down. Letting the firemen get the body, strap it to the stretcher, and hoist it vertically can displace things even further. And displacement can completely change the direction of our investigation."

"Shit, these guys are profes—" Aguiar starts to argue, but then notices the *we* in my previous sentence. I take his silence as consent. If I descend he's obliged to do the same.

I go to the team of firemen and announce I've changed my mind. Not only changed my mind but that we want to descend before any of them. Lieutenant Vaz doesn't attempt to conceal his surprise, but orders are orders, and orders come down the chain of command, however circumstantial. He orders a soldier to give me one of the safety harnesses. Aguiar also accepts one, wordlessly. A second soldier hands us helmets and gloves. A third checks the equipment and gives us rapid instructions. I take a deep breath. The smell of smoke is still in the air, though the mist has dissipated. I touch the folded paper in the pocket of my jacket. I begin the descent.

BLIND SPOT

BY Victoria Saramago

Tijuca Forest

nnie was recovering. Slowly, said some friends who obviously had no idea how much time a long and painful recovery process takes. Precisely because they thought Annie's world should have the same smell and texture as before, she found no solution other than to leave her life in Kansas and go somewhere far away. A place not totally unknown and that had some appeal for what others understood as tourism, perhaps, but that didn't recall the snow, the open fields where you could walk for hours without seeing a tree. Some city, maybe one in South America, about which she knew very little—*I'll always be a foreigner*, she reminded herself—but a city that would welcome her anyway. *A place whose language I'm not going to speak, because that will be easier, a city full of trees*. Like those long-ago days of childhood walks in Central Park where certain dense areas of bushes gave the impression of being far, far away in some forgotten land where the horizon of New York buildings could no longer be seen.

So Annie, upon arriving in Rio, had rented a room very close to the Tijuca Forest and indulged in long walks to the lakes and peaks. People passed by the trails and cascades with children and bottles of water, appearing to not have a care in the world. Annie envied them: they would return home after a few hours and not have some scowling guy offering them more blow.

But what Annie saw in front of her now was a coati. Not

very small and probably old, the coati, like all the inhabitants of the urban forest, was obsessed with a trash can. With its hind legs at the base and its tiny hands stuck into the opening that might be hiding the remains of cookies and sandwiches, the animal let its long, striped tail slide along the base of the trash can while it impatiently slipped into the orange box. Of course, the children and the tourists nearby didn't miss the opportunity. "A coati in the trash," they said, and smiled, though slightly perturbed by the intrusion of all that street garbage into the routine of a wild animal. As if they weren't precisely the ones, Annie thought, who made the trash can what it is. The coati, dizzy now, with a final effort succeeded in grabbing the contents out of the top part of the trash can— that is, an enormous wad of plastic bags, cups, and bottles smelling like a rotting picnic—which exploded and scattered onto the ground. The children clapped and the tourists accel-erated their picture taking until the animal left with its morsel and the audience dispersed in boredom.

Annie was disturbed. They're amused by the mess the coati makes and never think about the fact that it's not the coati who's going to clean it up. They find it reasonable, as long as they don't have to bother with anything besides trans-ferring the photos to their computers. Because some things had survived from the years Annie lived in Oregon, and this was one—walking angrily to the mess, she began picking it up item by item and depositing it back into the trash can. The cups with the remains of orange juice and the napkins with scraps of ham disgusted her, naturally, but caused noth-ing close to the shock she experienced when she discovered a human finger wrapped in a piece of paper that had fallen from a plastic bag.

She'd opened the paper carefully and, realizing that a new

phase was beginning for her, observed the relatively fresh, though purplish, index finger with its dark nail and the stump of bone emerging from the other end. Some dried bloodstains were interrupted by the folds of skin, as if the finger, after being covered in its own blood, were still able to move. Annie lightly nudged one of the stains, and the dark red skin came off in her hand, occupying a small area of her own index finger as if it had come from there. It was fascinating. She would never again see, for no reason, by sheer luck—or not exactly luck, but chance, improbability—what she was seeing now. A finger that no longer belonged to any human being, that would remain there, among the coati's paws and the remains of food, until garbagemen hauled it away and made it disappear. *This finger doesn't have an owner anymore*, she thought, *and it will be mine*. She rewrapped it in the paper and threw the rest of the refuse into the trash can. Walking with determination, holding the object between her fingers, with a challenging expression for any forest ranger who might have witnessed her actions, she headed for the park exit and then to Jonas's house.

"Want some more, Annie?"

It was almost ready when she arrived. Jonas was putting the finishing touches on the lines on the glass table and was rolling a ten-dollar bill to offer to the girl. Happy at the coincidence—"You always show up when I'm ready to take a hit," said Jonas, "you sense it"—Annie placed the finger on the other end of the table to avoid getting powder on it. She positioned the bill to snort the first line at the same time that Jonas noticed that finger in the napkin and wondered what the hell he was doing fucking and providing cocaine to a crazy gringa like her.

Deep in concentration, it was only after the second line that Annie perceived the puzzled gaze of the man before her. She smiled slightly, kissed him, and took the finger from him.

"I found it this morning on my walk," she said, while caressing the bloodstains on the dry skin and then Jonas's still-cool skin. "It was in a trash can."

The man listened to the rest of the story with a degree of skepticism. It was inconceivable that she actually wanted to keep the finger in the refrigerator. "Annie, that's part of someone's body."

She didn't seem very shocked. She wanted to find out whose finger it was, that was all. A nut job. Jonas hugged her tightly because after all she was sexy, though crazy, and he asked her to wash her hands before taking hold of his dick.

Annie agreed to this request, but she couldn't accept throwing the finger away. She preferred to find a plastic container for it and place it in the freezer. Then she commented that Jonas was a good person.

"I was very lucky to run into someone like you for this."

He felt it better not to ask whether "this" was primarily the amount of cocaine he had been supplying her in recent weeks, or the sex, or something else that he would never discover. In any case, Annie was well supplied with coke for the day, and with the finger comfortably in the freezer she felt at ease to pay with what might be the best blow job in Jonas's life. *They learn quickly*, he thought, *and know how to use it to their advantage*. Because Annie, seeing the right moment to repeat the question of half an hour earlier, swallowed the rest of the cum and began to speak as serenely as her state of lethargy would allow.

"You really don't know anyone who might know where the finger came from?" she asked craftily as if she were going to suck it again, and he had no way out but to sigh, stroke her hair, and reply: "There's a guy missing a finger who sells me blow. But it's his pinky, and yours is an index finger."

Even so, she seemed sufficiently interested, and before Jonas knew it he had promised to take her with him to the favela on his next buy.

He usually went up the hillside a few times a week. He tried to organize orders so he could go less often, but new orders could appear suddenly and he never wanted to miss the chance to make a quick deal. Especially now that Annie, having come into his life out of nowhere, consumed nearly as much as the powder ought to be generating.

But Annie was worth it. A bit weird with that talk about always recovering, true, but goddamn, what a body, and she knew how to use what she had, knew how to rub her hard nipples against him until he said, "Of course, sweetheart, we'll go up the hill together so you can see a man missing a finger while you hide your pet finger in your pocket."

It was a house like any other. As if at any moment a kindly grandmother would appear in the living room with a bowl of beans and chicken. Instead of that, two powerfully built men with all their fingers offered Jonas a taste of the new shipment. If he had been a gentleman and ceded the offer to Annie, she would have accepted. But he was the one who had to judge what he was about to buy, and she made an effort to keep quiet and concentrate on the fingers of the men in front of her while grasping the finger in her pocket. Smiling, one of the men came over and asked Annie if she loved Jonas. Because she didn't understand a word he said, she just smiled back as if she in fact did love him. Jonas, even with his back turned at the moment, was surprised by the question, and the sudden reminder of the blow jobs in recent weeks lightly stiffened his cock. The man then asked if she was afraid of losing him. Annie smiled again in her easy ignorance, but Jonas, distracted, didn't hear the question.

In the final analysis, it wasn't a good idea to stay in that country without speaking a single word of the language, and that was why Jonas brought up the subject when they were back at home and she was sucking him again.

"Are you sure you don't want to learn to speak Portuguese?"

His expression was too serious for Annie to simply smile and go wash the cum out of her mouth as if she didn't have to speak anything, not even Portuguese. So she became serious too and, a bit tired of so many blow jobs, replied: "I'm not going to take any classes."

And that was all. She could learn by immersion, of course. After years living in a country, even Hungarian can be learned, and Jonas hadn't needed to live in an English-speaking country to master the language and make himself understood so well with Annie. But it was an effort even for him. At that pace, in several months she wouldn't learn more than half a dozen key words which, if the necessity arose, wouldn't be enough for her to get by.

But Annie needed no rescue. What she needed was rest and the forgetfulness she found in those daily walks in Tijuca Forest. She needed to walk a lot, as much as possible, and take different trails every time, as if each one could neutralize, if only for a few hours, the wear and tear of that city, of the cocaine, of Jonas, and all the rest. Which is why she was anxious as she walked, because deep down nothing could any longer provide the initial relief and restore the feeling that, despite everything, she was recovering. Neither coatis nor severed fingers—even though that finger specifically had achieved its effect, like the rush the powder had afforded her weeks before when she met Jonas, and which had less and less effect after that first time. She walked faster and faster, aware of the animals and the trash cans, curious to return to the Borel favela, so near to the edge of the park, determined to find out how the hell that finger had ended up in the trash can. That was when she bumped into the park ranger.

He was a tall black man, and he was nervous when he came up to Annie to ask her not to walk by herself on those trails, it could be dangerous. Annie thought about smiling but remained serious. The man, not knowing what to do with the foreign woman, improvised with sign language while he went on explaining that she was a woman by herself, attractive, and the forest was large, too large—we do what we can to keep everything safe, but there are areas that can't be monitored, and if a man with bad intentions shows up (and here his pantomime was especially direct), he couldn't promise she would come out of the episode unscathed. After all, she was young and pretty and attractive, and Annie, seeing the man making those gestures, wondered whether she should take off her clothes right there and hope, when it was over, that maybe he had a bit of coke.

But no. She needed the solitude that one more random screw wouldn't give her. She approached him and, touching his arm, explained in English that she hadn't understood anything he'd said but that she didn't want sex. The man wouldn't have had to understand her words for his work responsibility to prevent him from grabbing the beautiful woman who, ignoring all his warnings, was approaching him. Even if it was difficult to contain himself. If they had met in some other setting, of course he would have taken advantage of the situation; and if she had the courage to let him see the severed finger, perhaps he could have even indicated to her where to look for its former owner. For there were many things in that apparently docile and cozy park of which Annie was unaware. And one of them was still the danger of walking alone on those trails during hours when few people were around, repeated the ranger dejectedly, until she grew tired and left.

At least it was Friday night and the weekend awaited them. Not that this dramatically changed Annie's situation, as she had nothing to do anyway, but it was pleasant to think that Jonas would be free the next day.

"I'm going to make a quick run up there for a last-minute order," he had said, "and then we can do a line and leave. Maybe we can go see those gringo friends from the bar we met a couple of weeks ago."

Annie wasn't good at meeting people in random situations and Jonas's friends didn't amuse her. Considering the few chances she had to speak with strangers, it was almost surprising that she had managed to even meet those gringos. It's worthwhile to invest in friendships, her mother had said a day earlier via Skype, concerned, and it was with that spirit that Annie decided to send them a message asking if they were up for a beer.

Jonas had left about fifty minutes before. According to what he said, he wouldn't be more than half an hour—his missions usually took about that long. Something unforeseen, maybe; it happens. I don't want to have to worry about anything, she said when they first met. Worry exhausted her, and she wasn't willing to be exhausted, never again.

"I've already exhausted everything I had, understand?"

Jonas didn't have to understand. He gave her what she

wanted, in exchange for what he wanted, and things were fine. With her, he spoke the English she was accustomed to hearing. With others, he spoke the Portuguese that she would never speak. Annie continued to be amazed at her luck in finding this available neighbor right after arriving in Rio, when she still hadn't known how to adapt to the city—but knew she was unwilling to do so.

An hour and twenty minutes waiting for him. The last line had been on Thursday, and all day Friday she'd been clean. She had tried calling, and nothing, not even a text message— even their friends hadn't answered. Should she go out looking for him? Brazilian men are fickle, she had heard someone say when she chose Rio. It wasn't enough. Not that he loved her and needed to keep her close at all times; he just wasn't the type of person to abandon her, especially after having agreed to a snort and her spending all day waiting for him to complete the routine.

Her cell phone chimed, announcing a message, and Annie jumped to open it. The friends: they couldn't make it that night, maybe tomorrow. The idea of the next night was still somewhat cloudy for Annie, who, without Jonas's arrival with more blow, couldn't visualize much beyond the next twenty minutes. The old house where she rented a room was empty, and if there were anyone to complain about the noise, Annie surely wouldn't listen to The Killers at such a high volume as she was doing right now. *Running out, running out* was an old song. She had now been waiting an hour and forty minutes, perhaps in vain, because Jonas might not be coming back. *Our time*, she repeated, imitating many others besides the vocalist, and how many others must have left the comfort of their beds to look for someone who, bearing something of value, doesn't come?

She waited another fifteen minutes before deciding. She

got her purse, took the finger from the freezer and put it in her skirt pocket, slammed the door behind her, and walked to the mototaxi stand. It couldn't be all that difficult to find him, and maybe she would discover the ex-owner of the finger as a bonus. The driver there wasn't one of the guys recommended by Jonas. She approached him nevertheless—she still remembered the name of the luncheonette at the top of the favela and with luck would recognize the spot. The driver left her at the exact spot she requested, but she didn't know which alleyway to take. Many people passed by, among them mothers bringing their children from school and bricklayers returning from work, and it was sheer luck that she recognized the man who days before had asked her if she loved Jonas and was afraid of losing him. The man seemed surprised at being approached by the gringa with her sign language and the few key words she knew in Portuguese: *cocaine* and *Jonas*. Guffawing at something, the man took her arm and led her to the house where she had been before.

There were lots of people. The guys from the previous visit and some others, women who seemed to be girlfriends, random visitors. If he was still there, Jonas was nowhere visible. The man Annie had met led her to a corner of the room and asked what she wanted. This time, she didn't have the strength to smile. The man spoke more slowly and she remained impassive, murmuring, *Jonas, cocaína, Jonas, cocaína*, enough for the man to at least imagine what she was after. He asked her to stay there and left for a moment. Even without understanding, Annie stayed. Her right hand in her pocket brushed against the loose finger. After a few minutes, the man brought another, precisely the one who, as Jonas had said, was missing his pinky. Surprised, she squeezed the finger in her pocket, and squeezed it more when asked something that she didn't understand, and went on with her sequence of *cocaine, Jonas*, and so on.

The man smiled at length. She wanted cocaine. The other told him that she was Jonas's girlfriend, and Annie didn't realize that this was the cause of the man suddenly raising his eyebrows, as if he smelled something wrong, and sending the other one away. Facing her, he gently took her two arms and asked her something incomprehensible. Immobile and still peering at him, she could feel, in place of his missing finger, the stump of skin caressing her. She would give a great deal to know how he had lost his finger, and even more to know to whom the finger she had found belonged. She almost took it from her pocket, to show it to the trafficker and wait for him to draw his own conclusions. Instead, she simply stared at him and repeated *cocaine, cocaine, cocaine*. There was no way he couldn't understand, and who knows why he decided to humor her.

After a signal to a third man, Annie within minutes had in front of her three lines of the best cocaine she had ever done. The boss was generous—he could only want something in return. At her first snort Annie saw it was a fine, very white powder, and it had an unusually good smell. So different from what Jonas normally supplied her with day to day, though a little more like what she snorted on the nights they had sex. Feeling her body move as if responding involuntarily, it was as if she were reconstituted to return to a situation now very far away in her life, the situation before everything happened. As if she no longer needed to recover, as if her life in Rio had magically worked out, as if the past could be expunged to make way for a present both solid and very fleeting, a present over which she would have the control she'd never had:

she felt her bones restoring themselves, the world regaining its colors, people moving about, and the extremely dark eyes of the man without a finger staring at her. *What do you want?* he seemed to ask and perhaps did ask. Annie would have so much to reply, but for now she thought of Jonas. Where was he? *You understand me*, her eyes said, *I know you understand me*, and he seemed undecided whether to take her at that moment, whether she was worth all the trouble she seemed to bring with her.

But no, perhaps he wasn't pondering anything, and Annie for the first time paid attention to her surroundings. On a bureau in the corner a forgotten cell phone was vibrating, announcing a message, a cell phone exactly like Jonas's. Whether or not it would be suicide for Annie to break through the blockade of the man's eyes and go to check who was sending the message, it no longer mattered to her—after all, she could do anything now. Determined, she went over and picked up the phone and opened it. The screen was scratched like Jonas's, and there were new messages. Since some of them could be the very ones she had sent hours before, she opened the first one: it was in Portuguese and therefore said nothing. She didn't have time to see the second one because the man with the dark eyes and missing finger grabbed the device and angrily shouted something that certainly wasn't an authorization for her to keep snooping. At that moment, Annie realized that nothing would be as easy as giving up for good. As calmly as if she had done this before, she took the finger from her pocket and almost rubbed it in the man's face. "Whose is it?"

His reaction only indicated that she had gone too far. He yanked the finger out of her hands and stared at it, looking a bit sad. He glanced at the finger in one hand, the cell phone in the other, at Annie's face, then back at the finger, mulling over his next steps. He wasn't furious but a little melancholy, and above all, startled: how the fuck had that finger ended up in the hands of that goddamn gringa who couldn't speak and didn't know anything about anything? Or maybe she knew and was trying to threaten him? Just let her try.

Grumbling, the man called one of the others. He was older, very skinny, and slightly bent over. Upon hearing the orders of the boss without a finger, he began smiling and Annie saw he was missing two front teeth. Still smiling, he took her by the hand, and she asked for the first time what she should have tried to discover from the beginning: "Doesn't anybody here speak English?" But those there who spoke at least at a basic level weren't the ones who heard Annie before she was taken to another alleyway and placed without resistance on the passenger seat of a motorcycle by the old man, who a few minutes later started the engine.

"Where's Jonas?" she shouted again. It was as if he were deaf. He drove at high speed through the forest and the sound of the engine drowned out the words, "Where is Jonas? Where are you taking me? Why?"

Without answers, they rode deeper into the forest. Little by little Annie could feel the air grow cooler, humid, like in the carefree mornings when she wandered the trails. The houses gave way to trees and finally to dense vegetation on both sides of the asphalt. She knew that many of the roads in the forest were outside the limits of the park itself and therefore remained open after visiting hours, even though it was all the same woods. The question was where the man was taking her. They could emerge in another favela on the other side of the city. They could stop right there, or in some other spot, God knows where. Annie tried to keep calm. She might never find out what had happened to Jonas or to the owner of the finger. Things of the past, like all the rest. She would have to recover from them like from everything else, like from herself if she were spared that night.

"Are you going to spare me?" she asked. The man grunted; it was useless.

If they could at least communicate. The park ranger had warned her. If she at least spoke Portuguese, she could find out what was going on, could have a history, cause and effect. If she had listened to Jonas, to the ranger, and later to the traffickers. If she listened. The bike's engine didn't completely drown out the crickets, a few night fowl that she had never heard before. In the Kansas fields so long ago she would know how to listen to them. In New York she hadn't heard anything, but that had been a long time ago. She could understand; if she spoke, if she listened, she might take off the blindfold.

A car passed by, its engine approaching and retreating. She could yell for help, in some form, throw herself from the motorcycle and run as best she could toward whoever had just crossed her path. She could throw herself from the motorcycle at any moment; what kept her tied there? She would come out a bit banged up, true, but it wouldn't be the first accident in her life. The man kept on driving, impassively. Annie yelled one last time, "Why?" And without reply they continued through the forest, deeper and deeper, the lampposts were becoming farther apart and the darkness of the trees, once so welcoming, was now only the darkness in which no one could see, speak, or investigate anything. The curves came one after the other and the roadway disappeared behind them in seconds, until they rounded one that suddenly ended in a small square. In the square was a car with its headlights off and some people inside who were surely having sex.

Unable to resist, the man braked, turned off the motor, and peeked in. Annie peeked as well and would never forget the two pairs of eyes suddenly staring through the glass, observing them in return, planning their defense. The woman's breasts, very large and sagging for her young age, swung lightly while the man, still in his shirt, kicked open the door and, holding an iron bar, came toward them. The old, toothless man was lost: he had to fight. With tears in her eyes, petrified, the woman opened the rear window to scream for help and gestured to the man who had been fucking her to let it go, get in the car, and flee. Because the stranger on the motorcycle could be armed, and was. Old, yes, but his criminal appearance left no doubt. The man who had been fucking the woman nevertheless advanced, and before seeing the old man take out his gun, Annie realized she wouldn't have another chance to get away. She ran into the woods before hearing the first shot.

The woods became thicker and opened briefly, only to close again. Annie tripped over a root, got up, and continued onward. *Go on*, she repeated to herself, advancing little by little. Faster at first to be sure she wouldn't be found, then more slowly because she had been walking for such a long time with no sign of the man after her, almost an hour, perhaps, moving aimlessly wherever it seemed easiest to walk, tripping again, getting scratched here and there, but what did it matter because it was what would continue to save her. It was obvious, she told herself, it was the dense woods that would welcome her once again, hide her and let her stay there, silent and covered with scratches, for as long as she wished. The treetops closed off the sky and cut her off from all sound, from the motorcycle and the footsteps of the man, yes, the trees shielded her from the two gunshots she had heard when still near the square; she had tripped over a rock and tumbled down a ravine, until a tree trunk stopped the weight of her body and she suspected that she had a broken arm. But no, she could still move it, along with her legs and all her bones. Only her forehead and shoulders were bleeding, and the rest ached. She rose carefully and saw she was in an area the man could get to quickly if he was crazy enough to jump. And if she knew a little about men, she knew this one wasn't the kind to plunge headlong into impenetrable woods. Even so, she walked faster and faster, without the courage to turn on the flashlight of her cell phone for fear it would give her away.

She only turned it on much later, having walked for a good length of time and wondering how long she would stay there, whether for a few hours more or for days or for the rest of her life, for the forest was the size of a forest, even if it was in the middle of a city, and she was the size of a person even if she wished at that moment to be the size of an ant or a coati digging its lair. The cell phone couldn't get a signal and the battery was almost dead, but its light helped a little, especially to tell the time: approximately three fifteen. Soon it would be dawn, and if the man didn't suddenly appear, she would have a better idea of where she was and what to do.

She stopped for a moment, sat on a rock, took a deep breath. If she only knew about Jonas. If she only had more coke. She needed to pull herself together. An opening in the canopy of trees admitted the sky and a few stars. A little bit of coke, just a sniff. It was tough thinking about it. She would get home and Jonas wouldn't be in the neighboring house, waiting for her with the lines already laid out. Jonas had to appear, and the thought that he might be dead or at least missing a finger impelled her to stand up and resume the trek.

* * *

It was beginning to dawn and her phone had died some time ago. Maybe she was exaggerating things. Jonas might already have texted her, might be waiting at home for her. But she might take days to locate him, even if she found a clearing soon, some open space in the vegetation. She quickened her pace, she was getting close. She almost didn't believe it. If she could get back to the park she was almost certain she would know how to get to her house. She knew the area well enough, every belvedere, every square, every nook. True, she could be a long way from the entrance, but it didn't matter. She walked farther and farther, almost ran, and finally spotted the square with the stone knee wall with its drawings of balloons, facing the city. It had to be the Excelsior belvedere, one of those she had visited most during the last several weeks. It was her territory and only a forty-minute walk to where she lived.

It had been a long time since Annie felt like crying. She did so at that moment, but controlled herself. She went to the wall and caught sight of the city from above; a light mist covered the peaks of Tijuca Mountain and the smaller Tijuca Mirim. Below, the start of morning merged with the lights of night, dotting the bay and the bridge to Niterói. The favelas were sparsely lit and Maracanã Stadium was visible. The streets were filling little by little with cars that would not come through those remote roadways in the heights of the forest, and the city began to revive, distant from the gringa covered with dirt and blood, her arm twisted and her skin gashed, the arrogant gringa who now wanted to speak Portuguese, understand what had happened, and, for the love of God, snort a little coke.

In the future she would understand. For now, she allowed the city to follow its routine after admiring it and grasping it as the city that would never be hers in its beauty and its small monstrosities, but no, Annie was exhausted and needed to sleep. Turning her back on the belvedere, she began slowly walking home. She ignored the calls from the guard at the entrance gate to the woman with blotted makeup and wearing a miniskirt who looked as if she had been raped by tree roots, who eventually climbed the steps of her own porch, opened the door, dragged herself to her bedroom, collapsed onto the bed, and closed her eyes.

She couldn't sleep, however. With her phone turned on and charging, there was no message from Jonas, no message of any kind. She thought of going to his house and ringing the doorbell, but he lived with his parents and she didn't have the strength to take a shower, tend to her wounds, and make herself minimally presentable for a possible encounter with his mother.

Instead, she telephoned. One call, two, nothing. On the third, someone answered and hung up immediately. That was suspicious, but Annie lacked the energy to try to do anything about it. She just sent him a message, *U alright? At home already? Pls tell me everything is okay*, and closed her eyes. She must have dozed, for she awoke with a small start to see a recently arrived message: *is good. i arrive my house. i love you.*

Annie refused to investigate. She could have wondered why Jonas had sent a message instead of answering the phone. She could have wondered why his almost native English had become transformed into that grammatical horror show. And why would he speak to her of something as alien to the two of them as love? But Annie didn't want to, couldn't investigate. She was spent. Satisfied with the rough draft of a reply, she ignored the scratches burning her aching arm. She couldn't do anything more, she could only ignore them just as she ignored everything else about Jonas, as she ignored the fate of the old man and the finger kept by the man without a pinky, the couple screwing in the car and her next snort, ignored everything because her body wouldn't let her anymore, and calm like the fields of Kansas after a snow, she closed her eyes and slept.

THE ENIGMA OF THE VICTROLA

BY ARNALDO BLOCH

Jacarepaguá

1.

Which came first, jacaré (the alligator) or Jacarepaguá (the place)?

In the bar where I was celebrating my fiftieth birthday, after extensive planning, I introduced the mystery that had engaged me since childhood, and whose solution I had found at last. All that was missing was to test the solution.

The first guest to enter the discussion was an ardent biologist, an experienced tender of turtles.

"The animal was there before man."

"So what?" I objected.

"So, before men, there was no such district."

"Who mentioned a district?"

"If it's not a district, what is it?"

"It's the word."

At that moment an expert in common sense intervened.

"First jacaré. Then Jacarepaguá."

"How do you know?"

"Everybody knows."

"Everybody who?"

"Everybody."

At the neighboring table a German linguist overheard everything. She said: "Excuse me for *brreaking* in, but *jacarré* came *firrst. Jacarrepaguá* was what the Tupi Indians called a lake of *jacarrés. Jacarré* means *alligatorr. Paguá* means lake. Consequently—"

A clamor erupted at the table: my friends were commemorating my failure.

It happens that the German woman was mistaken. Jacarepaguá came before jacaré. And, moreover, it *could* have come before, as befits the deductive method.

I drained my glass of beer with a slice of lemon in it and looked directly at the Teuton, who had hips the size of the bar.

"*Frau*, your explanation is illogical. There is no evidence that the Tupis named the lake before naming the alligator."

The German woman, who was pink, turned a deep red. "Senhorr, even if the lake was designated paguá before the *jacarré* was designated *jacarré, jacarré* only went into the lake after the existence of the two worrds sep-a-rrate-ly. So, jacarré-worrd already existed when Indian saw jacarré-animal go into paguá-lake. Only afterr, paguá-worrd joined jacarré-worrd in a new worrd."

Silence came over the audience, in criminological suspense.

"I could say, *frau*, in a philosophical sense, that the phenomenon may have existed before the word, therefore the word was already there, waiting for the fact. The nature of time is controversial."

"That is *absurrd, irrational*, because—"

"And I could raise another long, endless series of hypotheses, *frau*. As it happens, that's not the issue."

The woman, who had turned purple, widened her eyes. "And what is the issue, *senhorr*?"

I filled my glass. The lemon disappeared into the foam. "The issue is that there's a story that's not the story of biological, chronological, topographical, or etymological cases."

The German's eyes bulged out of their sockets. "And what *storry* is that, *senhorr?*"

"My story."

2.

Bbbbbbbbrrrrrrrrrrrrrrrm!
I'm so sick
Bbbbbbbbrrrrrrrrrrrrrrrm!
I'm neurasthenic

Bbbbbbbbrrrrrrrrrrrrrrrm!
I need to get help
Otherwise
I'm going to Jacarepaguá

The verses, wrapped in a dance rhythm, came from a Victrola that I never saw, only heard. Other verses came from it, from other records my mother bought in a store in Laranjeiras, including other verses from that same song, but lying in bed at the age of five, I focused on the floundering of the singer. Focused also on the word *neurasthenic*, accented on the last syllable to rhyme with *sick*.

And I focused, to the point of obsession, on that place: Jacarepaguá.

I didn't know it was a district. And to this day I still don't. I didn't even know what a *jacaré* was. And although my parents had taken me to the well-known Lagoa lake, the existence of *paguá* was beyond my contemplation.

But I guessed that the place, that place, Jacarepaguá, if you were to go there it wouldn't be anything good, which immediately aroused in me the desire to be there.

And that came to be the foundation of any future concern, plan, or action.

3.

It was the time for learning words, of asking *what's-that*, *what's-this*, *what's-whatever*. Away from the Victrola (which I never saw), I asked my mother what *neur-as-then-ic* was and she answered that it was a man who was nervous, and I asked what nervous was, and she floundered like the man's voice did on the Victrola.

"Loony," she finally said.

The explanation was convincing. *Loony*, about whose meaning I had no idea, clarified everything, sounded like something I had already understood about the song and matched everything else.

There was still the question of what Jacarepaguá was. But I would never dare ask. Jacarepaguá should be conquered without help, without explanations that weren't natural: any fact, word, map, or proof should spring from the days, like the word itself sprang from the Victrola that I never saw.

However, to move on, it was necessary for the jacaré to come. It came. The process of learning to read began, conducted by a teacher who not coincidentally was my aunt.

In my aunt's alphabet set, of her own design, the *a* stood for *ant*, a convenient thing, as it's easy to make the drawing of an ant fit inside of an *a* or even to draw the *a* as if it were the ant itself.

And so forth. The *d* was a strange set of *dice*, and the *e* was an *elephant* (don't ask me how), the *f* was a *flamingo*, and the *j*, the *jacaré*.

"What's a jacaré?" I inquired, and everyone laughed, as if they knew what a jacaré was. My aunt called on a cross-eyed

boy everyone thought was a genius. It happens that, in addition
to being cross-eyed, he also had a speech defect.

"*Jacalé* is an animal with a *gleeeeeeat* big mouth and *shaaalp*
teeth who stays in the lake lying in the sun."

It was the genius's turn to be the object of laughter.
My aunt got pissed and ended the class less than halfway
through the alphabet, which later earned her a warning from
the principal.

I went home looking through the school bus window at
the leafy trees in Laranjeiras, which gave off a hot breath of
late afternoon, and the sound of cicadas filled me with a bru-
tal sadness and the wish to die, especially since the sidewalks
emanated a bouquet of shit that battled with the blossoms
from every flower bed in the city.

At home, I dashed to bed in hopes of sleeping before dinner, but it was impossible. My mother had put on the Victrola
a song with hysterical syllables.

Mahna mahna
(ba dee bedebe)
Mahna mahna
(ba debe dee)
Mahna mahna
(ba dee bedebe badebe badebe dee dee de-de de-de-de)
Mah mama na mahna namwomp mwomp
Ma mo mo mana mo

I went to sleep and dreamed about my aunt turning into
a giant ant who emerged from a tree and exploded into al-
phabetic gas, leaving a stench of letters in the air. When the
smoke dissipated, Jacarepaguá materialized in a large gray
swamp where monsters with *enormous teeth* were eating one

another, forming a viscous mass that filled everything and went up their noses, mouths, and ears until embedding itself in the world's most godforsaken places.

I woke up and ran to my parents' bed in tears. Daddy was listening to the radio and Mom—where was Mom? I shouted for her but she didn't appear. It was only when I awoke the second time that my mother was at the foot of the bed with a plate of angel hair pasta and grated cheese.

4.

It took time, maybe months, for me to recover from that phonetic improvisation that, according to my mother, was an Italian tongue twister. I even came to forget the song of the *neurasthenic*.

I started having agonizing pains in my head and eyes. I cried and screamed. Mom dragged me to a macumba *terreiro*, I remember a dark room leading to another room separated by a beaded curtain.

An old man rocked me back and forth and gave me two punches on the ear that still ring today. Afterward, at home, my mother swung a chicken over my head.

But the bad luck, and the pains, won out, which made my mother resort to an extreme measure: to look for an optometrist. The man was shocked and, instead of recommending I see a psychiatrist, prescribed window-pane glasses, thinking it was an imaginary crisis.

The bad luck only lessened when Mom put two sambas on the Victrola. A samba-rock and a samba-samba. The samba-rock was luminous and lofty.

I live in a tropical country
blessed by God

and beautiful by nature
but what beauty
in February (in February)
there's Carnival (there's Carnival)
I've got a Beetle and a guitar
root for Flamengo and my girl's called Teresa

The samba-samba, on the other hand, tempered its haughtiness with the sun of a suburban and moderate Sunday.

Rio de Janeiro is still beautiful
Rio de Janeiro is still beautiful
Rio de Janeiro, February and March
hello hello Realengo
a really big hug!
hello Flamengo fans
a really big hug!

Both sambas had in common pleasant words like *February* and *Carnival*, but there was one uncomfortable word, *Flamengo*, our team's archrival, which I had learned when my father dragged me to a large stadium; I had a balloon filled with urine thrown on my black-and-white-striped Botafogo shirt. At the exit, Daddy tripped on a hole and fell into some mud. An older man helped him up.

When we got home, Daddy turned on the Transglobe radio that picked up stations from around the world and we listened to the Maré Mansa comedy group. The next day he brought corn on a stick from Guinle Park and we listened to Chacrinha's show.

The headaches got better and the glasses disappeared, along with the ill-smelling hen swinging over my head. As a consequence I came to like the chicken stew the maid, a woman who rooted for Flamengo, prepared on Saturdays and which I had found nauseating before.

At that time, fate revealed the first threads of a happiness that, if not possible, was at least visible. In the middle of the city rose a crooked architecture, and I always found odd that bus line with a sign saying, *Jacaré*.

I was relieved to discover that Jacaré was another place and not *that* one, and that there was even a neighboring district, Jacarezinho. In a book of native languages I found out that, in one definition, *jacaré* comes from *yacaré*, "that which is twisted, sinuous," like the Jacaré district, the destination of the bus that didn't go *there*.

The existential nausea, however, persisted, and the sight of my father sucked down into a muddy tomb comprised the worst moments of my night terrors even two decades later, when that stadium finally lit up, when Botafogo won for the first time in twenty-one years, and I clutched my striped shirt at my heart.

Jacarepaguá thus remained suspended over the territory of doubt, made up of vestiges, songs, and symbols.

The day I departed, Jacarepaguá would be ready. And I would be ready for Jacarepaguá.

5.

While I waited, bones, joints, skull, and nose grew. My dick, not so much. When soft, it resembled a mushroom attached to a blond sword. If I stretched the foreskin, it looked like it had arms. The nanny watched out of the corner of her eye. My little sister thought it looked like the Christ statue we saw from the window and wanted me to do it again.

"Do the Christ."

"No."

"Aw, do it."

I brought out the small organ and stretched the skin, and my sister laughed like mad. Once, when my sister wasn't there, the nanny, at the foot of the bed, came closer and suddenly rubbed her nose against the mushroom. I felt a sharp sting, different from the usual phenomenon that now and then overcame me.

That way, my dick even had a certain majesty, recalling a monk or an astronaut, and itched like the devil. With the help of a beige-colored soap that smelled of bleach, one day I had my first creamy, watery ejaculation, which had the same smell as the soap because the skin must have absorbed the acids listed on the wrapper. It was time to go to Copacabana, according to my uncle, who also arranged the address where there awaited me a woman who repeatedly washed her mouth in a basin located in a bedroom smelling of Chihuahua.

I was anxious for the great journey and in college I crossed paths with the loonies from the Pinel colony and greeted them intimately. They treated me like a longtime friend. I also learned that in a neighborhood in the West Zone, whose name I don't remember, there was a famous insane asylum that inspired an inane song at the start of the 1970s.

At the university there were people from all over— Copacabana, Méier, Sulacap, Quito, Leblon. There was a small lake where you smoked grass and an academic center where you smoked grass and a football field where you smoked grass and a dark parking lot where you smoked grass.

It was during a rainy night that I spotted, in that parking lot, *her* car; the key had fallen to the ground, the girl was groping on the pavement, the slit in her miniskirt was half open, her thighs marked from leaning against a low, jagged wall—I think there were even leaves with oily grime covering her skin.

Her hair was the color of vanilla ice cream, and she wore green high-heel shoes without stockings, tight, dying to come off. She owned a dingy white Beetle nicknamed *Roach*. I wanted to accompany her, but I lived a long way from *there*. When she told me where her house was, the blood rushed to my head.

"Where? You swear?"

"Yes."

"Will you take me there?"

"One day. But it's still early."

"Want to go for a ride?"

At the top of the Vista Chinesa I tested the soles of her feet to see what she was like, and her soles were bloody and covered with talcum. I coughed and came on the sole and made the talcum into a holy paste with which I anointed my mouth and I think the paste never came off.

The next Saturday we went to the Reserve, a beach area, deserted, taking a bottle of coconut cocktail from Oswaldo's bar. From the sand we returned to the smooth leather of the Beetle and she steadied her ass in the space between the front seats and asked me, in the backseat, to stick it in her pink aureole under the weak light.

Afterward we continued, with her at the wheel, along the Bandeirantes highway. Groggy from the drink, I saw an unknown city go past: a dirt road that in the dark seemed like an Indian village, half inhabited; a winding mountain range; and a long-deserted avenue. The next thing I realized, we were *there*.

6.

Bbbbbbbbrrrrrrrrrrrrrrm!

I'm so loving
Bbbbbbbbrrrrrrrrrrrrrrrm!
Whoever tried me liked me
Bbbbbbbbrrrrrrrrrrrrrrrm!
I gotta take care of myself
Otherwise
I'll end up in Jacarepaguá

I sampled all her fruits, including the ability to look at the sky through a telescope, and the art of screwing on a roof, fucking in the woods, fornicating on the ground where ten dogs roamed loose.

From time to time some of them would kill each other and we heard their doleful yelps there inside, in the spacious semiabandoned house on a vacant lot. But on the following day it would seem like there was an extra bevy of dogs, adult offspring that death added instead of subtracted.

She said she had a mother and no father, but I never saw her mother, although there was a bedroom whose door never opened. The area around that place had roads with strange names that multiplied like parasites, *ironwood, arroyo, tindiba, gerenguê, cafundá, boiuna, curumaú, catonho,* and *marshal miguel salazar mendes de moraes.*

Another road was said to lead to Grajaú, but how can you go from an improbable place like that to an established, famous, treelined district?

At the top of the *hill* was a cabin that might function as an establishment, but I never saw anything around there, although there was an indistinct movement of bodies to which the girl referred and which I glimpsed in flashes.

One day, the girl had a dream. That from the hillside, instead of all of Rio de Janeiro in view, there was only a foggy swamp, and on an especially dark night she went looking for me, descended to the swamp, and after searching through it pulled out like a root my still-fresh hand, ejected bleeding from some random spot.

I thought the dream was a summons, that I should take a stand by acting or making a pact. I heeded the summons at once.

"Tomorrow I'm going up there. The place in the dream."

"Because of me?" she asked, rubbing her heel between my iliac and sacrum.

"Tomorrow," I promised.

I have no idea how I got there. I know that up at the top I felt like releasing the steering wheel of the Passat 1.8T and letting the fragments from the collision with the rock scatter into the fog, and that my hand was the only whole, intact form to repose in the swamp and later disappear under one final bubble of air.

However, things didn't happen that way. The truth is that I skidded, flipped, was blinded by the fog until, lacking hope, I ended up at the foot of the quarry, in its arms, and the dog pack howled at the moonless sky and the Victrola was playing Pink Floyd and in the darkness of the bedroom that had a phosphorescent vault on its ceiling we made love.

7.

I was in Jacarepaguá. The sky, the quarry, the roads, the cabin, the fog, the swamp: city-word. One night I think I actually found myself amid a group of humans, at the counter of a bar in a Scandinavian restaurant. We had a strong drink made of Nordic herbs.

A gentleman, thin like an umbrella, tall as the ceiling, bent down to give an urgent warning.

"The airplane. Be careful with the plane," he said, displaying his infinitely long finger. He bowed and left the bar.

That night we made love for a long time and without protection, as we always did five days before or after her period.

On a foggy Sunday she said she was leaving and would be back the next day.

"I'm going by bus," she emphasized, without my having asked and without her saying where she was going.

I waited for her in the same place, covered in the smoke of four packs of filterless cigarettes. When she returned, we went into the quarry and rubbed ourselves against the walls of a cavern, hearing distant drops of water.

Her belly began growing three months later.

She loved dogs. The animated creatures.

I wanted nothing of any kind that might take me back to life in the city, to pin me down, nothing—a child, a saint, an envoy—that would remove me from here.

"I'll get rid of it," she said, impassive, but there was a shadow.

So, I returned to Copacabana and settled there. I didn't go back to the university. For a time *Jacarepaguá* became a forbidden word. By phone I learned that *she* dreamed about the fetus as an angel, the ectoplasm pursued her, stuck its fist in her navel, and abraded her breasts.

One day, in my sleep, the umbrella-shaped man returned to me. I woke up and called her.

"The airplane."

"What airplane?"

"You didn't go by bus."

"Yes I did."

"You didn't."

"I did."

"You went by plane."

"No."

"Yes."

Planes are pipettes of uteruses, centrifuges of ovaries, graters of placental walls.

She left. And took the city with her.

8.

I know they love me,
but for marrying
and I tell them to wait for me
because after the party ta-ra-ta-ta
Bbbbbbbbbrrrrrrrrrrrrrrrm!

One day six or seven years later, I had taken every kind of drug known to man, got my father's Maverick, and drove up the sierra, down the other side, and stopped in front of the house *there*, still intact. I saw the Beetle, but by now it was decomposing and ready for the junkyard.

The surrounding region was becoming a favela and the house was already part of the complex. It looked like no one was there anymore, except for a dog, the patriarch, who in earlier days almost spoke, shouted my name. He recognized me and tried to shout and speak but only succeeded in emitting a weak and screechy whistle.

From the house a fat woman soon emerged, dragging herself.

One hand pulled a boy who looked a lot like me in the time when I listened to records on the unseen Victrola. The other hand carried a box, supported at the waist. The fat woman had crooked teeth and a neck covered with pockmarks.

The boy looked at me, opening his eyes wide and covering his mouth as if about to vomit.

I felt my throat convulse and my intestines tighten.

The woman stared deeply into my eyes as far as my throat, and in her eyes I recognized a glimmer. A voice of gales whirled through the mountain range of her teeth. "*You took a long time to come back*," said the voice.

Everything spun.

The boy ran into the house. I thought I heard the hoarse growl of the dog and a tearing sound of lacerated viscera, an echo.

The next instant, she was no longer there. In my hand, the box she had brought moments before.

There was no house, quarry, or valley. Only fog. The ground was mud, like the mud where the body of my father was almost lost.

I opened the box. In it, the hand was still fresh and smelled of sulfur.

9.

I thought that all my friends, or whatever they were, would enter into logical considerations and rationalizations, led by the *plot*, avoiding the truth. That they were going to ask whether the fat woman was really *her*, whether that boy was my son, or whether the son was me myself on the wrong side of a dream. Whether the hand was mine (and whether it was the right or the left) and whether upon receiving it in the box I had both of mine intact or was missing one. If there were a psychoanalyst in the bar, perhaps he would want to know if the fat woman was my pregnant mother. Or if that man (me) was the son of another man (me), a policeman killed by a drug trafficker (me) found at the foot of the sierra with a hand cut off, being that my hand of *his* ended up in the hand of *her*, that I had received the double hand as a trophy, that I was the perpetrator of those happenings, assassin of the fetus, son of Jacarepaguá, and that it would therefore be the son I never had, properly or improperly, the incarnation of an angel. Maybe someone versed in the lines and history of the city might argue that, in the ultimate analysis, Jacarepaguá isn't a district, since with the growth of the West Zone it transformed into a *collection* of districts, a region, a city.

But no.

Instead of that, a solemn and moving silence filled the bar. It was no longer a silence of criminological suspense but a silence of empathy, compassion, and even submission. The waiter bringing the birthday cake retreated, took it back to the kitchen, and, I think, never returned.

The German linguist, in turn, was holding her head low in such penitence that one could say the entire weight of the world was resting on her shoulders, which would be, deep down, the dream, or the reality, of every German, every Frenchman, every European, all of us on their backs, on our neighbor's back, and the neighbor on the back of the dog.

I left money on the table (just my part) and got up, heading out into the empty streets.

When I was about to reach the foothill, behind me there was some kind of procession. I think I even saw a candle.

I went on walking, at the head of the line. Sometimes I'd risk a sideward glance, but I grew tired of checking to see if there was still a cortege.

Frequently I felt, at such times, that I was walking in circles, or spinning like a record around a tree, following a curve, an axis, in a lighted courtyard redolent of bygone rose apples, at the hour of a sunbath, and afterward everything vanished for a time; I'd feel a sharp pinch in the wrist and fall into a sleep as deep and as cloudy as death, in a sterile bedroom.

When I awoke, the story would begin again, and I'd await, attentive, for the next intermission.

PART IV

RIO BABYLON

TANGERINE TANGO

BY MARCELO FERRONI

Barra da Tijuca

I could have called it a premonition, but I don't believe in that, or in luck; in fact I believed in few things other than some money at the end of the month and a decent place to sleep, maybe someone beside me and a bit of happiness. I believed in what I didn't have and laughed at myself at the counter of that hotel made of plaster and granite, of plywood with a veneer imitating hardwood, plastic plants in cement pots, lustless leather sofas. A steady bureaucratic rain was falling; I leaned against the counter and observed the curtain of thick drops that descended the narrow roof of glass a few feet beyond the automatic door. This city sucked up my air, this city of false appearances and low ceilings, this city whose buildings were neoclassical aberrations under a leaden gray sky, a São Paulo simulacrum of hell, while the receptionist—braces, the face of a kid—waited on the phone for my author to answer. I didn't hate just the city, I hated my job, and before I could go back to cursing myself she passed slowly by outside. The automatic door opened and closed while she moved along the sidewalk without coming into the lobby. She had yellowish-beige skin, and her slightly flaccid arms emerged from a modest black dress that descended a little below the knee. Black shoes with medium heels, discreet legs. She rested her cheek on the phone in her left hand and in the right balanced an umbrella, which suddenly swept my senses into a celestial premonition (but I don't believe in that), each of the umbrella's colorful segments a portrait of Rio de Janeiro—Christ the Redeemer, Sugar Loaf, another showing Maracanã, still another the beach and the wave-patterned sidewalks—and I thought I could be in a better place, warmer, where people smiled like that girl with large white teeth. She continued to the edge of my field of vision and disappeared into a service entrance.

"What did you say your name is?" the receptionist asked me.

"Mariconda. Humberto Mariconda."

I waited a bit more. My author sent word that he'd be down any moment, but the moment didn't come. Behind the receptionist hung a panel with the name of the hotel, and farther back, in the rear, where the office must be, she reappeared, without the umbrella or the phone, but still displaying her teeth in a half-smile, and only then did I notice how round her eyes were, and she raised them and looked at me. She was plump and diminutive at the same time, her dark hair tied in a bun, bare shoulders with small variations in color, and my God I smiled at her and her entire face opened up. She was about to say something but saw that her colleague was already taking care of me, then lowered her eyes to the computer monitor and started typing.

I could have said so many things to her. If she were alone. If the guy beside her weren't looking at me the way I was looking at her. If the elevator bell hadn't dinged and a man as shapeless as melted Camembert hadn't emerged, accompanied by a blond woman who seemed like a collage of several faces, new and old, put together by a child in an art class. They didn't notice me when I stepped forward with my best smile to escort them to the taxi waiting in the street. I started to help him, but he grunted, pulling his cane away.

That was what I was doing lately, greeting authors who

didn't want to be greeted *by me*, who would like to be successful with another publishing house, lionized by more relevant people, selling out entire printings of their tired novels, but who one way or another had fallen into the well and felt it was our fault, always our fault.

Natsume, my editor, assigned me the unpleasant duties only because my behavior was more stable than that of Rose, the publicist—a lady as old as our dot matrix printer—and because I was the only one there who could manage more than three sentences in English.

Seven months later, there I was again, playing the same role in another city, imparting concrete form to my premonition (though I don't believe in that), leaning against a slightly larger counter in a more spacious lobby, monumental without having anything to be proud of, the salmon-colored walls with high-relief plaster waves, uncomfortable sofas, old palms, and carpets that made an effort to instill a warmer atmosphere in that third-rate Persian temple. I could be in the outskirts of anywhere in the world, except for the strip of ultramarine blue beyond the avenue, which merged with the turquoise sky at the horizon whenever the smoked-glass double doors opened to admit the fitful service of the porters.

Hours earlier, from the window of the plane, I had seen that same sea, camouflaged by a diffuse fog, and the images of a distant umbrella: Christ the Redeemer, Sugar Loaf, the whitish Maracanã Stadium, and the circular shores of foam, sand, and buildings. All of that dissipated in the heat at the airport, the chaotic wait to get a cab, where the attendants laughed among themselves or spoke on cell phones while men in suits broke in line. I left in an old Santana with dark windows and damp seats, clutching my backpack, and we plunged into the other end of the city, in heat that would strip the bark off trees (the air-conditioning went out today, the driver said, without the slightest effort to sound convincing), stuck on the congested highway on the way to Barra, amid nightmarish hovels and prisonlike walls that reminded me of the stories of people from São Paulo who get lost upon arriving in Rio and end up in a favela where they're robbed and ultimately shot.

I wasn't shot; I didn't go where I shouldn't; I didn't flee from gunfire or have a gun stuck in my face, and yet a day later there I was, with an enigmatic girl, sandwiched between sun and cement in an enormous parking lot in Barra, with our author still missing in some part of Rio, and her and me fleeing hand in hand from a police car, with her sweaty and leading the way, without listening to my pleas, until she stopped suddenly and let go of my hand, took three steps, and stopped again, as if in a trance, her straw-colored hair tousled around her freckled face, squinting against the brightness, she began to rock lightly, panting, more whirling than turning now, among the white stripes like ancient inscriptions on the scorched pavement. Then she opened her trinket-colored eyes that glowed against the sun, she moaned, and my heart almost burst. With quick steps I covered the distance that separated me from her and caught her before she could fall, near a concrete gutter. She held onto me as best she could—her thin arms had almost no strength—and stuck her face in the hollow of my shoulder and I ran my hands over her tangled hair, she made an effort not to faint and then whispered in my ear, *I know what happened to him, I know.*

It took me some time to identify the color of her eyes, and what they seemed to be saying when she stared at me with dry lips and an expression of discontent. She paid no attention to me, or pretended not to, the first time I saw her, coming out of the elevator in dark glasses, tapping disinterestedly on a cell phone. She came just behind the person I was really there to greet. She vanished, probably accustomed to his small displays, as soon as he stepped forward and occupied all the available space, agitating the air molecules around him. His name was Greg Nicholas, MD, and he was in every sense just who he appeared to be. Compact, tanned, with dark hair clinging to his scalp like a new doormat. He wore beige pants, hitched a little above the waist, and a blue shirt that emphasized his well-defined pecs. A small silver chain hugged his powerful neck. He had a square chin, hard professional eyes that shone mechanically when he saw me. He extended his hand, which I shook, but it was like grasping a stone, a stone that in turn shook back. He gave me a lingering look. "How are you?" he said, and took from his pocket a blue pen, which he presented to me as a gift. *Greg Nicholas Institute of Positive Knowledge*. I smiled, looked at the pen again, got confused a bit at the greeting, the sweat running down my back wetting the waistband of my loose-fitting jeans.

With the nervous muffling of my ears I didn't notice that there were others with me: two onlookers, the manager, a very young journalist, and a platinum-blonde in dark glasses with her likely driver, a scowling unshaven guy in a suit too big for him. The blonde advanced and to the sound of tinkling jewelry extended her slender fingers, which Greg took delicately. "How are you?" he said, with slightly more warmth, and a sly smile appeared in the right-hand corner of his mouth. He handed her a pink pen, without breaking eye contact. I began to explain that I was from the publishing company, that I— the blond woman had started talking over me, in Portuguese (while I was getting tangled up in schoolboy English), about how honored she was by his presence and how she was sure he wouldn't be so unkind as to decline the invitation to dine at her house that evening.

Greg Nicholas enjoyed considerable success in Brazil with his method of losing weight: *You Can Do It—How to Lose Those Extra Pounds by the Power of Thought.* It had been launched by our publishing house without much fanfare—marketing was an alien concept to Natsume—and no one could explain how it had been successful here when that hadn't been the case anywhere else in the world. Two months after publication, among our other random titles (*The Ten Cruelest Leaders in History, 101 Microwave Cupcake Recipes*), Greg's book had slowly begun climbing the list of best sellers, settled into a solid sixth place in the self-help category, and stayed there. His method, according to the website of the Greg Nicholas Institute of Positive Knowledge, had been adopted by the rich and famous, among them the actress Lindsay Lohan and one Mimi Lesseos, a longtime wrestling star and stunt double for the protagonist in *Million Dollar Baby*.

I know this because I wrote the text for the book's flaps, and both names were important to sweeten the press release. To cite the lead paragraph of my text:

> *Greg spent two months in Tibet, where he learned Buddhist monks' age-old technique of concentration. By studying the energy that flows from our mind and courses through our body, Greg developed ten steps to channel this positive energy into radical weight reduction. Tested with patients around the world,* You Can Do It *is revolutionizing Western medicine.*

Greg currently lived in Belize, where he conducted cutting-edge research at his institute. I didn't know anything more, and I wouldn't have access to him during his stay in Brazil. His schedule was rigidly controlled by the girl who, while Greg was led by the hand through the lobby, stared at me with anger and incomprehension. It took me some time, lost in those eyes, but I was finally able to identify their hue. They were amber-colored, a bit yellowish. Her name was Ellie.

She had scheduled three heavily packed days for Greg Nicholas. That afternoon he would give his first interview. Afterward, he would take part in a fitness and health program and continue, in early evening, to the main event: a debate in the grand salon of the book fair with Tatá Mourinho, a journalist and student of female behavior; Laura Ruiz, nutritionist to the stars; and the retired judge Gilberto Mendes Albuquerque (Mendes Albuquerque had written a folkloric saga with spicy elements). Later Greg would sign copies in our tiny booth, with me beside him preventing access from the fans. In the days following, he would have two more interviews; visit the TV Globo studios, where he would demonstrate live one of his mentalization recipes—as he called them—and give an exclusive talk for subscribers to the newspaper O Globo; climb up Rocinha with a TV crew, where he would watch a show of children's capoeira; eat feijoada in the company of a society columnist; and conclude by autographing his book at a shopping center in Barra before embarking for Belize, with connections in Panama.

In the few minutes he was unaccompanied in the VIP section

at the book fair, Greg sat at a small table and ate compulsively from a bowl of colored peanuts while his assistant was stern, very stern with me. She wanted to know who the devil that woman was who had spoken to Greg earlier, and what was that dinner invitation that Greg had been forced to accept, and said Greg didn't like being harassed by unauthorized individuals, Greg needed his rest, Greg wasn't comfortable with the pillows at the hotel, Greg's towels weren't as she had specified (one of the things Natsume had cut from the budget), Greg needed a neutral room to radiate his positivity before the talk, Greg found it very annoying not to be able to use his PowerPoint presentation, and Greg was upset at having to share the stage with three other people. I merely looked at the horde of uniformed schoolchildren down below, sweeping through the booths like termites, asking myself why I had accepted such a job.

"And I haven't seen our book displayed anywhere till now."

She said something else that I didn't entirely catch. That accent of hers—which was perhaps only the English spoken by a native—was sometimes impenetrable for me. Nor did she understand what I was saying, and we stood there looking at each other, not understanding, frustrated.

I phoned my boss. Natsume was one of those diabetics who drink out of foolhardiness, and I knew that at six o'clock, with whiskey fermenting his brain, he would be mildly ill-humored.

"The assistant complained about the towels," I said.

"What towels?"

"I think she's going to notice the car we rented this morning isn't armored."

"What car?"

"A platinum-blonde intruded into our conversation and invited Greg to dinner."

"What blonde?"

The panel, needless to say, was a mess, the way events tend to be in my presence. They put Greg at the end of a long table with a white cloth, and it was obvious that the ladies and teenage girls in the audience of two hundred—more packed than I'd ever seen at a book fair—were only there to see Greg. The moderator was an environmental journalist and insisted that each panelist, himself included, say a few autobiographical words before Greg. Greg fidgeted so much that his legs made the table shake—he was a veritable reservoir of positivity. When he finally took the microphone, he leaped up because he was incapable of giving a talk sitting down. What happened next was monumental. Racing from side to side, interacting with the audience, which didn't understand a word he was saying, Greg told his story of self-awareness, of how he had been a poor child with no prospects, and how early on he discovered the gift of channeling positive energies to overcome barriers. Greg questioned people, Greg made them laugh, Greg summoned a woman from the audience, Greg did push-ups, Greg threw out fistfuls of colored pens, Greg drew applause that raised the temperature of that enormous sardine can by several degrees. The other panelists were as astonished as I was. At the end of his talk the stage was invaded, and only Ellie's brute force allowed him to be led down the crowded corridors to our booth where, I should add, a plywood wall was knocked over during the autograph session.

I was wiped out, I needed a shower, I cursed our publicist for having learned English on cassette tapes. Only one other person didn't try to get closer: the platinum-blonde, all in white, fiery lipstick, heavy eye shadow, whose gaze focused unwaveringly on Greg's every action as he signed copies on the plastic table. Her and the unshaven guy in the overly large suit. Two people, then. Three, actually, because another guy was there, a guy with a foreign air about him, now I remember: tall and thin, very straight caramel-colored hair parted in the middle, prescription glasses with round frames, beige linen jacket. Standing a bit away from us, as motionless as a lizard.

We would see him again a few hours later, at the dinner in Greg's honor, which I was forced to take part in. Ellie was nervous about anything outside the schedule, too nervous, and I had to spend a few hours in the lobby of the Windsor Barra, wearing the same clothes from the afternoon, still with my backpack because I hadn't had time to check in to my own hotel, which was apparently a long way from there—more of Natsume's stupid penny-pinching. In fact, it was so far away that the cabbie laughed when I gave him the address: Aterro do Flamengo. Even if Greg pumped iron, took a bubble bath, clipped his nails, and fixed his hair, there was no way I could go and be back in time to meet them.

We left at ten p.m. Ellie had tied her hair in a bun, light makeup, black silk pants, and a white blouse, and Greg was wearing the same beige-blue combination immortalized in his photo on the book jacket. The taxi driver passed through dark, empty treelined streets with high fences in what could well have been São Paulo and turned onto an avenue with unfinished buildings, colored posters advertising something of low quality, and fallen boarding swollen from humidity that revealed machines and rusted girders. Instead of taking the tunnel, the driver hung a right onto a narrow street and stopped at an iron-gated entrance whose green bars rose in waves to form a design of delicate leaves. We waited for a reply. Greg fidgeted every time he shifted on the vinyl seats, and he didn't fidget just a little. The gate opened. Then we began going up.

The houses got larger the farther we went, and we stopped near the summit, in front of a two-story mansion that attracted attention not because it was imposing, nor because of the lights or the palm trees at the entrance, but because of the colors. Dark green, grenadine red, dark green, grenadine red, grenadine red, grenadine red, dark green, every wall, every window, every balcony painted with the colors of Fluminense's jersey as if the owner was obsessed with it, or honoring a vow. Nothing else could explain such absence of taste.

I left my backpack with an attendant. The house was full. Greg was immediately surrounded by four women of indeterminate ages and was in his element, gesticulating, communicating with winks. He distributed a few colored pens, the women laughed, one of them raised her dress to show a muscular thigh compact as a chicken drumstick, and I recognized the hostess because she was talking the loudest; this time she was wearing a vivid orange miniskirt and a pink, brown, and gold leopard-patterned blouse. The battle between colors in such a short expanse of cloth was terrible.

"Try the caipirinha," I told Ellie, who had been forgotten in a corner. I had already gotten a drink, sake with red fruit, and was amused to see the same guy with the oversized suit behind the fruit table, grinding sugar in a glass. "I thought you were the driver," I said.

He filled the glass with booze and stuck a colored straw in it without looking at me. "And I thought real men didn't drink sake caipirinhas with red fruit," he replied.

The blonde followed Greg wherever he went. When Ellie returned, I commented that I hadn't seen Mr. Platinum-Blonde anywhere. It was obvious, I said, that a house with

those colors demanded a man. A rich, truculent man. Ellie didn't hear me, or didn't understand. She was looking a
bit paler. She held her untouched caipirinha in both hands,
which were now shaking. She said, "We need to get out of
here. *Now*." That was when I saw the guy again, leaning
against one of the plaster Greek pillars. The same hair parted
in the middle, the same linen jacket. The same lizard-like
eyes, which he kept glued on Greg.

She pushed through the guests to pull Greg away and in a
short time had disappeared. I finished my caipirinha, grabbed
a beer, and went out a glass door into the night. The pool and
terrace were on a level below the house. I descended the metal
steps, crossed the lighted patio, and headed to the glass parapet. My God, the view was magnificent. To the left, a concrete
elevated roadway lit by car headlights followed the curve of
the mountain and hovered over the sea. Even at night it was
possible to see the violent crest of waves crashing against the
rocks down below. I looked at the dark water. Looked directly
at the cliff beneath my feet. The ground disappeared suddenly
amidst roiling black treetops and a chilling discharge rose between my legs. I moved away from the parapet, which suddenly seemed too low. I turned back toward the house, three
stories above, also painted in the insistent dark greens and
grenadines. In the brightness of the glass door I recognized the
spare silhouette of Ellie.

We took a cab back, in silence, Greg with a smile trapped
on his lips, squirming as he did on the earlier trip. His yawns
didn't convince me. I left them at the door of the Windsor
Barra, Ellie and I reviewed the itinerary for the next morning,
and Greg went through the automatic door without waiting
for her. It was the last time I saw him.

* * *

I found out that he had disappeared the next morning when I answered the third or fourth call on my phone. It was ten thirty and I had ridiculously lost track of time. To be expected, since I had gotten to my hotel, the Mengo Palace, at almost three a.m. after crossing the city in a ride that cost over a hundred *reais*, which I had to pay out of my own pocket. I entered the mirrored lobby, with its slight smell of must, and realized I had left my backpack at the home of the platinum-blonde. I got under the poor electric shower, lay down on the bed with my underwear inside out. The air conditioner rattled like a jalopy, someone laughed loudly all night, and the sound of buses cutting across the Aterro seemed to materialize itself directly over my bed.

It was Ellie on the phone, and from what little I understood she was saying that Greg hadn't come down for breakfast, wasn't answering calls, hadn't gone to the gym or left for a run on the beach. The manager had just opened the door to his room, and Greg's bed hadn't been slept in.

On the way to Barra I called Natsume.

"Greg has disappeared."

"Did he sell a lot of books at the talk?"

"You don't understand. Greg has *disappeared*."

"Rose asked for five autographed copies, for us to promote on radio."

"You don't understand."

I was escorted into the Windsor Barra, through the lobby to a sliding door in the rear that opened onto the Emerald Room. They had pushed back the chairs and she was in the middle, among unfriendly types. She was blowing her nose into a tissue and her eyes were puffy. One of the guys, tall and paunchy, with gray hair forming small greasy waves on his shirt collar, came up to me. He wanted to know my name and what I did, and the way he asked the questions made me want to confess to anything. My hands were shaking.

I needed to sit down; I pulled up a chair beside Ellie. She had already tried to explain what she knew. Greg's real name was Gregor Nikolaidis. "Did you know that?" the policeman asked me with a sarcastic smile. No, I didn't. My head hurt. Greg, or Gregor, was in Belize because he was being investigated by the IRS in the US. Greg, or Gregor, could no longer live in Europe, wanted on a series of charges. The cop turned to his colleague, who was eating cupcakes from the hotel buffet.

"Macedo, can you remind us what he is accused of?"

Macedo swallowed quickly, wiped his mouth, and took a small notebook from his pocket. He read before speaking: "A bit of everything. Use of false identity, larceny. He swindled a rich widow, the family found out, and he can't set foot in Italy anymore."

"A rich widow, huh?" said the other, feigning interest.

"That's what it says," replied Macedo.

"How do you say *estelionato* in English?" asked the gray cop.

"I used to know, but I forget."

The gray cop turned to me. "Right. Swindling, tax evasion, extortion, and a lot more, my friend. Heavy stuff. So it's better for you to tell us."

I described our trip to the green-and-red house; the cop said he already knew that part. "This woman here can't stop talking about the house and the people there, but I want to know what happened *afterward*."

"Maybe she doesn't know," I said.

"You think I'm a fool?"

Macedo answered his cell phone, whispered something

out of the corner of his mouth, and hung up. "A representative from the American consulate is on his way."

"Shit," said Gray. "Bucetinha said he's going to take over the case. What he wants is to get on TV. This time he's not going to." They exited the Emerald Room hurriedly, leaving us in the custody of Rejane, a dyed-blonde, her huge ass stuffed into white jeans under which I could see the outline of her thong. She sat across from us, leaning against the back of her chair, her legs apart, and said she still needed to clarify a few things.

Ellie's chilly fingers found my hand. An electric shock ran through my body. Those fingers, those gnawed nails.

Rejane wanted to know: "Does this visualization really work? I mean, do people lose weight by the power of thought?"

My boss to me: "The Internet is saying our author disappeared."

"Can't talk now."

"Our book orders are doubling. Keep him disappeared awhile longer."

"Look, I don't think you understand—"

"We're going to hit number one. It's you who doesn't understand."

Lindsay Lohan, from house arrest, had just sent word that she didn't know Greg Nicholas, had never been treated by him, was unfamiliar with his method, and had never been in Belize. A similar statement from Mimi Lesseos was expected at any moment.

Rejane spoke for a long time on a pink phone, pacing around the Emerald Room. Then she took a black automatic from her purse and checked to make sure it was loaded. We proceeded down dark corridors, crossed through the kitchen, and found ourselves before a side door. "Why are we leaving out the back?" I asked, but she didn't answer. Belatedly I understood that we were throwing the representative from the consulate and that Bucetinha guy off the scent, while Gray and Macedo tried to solve the case.

We took the same busy avenue as the night before, in the opposite direction, and got stuck in traffic. The air-conditioning wasn't working, and Ellie began saying she wasn't feeling well. She asked Rejane where we were going, and the woman, in mirrored sunglasses, simply looked at her in the rearview mirror. We inched our way through a collection of shopping centers that ended in epic fashion with the Statue of Liberty pressed between bluish glass and beige mortar. Ellie stared like a blind person who has recovered her sight. Rejane spoke again on her pink cell phone. No, no one had seen her leaving the hotel; yes, she had turned off the radio and the vehicle's GPS. Yes, she would keep moving, but they didn't have much time. "Macedo, where are you guys?" she said. "No, I think the victim was only supposed to go to Rocinha this afternoon or tomorrow. You shot at who? How? What're you doing there?"

We slowly made our way through an endless traffic circle where a huge concrete box, at least five stories high, was being constructed, a mixture of Trojan horse and smokehouse. We passed by neoclassical-style buildings, like those I saw in São Paulo, in the middle of empty lots that in a matter of months would be occupied by new neoclassical buildings. "I need to get out of here," said Ellie, turning the door handle. Rejane looked at us again and said she would stop. She drummed on the steering wheel. She picked up her phone but wasn't able to complete the call. She sighed, thought. We crossed under red pennants at the entrance to Makro and pulled into its parking lot, almost empty at that time of day. Rejane hesitated about which space to choose and stopped between two of them. She left the windows half rolled down and took the car key. She told us to stay there and abandoned us like children.

That was when Ellie began to cough and clutch her neck—"Air, air, air"—and tumbled out the door.

I held her as we kneeled on the hot concrete, and I could feel her breath warming my shirt. She repeated that she knew what had happened to him. I asked if he was being hunted, whether he had gotten into something bigger that not even he, Greg, understood. She shook her head. No, no, no. She said I had to go back to that dark-colored house at the top of the hill. Then I remembered the strange guy and his glasses, his straight hair. I tried to describe him to Ellie, as I held her tighter. A security guard came by on a motor scooter, but we didn't move. I tried to kiss her but Ellie said, "No," then added that she had been trying to explain something to those cops from the beginning. The man, the man with the caipirinhas—

"A bit ill-humored," I said.

"Didn't you see the gun under his jacket?"

Only then did she look directly at me with those startled amber-colored eyes. In the distance I saw Rejane lugging a large package on her shoulders. Halfway to the car she stopped, noticing our flight. She put down the box, looked around, took out her phone. We didn't have much time. Ellie squeezed my shoulders and looked at me intensely. She said I had to go there, to that house. That I had to *find out*. I pressed her about the snakelike guy with the parted hair, who seemed to be working for someone, who hadn't taken his eyes off Greg.

"He may be from some criminal organization," I said.

That somehow broke the spell that bound us. She dried her nose on the sleeve of her shirt and got up. When she spoke, she radiated disappointment.

"No, Humberto, he's not *after* Greg. He's not violent. He's not a gangster. He's an editor, like you."

The policewoman had spotted us. She waved, ordering us to come back.

"Another editor?"

"Your competitor. With whom Greg was going to sign for his next book."

"Next book?"

"I'm sorry."

I heard only the silence of heated concrete. Ellie called to me. Ellie tried to touch me. I was just a shadow moving on the ground to the car, to the open trunk, where Rejane was attempting to insert a monstrous box. I looked and didn't understand. A portable barbecue grill.

"My boyfriend's has a hole in it," was all she said.

Betrayed. That was how I felt when I rang the doorbell of the house at the top of the hill. The sun was starting to go down, but it still burned my neck. I was tired from the inter-rogations in the afternoon, tired of the police. Our arrival at the 16th precinct hadn't been pretty, to say the least. Jostling and pushing. The gray detective, bandaged, arguing with an-other investigator. No sign of Macedo. Some guy with a pink little mouth shining in a curly goatee was giving an interview on TV. They had placed a coat over Ellie's head and pushed her down a hallway filled with photographers as if she were a suspect. And still no sign of Greg. I just wanted to get my backpack and take a shower before returning to São Paulo.

I explained on the intercom what I had come for. I explained it again to a uniformed maid who led me to the empty grand ballroom, said that madam had just woken up, and left me there. Only then did I observe the room in detail. A spiral staircase rose right in the middle of the windows, blocking the view outside. Greek pillars led nowhere. On the wall, a framed jersey from the Fluminense football team vied for space with an abstract canvas of childish bad taste. In the photos on the chest of drawers (Bariloche, yachting, carnival) I finally saw Mr. Platinum-Blonde. Gray-haired, stocky, he could have been her grandfather. Since the servant hadn't returned, I decided to go down to the swimming pool.

The view was even more impressive at twilight. She was in a lounge chair down below.

The light blinded me momentarily. Her wavy hair shone. She was wearing a white beach skirt over a white bathing suit and white sandals with ruffles and heel. She was lying on her side, her languid legs resting on each other. Her eyes disappeared behind very dark glasses. She looked at me, I think, but said nothing. I sat in the lounge chair opposite her. She removed the cigarette holder from her lips and blew smoke into the air, framed by the indecent blue of the sea.

"Ah, the messenger boy."

"The name is Mariconda. Humberto Mariconda."

"Do you like the house? Is that why you came back?"

I looked around, blinking my eyes. "To tell you the truth, the colors don't go very well with this little paradise you have here."

She raised the holder to her mouth, examined me for a moment. "My husband, Mariconda. He's a fanatic."

"Is that why he's never around? Traveling with the team? Does he visit the dressing rooms? Young men changing clothes?"

She smiled as if not smiling. "The police were already here trying to intimidate me. You're not going to do it."

"Ah."

She released the smoke. I spoke again.

"And where can I find Mr. Platinum-Blonde?"

She thought a bit. Making the connection with the name was difficult. She smoked. She understood. "That's none of your business, darling. That's a problem between him and me."

I got up and walked around her lounger. The sea was calling me, the trees clamored down below. I felt the same chill as the night before. Something gleamed through the foliage. In the indirect light of sunset little colored streaks striped the grass, emerged among the rocks. The hot wind whistled in my ear. I realized I was alone, completely alone, and that Ellie was right. I needed to hold on tight to the glass parapet.

"I noticed your gunman isn't here."

"He's not *my* gunman."

"Where is he?"

"Ask my husband, if you find him."

She seemed to be in a bad mood. I looked at the abyss again, then at her. "You thought you'd have the night just for yourself, with your husband away."

Now she showed a hint of a smile mixed with impatience. I went up to her again and sat down with difficulty. My back tingled. She shuffled her funereal legs. She was facing a terrific hangover, I now realized.

"Greg came back here late that night and you thought you'd have a great time. But the guy making the caipirinhas spoiled everything, didn't he?"

"I don't know what you're talking about," she said, looking bored.

I pointed to the parapet. "He should have removed the

pens from Greg's pockets before throwing him down there."

She touched her hair. Sighed. At no time did she make a move to rise, or look behind her. She said I was being a bit ridiculous.

"What's ridiculous is this house. Those colors," I said.

She sighed and laughed. I stood up, feeling a chill in my spine. I suddenly felt fragile, exposed; thousands of needles pricked the nape of my neck. Then she spoke.

"Don't worry. He doesn't own me, and he'll get what's coming to him."

"Are you going to bring in the police?"

"What do the police have to do with this? Much worse, dear. In a week all this will be a different color."

"Color?" I said between my teeth. I couldn't say anything else.

"Tangerine tango. *The* color for next summer. It will go well with the palms."

The maid descended the stairs with a tray of drinks. My backpack wasn't anywhere, and the sea had taken on a carnivorous blue tone. I looked at her again in the lounge chair. I understood that she had just planned that revenge, and her body emanated an opaque glow of satisfaction. I barely remembered why I was there, and she had no intention of reminding me.

THE WAIT

BY FLÁVIO CARNEIRO

Downtown

> *The lover's fatal identity is precisely this: I am the one who waits.*
>
> —Roland Barthes

I t was an ordinary day, a Monday like any other, even the hangover was the same. It was a little past noon and the sun seemed to flood its full intensity on my head as I entered the old building on Rua da Relação.

"It's not working. I already called maintenance," said the doorman without taking his eyes from his newspaper.

"That thing ought to be retired for good," I replied, looking at the elevator, which was always out of order.

I climbed the stairs thinking that my life wasn't going very well. An aching head, the heat, and that infernal din from the building, half commercial, half residential. I went from the first to the fifth floor hearing children crying, neighbors arguing, loud music, and the irritating sound of some idiot drilling into a wall.

My office door needed serious repainting. I stood there for an instant, the plaque in front of me reading, *Detective André—Investigations*.

I don't really know if what I felt was what mystics call an epiphany, I don't understand such things, but maybe it actually was that, an epiphany, a revelation. As I looked at the plaque it was as if a voice was telling me in an ironic, slightly diabolical tone: *Wake up, brother, get out of this morass.*

I solved problems for everyone, recorded adulterers in the act, uncovered insurance fraud, assisted cuckolds and lovers with equal competence, and was still down in the dumps, living in a matchbox in Copacabana and working in a horrific office in a horrible building in the center of a city that seemed more and more hostile.

"Excuse me, are you Detective André?"

I turned toward the voice. "Yes."

"Can we talk?"

I opened the door and motioned the woman inside. I went in immediately after her, offered her an armchair, and opened the window.

Sunlight illuminated the spot where she was sitting. My desk was in shadow. I could turn on the light but I preferred it like that. I had read in a story by Machado de Assis that it was the way a certain card reader received her clients. The fortune teller in the shade, the client in a kind of spotlight like in a theater. The card reader could judge the customer's face while shuffling the cards, without letting herself be seen clearly.

"How can I help you?"

She was a beautiful woman. I had noticed her perfect body when I saw her from behind, slowly entering the office. She was wearing a short knit dress, dark red, almost wine-colored, contrasting with her very white skin. Her small dark eyes took on a glow when she started to speak.

"Forgive me, I don't know where to begin, I've never been in a detective's office."

"There's always a first time."

She smiled, with a somewhat forced shyness.

"You can begin by telling me your name."

"Marina."

The office door opened suddenly and she was startled by the noise.

"Am I intruding?"

A rhetorical question. Whatever my response, Fats was going to come in and remain in the room. An old friend, he knew all there was to know about crime fiction. He owned a used-book store on Rua do Lavradio and in his free time helped me with investigations. Though he didn't call it helping. He called it advising.

I introduced the two. He greeted her with a smile. I knew that smile; Fats is a perv, and I believe he thinks the same about me.

He pulled up a chair, turned it around, and sat down, resting his arms. It was a studied move to impress the woman, as if he were one of those hard-boiled types in a gangster flick. All that was missing was to chew on a toothpick and spit on the floor. Marina ignored him.

"I came here because I'd like you to locate a person."

"A person."

"Yes. A man."

I waited. She lowered her eyes and crossed her legs. She rested one hand on a knee. She had long, delicate fingers, a pianist's fingers. I noticed the wedding ring.

"Your husband?" I let fly.

"No, it's not my husband. My husband knows nothing about it. And he must not know."

"I understand."

She fell silent again.

"Want something to drink, dear? Water, soda, beer?" Fats asked.

"Water, please."

Fats went to the minibar and opened a bottle of mineral water. He poured it into a glass and handed it to her.

Marina looked at the bookcase that occupied the back wall of the office. "You enjoy reading, I see."

"Yes."

She got up and went to the bookcase. She had long, straight black hair and was wearing high heels and walked as if she were barefoot, light as a feather.

She ran her eyes over the books' spines. "There's nothing but crime stories here!"

"Anything wrong with that?" I asked in a joking tone.

"No, of course not. It goes well with the office of a private detective."

"Most real detectives don't like to read. I think I'm an exception."

Fats went up to her. "Let me show you something," he said, picking up a book and handing it to Marina.

"*The Maltese Falcon.*"

"Have you read it?"

"I don't like crime stories. And Hammett is far from my favorite writer."

"You know there's a character in this novel, a woman, who's very much like you?"

"Is she?"

"Her name is Brigid. Her real name, I mean. She uses other names as well."

"Hmm."

"Don't you want to know why she resembles you?"

"No," she replied in a dry tone, and sat down again.

"Who's the man you want to find?" I asked, making no effort to conceal my impatience.

"Actually, I don't know him. I don't know his name or

what he does in life. I've never spoken with him. He must be five-eleven or a little less, short black hair. Dark skin, I think."

"You think?"

"I've never seen him up close, only some distance away, and at night without much light."

Fats looked at me and raised his eyebrows.

"It all started two weeks ago. One night as I was leaving work, I sensed someone was following me."

"Where do you work?"

"At the National Library, in the rare books section."

"And where do you live?"

"Right here in downtown. On Avenida Calógeras, on top of the Villarino. Are you familiar with it?"

"The Pan América Building. I had a client who lived there."

"Quite a coincidence."

"Yes, it is."

She paused, her gaze a bit distant. I would have liked to know what she was thinking at that moment. It was a brief pause, just a few seconds, then she looked at me again and resumed her account.

"I always walk home and nothing had ever happened to me. You know, it's nearby, a ten-minute walk. But that night I felt something odd, I was certain I was being followed. And I admit I was afraid to stop and look back."

"What did you think might happen if you looked back?"

"I don't know. Obviously nothing was going to happen, the street was full of people, but I was scared. I walked a bit farther, and when I was near my house, I had to stop at a traffic light. Then I looked, and there he was." She took another sip of water. "He had a newspaper under his arm. He was wearing jeans and a white short-sleeve shirt. He stared at me."

"Was he a hunk?" asked Fats.

"What?"

"Was he good-looking?"

"He wasn't ugly."

"Was he good-looking or just not ugly? They're two different things."

She didn't answer.

"And what happened after that?" I asked.

"I kept on walking, fast, until I entered my building. I don't even think I said hello to the doorman, I went straight upstairs with a flutter in my chest. I got into my apartment and lay on the sofa for a few minutes, without turning on the lights. Then I went to the window, opened it, looked down, and there he was, on the sidewalk."

"Looking at you."

"Exactly. He was leaning against a lamppost, the newspaper under his arm, looking at me. I noticed he was carrying a leather pouch on a strap. He didn't seem scary and he wasn't smiling, just looking at me. I closed the window. I took a shower and after dressing went back to look at the sidewalk. He wasn't there anymore."

"But he came back the next night," Fats said.

"How do you know?"

He smiled.

"Yes, the next day he followed me again. I didn't even need to look back to know he was following me, my intuition told me he was there. In the middle of the street I turned around and stared at him. He was still in jeans and a short-sleeve shirt, blue this time. The scene was almost the same as the first night, and I was impressed. The same neutral expression, the pouch, the newspaper under his arm, not moving a muscle, just standing there."

"This time you took a long look at the guy, it wasn't as rushed as the first time," I said.

"I didn't feel any fear, you understand? The first night I was a little frightened, but not this time. He had a serene expression, calm. He didn't look like a criminal. He seemed to have something to tell me but he didn't say anything."

"Did it enter your mind that he might be interested in you?"

"Of course. But then why didn't he come closer, speak to me? I turned my back and went home. And the same thing happened again."

"You opened the window and he was on the sidewalk."

"Yes. Leaning against the same lamppost, with the same demeanor, the same expression."

"Did you see when he left?"

"No. As long as I stayed at the window he remained on the sidewalk, in that same spot."

"With the newspaper under his arm."

"Always with the newspaper under his arm. I closed the curtains and when I went back to the window, later, I didn't see anyone on the sidewalk."

"Let me see if I can guess," Fats said, pouring a cup of coffee. "On the third night, everything happened again, the same script: he followed you, you stared at each other, afterward he stood on the sidewalk contemplating you."

"I don't know if *contemplating* is the right word. He was looking at me."

"No, my dear, he didn't look at you. There's a big difference between looking and contemplating. That guy's not one for looking at a beautiful woman. He contemplates. He's the sophisticated type. Sick, maybe, but who isn't?"

She laughed for the first time. She had a lovely smile. "You're kind of crazy yourself, aren't you?"

"Could be. But I've got that guy's number. I know what he's like."

"I don't think so," she said with a touch of irony. "I haven't told you everything yet. He continued to follow me for several nights. More than once I felt like going up to him and just asking what he wanted from me."

"And why didn't you?"

She took a deep breath. Then she said in a soft voice, almost a whisper: "Because I was enjoying it."

Fats and I looked at the woman sitting before us. I should say, rather, not that we looked but that we *contemplated* the woman.

"I was afraid of what might happen if I went up to him. I don't know, I thought he might get scared and run away."

She looked like she was about to cry. Marina straightened her body, sat up erect in the chair, and held back the tears.

"One day, at the library, a girlfriend showed me a book. By a French writer, Roland Barthes. You surely don't know him, he never wrote a crime novel," she said with a small smile.

I chose not to respond.

"I took the book home. It was a book of fragments, notes about things relating to love. And there was a very lovely story in it, about a mandarin who falls in love with a courtesan. The mandarin declares his love and the courtesan tells him: *I will be yours if you wait for me a hundred evenings in my garden, beneath my window*. For ninety-eight evenings he waits for her, in the garden. On the ninety-ninth evening, when she is ready to give herself to him, he leaves and never returns."

"Dirty trick," says Fats.

"I think I will accept a beer."

"Coming up," I said, getting two. I gave one to Fats. I didn't want to drink, not just yet.

"I copied the story of the mandarin from the book. I copied it on a sheet of paper, put it in an envelope, and one night when the man was following me, I dropped the envelope on purpose. And hoped he had seen it."

"You dropped the envelope the way a woman in love drops a handkerchief," Fats said, and it didn't strike me as a provocation.

"I went on walking, following the nightly ritual. I went up, waited a bit inside, opened the window, and saw him on the sidewalk looking at me as always. Except that this time there was a small difference, a new detail. He took the envelope from the pouch and held it up, as if to say: *Here it is, I got it.*" She drank the beer, slowly. Then she placed the glass on the table and said in a firm voice, "It was the last time I saw him."

I got up and went to the window. There outside, people were moving hurriedly, car horns were blowing, a workman was trying to control a jackhammer. He was small and thin; they shouldn't have given a guy like that a jackhammer, I thought.

It wasn't the only odd thing in the city. Rio is an unusual place, full of surprises, and downtown is the best example of that. To start with, downtown isn't in the center of the city, it's at one end, along the oceanfront. If it were truly central it would be right in the middle, not on the edge of the beach.

"Do you have any idea where he waited for you to leave the library?" I asked, returning to my chair.

"He always waited for me at a sidewalk table, at Amarelinho. Every afternoon when I would leave the library, there he was. I would walk down the steps and head slowly toward home."

"Slower each time."

"That's true, slower each time."

She stared at me. The story she had to tell had been told and Marina awaited my reaction.

I lowered my head and shuffled some paper on my desk. Bills: lights, rent on the office, condo fees.

"All right. I'll find that nutcase for you."

After she left I didn't stay in the office for long. I made some phone calls, saw a client, and around four o'clock closed down. I decided to focus on Marina's case. She was paying well—Fats set the price this time. And it was hefty.

"Nothing like mixing work and pleasure," he said as we sat at a sidewalk table at the Amarelinho, across from the National Library.

I thought that was where we should begin. Not that we expected to find the guy in the most obvious place. We knew he wouldn't be at the Amarelinho. But Fats thought that, before anything else, we should try to better understand, or at least speculate about, what he was up to.

"We have to put ourselves in his position, right, André? It was from here that he watched Marina every day. Remember the lesson of a master, Chesterton's Father Brown: it's necessary to put oneself in the place of the criminal, it's necessary to think like him to predict what he will do next."

"The guy's not a criminal. It's no crime to follow a beautiful woman in the street."

"He did more than that. The scoundrel broke the heart of a ravishing woman. And I should add: a ravishing married woman."

"Pay attention, Fats, we're at the Amarelinho, the way you wanted, and we've just ordered a fourth round of beers. Is that enough to put ourselves in the place of the guy or do we need to get completely plastered first?"

"It wouldn't be a bad idea. But it won't be necessary, since I know why he stayed here."

"So talk."

"The guy's a professional observer."

"Huh?"

"Just what I said. Remember that story by Poe, 'The Man of the Crowd'? The guy in the story, the narrator, was methodical. He would sit in a café in London looking out at the street packed with people. And he cataloged each type: merchants, lawyers, public servants, prostitutes, pickpockets, noblemen, and loan sharks; he would classify everyone. Our man is like that too, he's no amateur. He has a method. And like Poe's character, he starts by carefully hiding his observation point. A café in downtown London, a table at a bar in downtown Rio. See the parallel?"

"Go on."

"From here, maybe from this very table where we're sitting, he could observe at will, without really being seen. People of every kind pass through this square; Cinelândia is a kaleidoscope of humanity, if you'll permit me a poetic image. Tourists, beggars, politicians, artists, con men, professors, students, drunks of every kind, and of course beautiful women."

"Like Marina."

"Yes. Imagine the guy sitting here, right across from the library. At six in the afternoon he sees her descending the stairs, a beautiful young woman, tall, elegant, wonderful, a goddess. He follows her with his eyes, intently. And then he thinks: *Tomorrow I'm going after that woman.* The next day, at the same hour, he begins his game with Marina. And the rest, we already know how it was."

"And why do you think he gave up?"

The waiter arrived with two more beers.

"Marina sent a message: she didn't want him to act like the mandarin in the story. She was in love with him and hoped one day he'd speak to her. The waiting was proof of his passion. The guy understood that and chose to leave. He knew that if he continued the game, sooner or later he'd fall into the trap."

"What trap?"

"The trap we all fall into, we romantics, those perpetually naïve about love. You, in fact, more than me."

"What trap?" I asked, trying to sound bored.

"The same as ever, since Adam and Eve. The trap of commitment."

"You think Marina acted hastily."

"Of course. She didn't know how to wait long enough. Marina scared the nutcase and he hit the road. When she copied the passage from the book and then purposely dropped it, she was telling him: *Don't be like the mandarin, don't go away on the last night.*"

"And he did."

"Right. These things happen."

From the Amarelinho we went to Marina's building, following the route she said she took every day. We crossed Rio Branco, took Pedro Lessa to the end, turned onto Graça Aranha, which joins Calógeras, and after a ten-minute walk we were there. I remembered the Pan América well. The apartment of my former client faced Avenida Beira-Mar and had a dazzling view. Marina's faced Calógeras.

"This is where he stood, contemplating Marina," Fats said, leaning against the lamppost.

We stayed there for some minutes, looking for I don't know what exactly. The doorman began regarding us suspiciously. I thought it best for us to leave.

We then began our rounds through the bars, as planned at the table at Amarelinho. That night and the following two nights we made our pilgrimage to the downtown bars in search of the man.

Rio is a city constantly inviting people into the street, and downtown is no different. I would meet Fats at the end of the day and we would hit the dozens of bars scattered along Rua do Lavradio, Lapa, the narrow streets leading to Cinelândia, the venerable Rua do Ouvidor and environs.

Those were long nights, I must say. And we didn't find the guy.

"Patience, André, we have to be patient. I have the feeling we'll find the man tonight."

"You talk about method but don't have one, you know that?"

"Trust me, little brother, today we'll find that sly fox, trust me."

It was eight at night when we entered Arco do Teles. I checked to see if our friend was in any of the bars.

"A change of plan, André," Fats said, taking my arm. "Next stop: Bar Brasil."

"You think he might be there?"

"No. But I urgently need to eat a *kassler* with potatoes."

"You shouldn't eat pork ribs. They're fattening."

"I'm already fat, have you forgotten?"

Deep down I knew my friend didn't want to go to Bar Brasil just to devour his favorite dish. He had something in mind that he didn't want to tell me just yet. Fats is like that; at times he thinks he's Sherlock Holmes hiding some thought from Watson in order to enhance his brilliant deduction at the end. Watson in this case was me.

We walked to Rua Mem de Sá. I enjoyed walking at night

in those streets. The infernal daytime bustle with people scurrying like ants gave way to a different lineage, the bohemians. And walking at night lets me see more calmly the old houses, the buildings from the time of the empire, the signs of another era written on the streets like a book open to whoever wants to read. I wanted to, I liked reading the city, especially downtown, where everything is written.

We got to Bar Brasil and chose a table at the rear. The waiter quickly brought our dishes. Fats went with *kassler*. I ordered meatballs.

"Okay, out with it. Why Bar Brasil?"

He pretended to be startled. Then he smiled. "Elementary, my dear boy. We've been roaming around for three days. We've been to practically every sidewalk bar in the area. If he's not in any of them it's because we've been looking in the wrong place, understand? It boils down to this: the creep doesn't want to be found. He doesn't know that Marina put a detective on his tail, but to be on the safe side he decided to change his strategy. No sidewalk bars now, no showing himself. *I'm going to a quieter spot, where I can contemplate women without a lot of people around, my way.* That's what he thought."

"Then why didn't he change neighborhoods?"

Fats cut off a generous piece of rib and chewed on it.

"Get one thing through your head, André: the man is methodical. He likes this area and doesn't want to leave it. It's his territory, understand? The guy knows the streets, the alleys, and the bars downtown the way you and I know our own faces in a mirror. It's his home. It's not just the setting for his life story, it's the story itself. And listen to what I'm about to say, listen carefully: it's from the village that you see the universe. Learn from that, my friend, learn."

"You read that somewhere."

"No I didn't."

"Yes you did."

"All right, it's from Alberto Caeiro. I mean, I adapted it a little."

We fell silent. The waiter brought two more beers.

"How is it you know so much about a guy you've never met?"

"They're merely hypotheses. And don't forget: *What songs the Syrens sang, or what name Achilles assumed when he hid himself among women, though puzzling questions, are not beyond all conjecture.* Sir Thomas Browne."

"I think you chose the wrong profession. You should've been a literature professor."

"If I'm going to starve to death, I prefer being the owner of a used-book store."

"You're not exactly starving. Not in the least."

"A figure of speech, if you understand me."

"What I understand is that everything's very good—cold beer, tasty dishes—but where's the guy?"

"He just came in."

It was him. Medium height—Marina had said five-eleven or a little less—short black hair, dark skin. Jeans, white short-sleeve shirt, the newspaper under his arm. Even the leather pouch was there, on a strap. It could only be him.

"I don't believe it, Fats!"

"Now you see. I told you to trust me, it was just a matter of time."

The guy came in, took a look around, said something to the waiter, and chose a table near ours. He placed the pouch on a chair and sat down in the other. From where we were, we could see him in profile.

I called Marina.

"We found your friend, he's just come into Bar Brasil, on Mem de Sá. Do you know it?"

"Yes. I'm on my way. Don't let him leave."

"Hurry up. I don't know if he's going to stay here for long."

I hung up.

"Look, André. He's pretending to read the menu."

"He *is* reading the menu."

"No he isn't. I saw when he opened the menu without looking at it. He merely opened it for show. And he's not turning the pages; he merely opened it and left it open, to fake it. See? He's looking in our direction. At the table with the women."

At a table across from us, three women were taking loudly and laughing.

"What can they be laughing so hard about?" I asked.

"They're beautiful, young, and judging by their clothes they have money. Do you need any other reasons to laugh about nothing?"

"And which of them will he choose to follow?"

"He's not thinking about that yet. He just got here, he's analyzing the terrain. And it won't depend solely on his choice. It'll depend on how they leave the bar. They may leave together and get into a car nearby. That would be it for the loony. Or it may be that one of them leaves before the others, walking toward the subway, for example. That would be ideal for him."

"I just saw him give the waiter his order."

"Excellent, it means he's going to stay for a while. At least until Marina gets here. Where was she—at home?"

"I don't know."

"With her husband?"

"I have no idea, Fats!"

"I was thinking: it would be funny if her husband followed her when she left."

"The husband following his wife who's following a stranger who was following her."

"Yes, like those Russian dolls, one coming out of the other."

"Look what the guy ordered: kassler with potatoes. What else do you two have in common?"

"I don't know, but I'll find out very soon."

"Find out how?"

"I'm going to talk to him. Or rather, we're both going to," Fats said, standing up and taking his glass of beer.

"What? You're going to spook the guy!"

"Come with me."

I grabbed my beer and we went to the other table.

"Everything okay, boss? All right if we sit here?" Fats asked.

He raised his head and looked at Fats, then at me, without a word. "No," he finally answered, returning to his food.

"Why do you follow women?" Fats demanded, sitting down at the table. I sat too.

He gestured to the waiter, asking for the check.

"Take it easy, we're good people, we just want to talk."

"Who are you two?"

"A female friend of yours hired us. We're detectives."

"From the police? I haven't done anything wrong."

"We know that. And we're not cops."

"I don't have a female friend. You're crazy."

"*We're* crazy? You go around following women in the street and run away when one of them wants to speak to you, and we're the crazy ones?"

The waiter brought the check. Fats grabbed it.

"Leave this to me, I'm treating. And bring three more beers, please."

I thought the guy was going to split, but he surprised me; he stared at Fats for an instant, then nodded and said: "This city is like an insane asylum."

"May I?" I asked, pointing to the newspaper.

"Of course."

I looked at the date on the front page: it was from last week. He understood.

"I don't like reading newspapers."

"Then why do you always have one under your arm?"

"To give the impression that I'm normal."

I found that humorous. I got the impression that this nut was pretty cool. In different circumstances we might even have become friends.

The waiter brought the beers. We drank in silence for a bit.

"Who hired you?"

"Her name is Marina. The woman from Avenida Calógeras who you followed for a bunch of nights."

"Marina. A beautiful name."

"And a beautiful woman as well."

"Without a doubt. A pity she's so unhappy with her husband. She deserves something better."

"How do you know she's unhappy with her husband?"

"It's just a hypothesis."

Fats laughed. "Why do you follow women if you don't want to be with them?" he asked.

"What makes you think that's any of your business?"

"I know it's none of my business, but you could tell me, couldn't you?"

"No."

"How do you choose them? What are your criteria?"

The guy finished his beer. He drank rapidly, and I took

that as a sign he might bolt at any moment. Sitting down at his table had been a terrible idea. Curiosity is Fats's weakness, and it would be to our detriment.

"I follow women who want to be followed. I can see it in their eyes, the clothes they wear, the way they walk—I know when they want a little adventure. Those three over at that table, for instance. None of them are any good."

"Why not? Because they seem happily married?"

"No. They have lovers. They're too happy to just have good marriages. They probably love their husbands, fine, but they have lovers. They don't need another adventure."

I was still thinking about what he had just said when the guy left. There was no way to stop him, it was all very sudden. He took the pouch and the newspaper and left.

Seconds later, Marina entered the bar.

"Where is he?"

"He just left."

We went out onto the sidewalk. We could still see the guy, walking along Mem de Sá toward the Lapa Arches. Marina could catch up to him if she so desired.

"Now it's up to you, angel."

She kissed me on the cheek. And went after the crazy man.

"I don't like happy endings," Fats said, standing beside me.

"We don't know what the ending will be."

"Want me to tell you?"

"No."

THE STORY OF GEORGES FULLAR

BY RAPHAEL MONTES

Copacabana

I didn't know he lived in Copacabana. What I mean is that it wasn't premeditated, you know? We moved in September of the year before last; my parents chose the apartment, I just went along. I don't have much say there at home. If it were up to me we would've stayed in Méier, my friends are all from there. I studied for nineteen years in the Venceslau district, and I never liked the beach—I didn't find the slightest attraction in living in Copacabana.

Our apartment is at the corner of Ministro Viveiros de Castro and Duvivier. My mother loves living in the South Zone, she talks about it all the time, how she's come up in the world, how she struggled to get where she is, and how what she wants now more than anything is to be happy. The corner is near the Arcoverde subway station and she almost never uses the car—she hates to drive.

The street is treelined, quiet with a few hotels, quite attractive with their mirror-glass façade, that, according to her, provide greater security. And everything is nearby (as she says with pride): supermarket, luncheonette, flower shop, manicurist, cybercafé, a dance studio, a bakery, and *three* gyms. I even signed up for the cheapest one, though I definitely don't have the patience to work out.

So . . . on Thursdays there is a street market with fruit, vegetables, and fish over on Ronald de Carvalho. I always have to go with my mother. It's close, but she insists I keep her company and take the cart. We get there toward the end, to pick up the leftovers; my mother thinks she's the world's greatest negotiator when she buys four limes for a *real*. Be patient. I'm mentioning the market because it was there that I first saw Georges Fullar. It wasn't until then that I found out he lived in Copacabana. When I laid eyes on him I was paralyzed—my mother was sticking a few grapes in my mouth to judge if they were sweet but I barely noticed. Hey man, put yourself in my place: you're at an outdoor market and you see your idol a few feet away. Georges Fullar in Bermudas and slippers carrying a bag of bananas. Can you believe it?

What? You don't know who Georges Fullar is? Only the greatest writer in the country. *Sordid Harvest*, you read it? A classic. He's been mentioned for the Nobel Prize. Georges was a philosopher and an academic. That was back in the 1950s. During the dictatorship he fled to Europe and began to write in order to survive. He wrote a few unimportant detective novels under a gringo pseudonym. You know, the ones they sell at newsstands printed on cheap paper? Georges wrote dozens of them. Extremely hard to find nowadays. I bought three in a used-book store, written in French, but I don't understand French. I keep them just to have them.

When he returned from Europe Georges published *Sordid Harvest*. It was a smash. It's a political novel but also a work of suspense. You can't stop reading it. It's not shallow or pseudo-intellectual, you know? It has incredible profundity, a power I can't explain. It's told from the point of view of a political exile. It's the best crime novel I've ever read. *Sordid Harvest*, make a note of it. Later you can look for it. It's really good.

I had to go after Georges. At the market, I mean. He was tall, bony, and had a head of white hair, easy to follow. He moved somewhat aggressively through the crowd, and the funny thing is that no one recognized him. The greatest writer in Brazil buying half a kilo of fish like he was just another guy. I don't know how long I watched him. I saw when he finished shopping and headed down Ministro toward our building. He entered the lobby. Jesus, beyond living in Copacabana he was my neighbor! Me on the fourth floor; him on the second. Only two floors between me and the baddest dude in Brazilian literature. I almost flipped.

I told you, didn't I? I'm a writer too. I've got a couple of novels put away in a drawer somewhere. I've never tried to publish because I feel I'm too young. A writer's got to be old, you know? Have experience. I like my work, but nobody writes anything of value in their early twenties.

But what I was saying is that I couldn't get Georges out of my head. I told my mother, and she insisted I call him on the intercom and explain my admiration for him and all the rest. I was against the idea, I didn't want to be a nuisance. I tried to forget about him.

Copacabana is the world squeezed into a single district. Families, whores, street vendors, drunks, old ladies, nannies, gringos, lottery-ticket sellers, and actors are constantly rubbing elbows on the sidewalks of Portuguese mosaic stones. Some weeks later, I was returning from college when I saw Georges having lunch at Galeto Sat's, right at the beginning of Barata Ribeiro. I wasn't planning to eat out (actually, my mother was at home waiting for me for lunch), but I couldn't resist and went in. I sat at the table next to him, ordered Cornish game hen, potatoes, farofa, and a beer. I ate slowly, watching Georges gnaw on chicken bones and thinking: *Man, the greatest Brazilian writer gnawing chicken bones right in front of me.*

He had already finished eating when he started a conversation. You may not believe it, but that's exactly how it happened: *he* started a conversation with me. "You're the new people on the fourth floor, aren't you?" I nodded and replied that he lived on the second. He smiled, even though his eyes remained very hard. Georges had grave, always deep eyes, a characteristic of a talented writer who is ever observing the world around him. He added some complaints about the building—he had lived there for thirty years and the new super, a woman, was a cow. A cow. I wasn't expecting to hear Georges Fullar call someone a cow. I let him go on talking about water leaks, and the problem of having the subway station so close. In addition to being a talented writer, Georges was old and, you know, old people love to complain about life.

Soon afterward, he invited me to sit with him. He asked my name, and then I made a mistake: I introduced myself and confessed I knew who he was, that I had read *Sordid Harvest* and that it was my favorite book. Man, Georges's expression changed immediately, and now it wasn't only his eyes that were hard. Much later, after we became friends, I understood his reaction better: he didn't like to talk about his work or his life. That was why he lived alone. He had no maids or servants, no children, not even a pet. Really solitary, Georges. It was only when he drank that he talked and opened up.

"Literature is like a steak," he once told me, when I asked why he hadn't written anything since *Sordid Harvest*. "Would you rather eat a steak or talk about a steak?"

"Eat a steak," I answered.

"The same is true of literature," he said. "Talking about literature doesn't hold the slightest appeal."

We spoke very little about it; he left no opening. There were nights when we drank wine or whiskey, and then there was a way to initiate a few conversations about literary criticism, methods of writing, theories (Georges detested rules), and literary festivals (he also hated literary festivals—a gathering of people to talk about steak).

From time to time a journalist or literature student would show up looking for an interview, an opinion, or even a photo with him. They were all shooed away. Georges wanted to be forgotten by the world. And little by little the world did forget him.

You must be wondering what we talked about. Georges loved talking about women. Beauty, gentleness, maternal devotion. He was enchanted by that and also by their scent. He was a bit of a pervert, Georges. As well as cultured, obviously. We would usually meet on Tuesdays and Thursdays; he would come down from his apartment and we would order sandwiches from Cervantes. It was one of Georges's vices: the ham-and-pineapple sandwich from Cervantes. We would eat and gorge on wine. The guy knew a lot about wine. And sacred music. Cinema, cuisine, and sculpture too.

We visited the Drummond statue in those days, there at the end of Copacabana. He pointed to some tourists who were posing beside Drummond. "I'll bet those sons of bitches have never read a single poem of Carlos's," he said. "Life is really shitty, you write and become a statue for a bunch of scumbags to take a picture with." As we were leaving, some idiot tried to cornhole the statue and guffawed. Shitty, huh?

He never came to our home. I invited him once, he said no, and the subject died there. I also never asked him to autograph my books. Because writers are like that: the more adulated they are, the more they disdain people. He liked me because I didn't pester him, didn't ask questions, didn't push. We met for months without my telling him that I also wrote.

Understand, it's not like I hid anything. I just didn't think I had the right to talk about it with him.

But there came a night when I told him. It was a Thursday, I think. That was some time ago. Georges and I had killed two bottles of wine and several sandwiches. He was on the balcony of his apartment, sitting in the rocker, and began speaking of the period when he published *Sordid Harvest*. He told about the launching, the criticism in the media, the prizes, the glamour, and concluded: "The literary scene is so full of shit." He used a lot of four-letter words, Georges.

That was when I came to feel at ease talking about his book, the impact it had on me, about violence, the honesty I saw in the protagonist's voice . . . He interrupted me, agreed, and said that was why he had stopped writing. "I don't know how to be honest anymore," he confessed. He himself had experienced everything depicted in *Sordid Harvest*, which is the reason the book was so authentic and vibrant.

"The writer needs to live what he writes," he said. "What am I going to write about? A decrepit old man who screws whores and strolls along the beach in Copacabana?"

He was talking about self-fiction, you know? It's the latest thing. Nowadays almost every book has a writer as protagonist. It goes like this: writers writing about writers who don't publish; university professors writing about university professors in midlife crises; scriptwriters writing about scriptwriters who work hard and earn little.

"They never stop that mutual masturbation," Georges said. "Gravediggers, firemen, garbagemen, and cabinet makers should be characters too."

It was then that I said I was writing a book. Four friends sharing an apartment in Copacabana. The main character was a food lover. And there was a hooker named Cora who was a strong female character. He loved the hooker. And loved the idea. In later meetings we didn't even need to drink in order to talk about my book. He would show up and ask right away how it was progressing. He never offered to read a single page. He just liked to listen and put in his two cents' worth.

Near the beginning of the book there's a scene where the protagonist hires a hooker for his virgin friend. That part kind of stymied me. I didn't know much about hookers. Georges understood right away. The next Tuesday, when I got to his place, he had company.

"This is Suellen," he said. She was a short, busty woman with curly hair that smelled of shampoo. She was chewing bubble gum and wearing shorts that showed the panties up her ass. I wasn't taken with Suellen in the least. She was sexy, but her style didn't turn me on at all.

Georges told me to make some caipirinhas in the kitchen because Suellen only drank caipirinhas. As I was squeezing the limes, he came in and said I was going to screw her. I was against the idea, but he said it was already paid for and I needed to screw a whore to write the scene authoritatively. Did I want to be a decent writer or a hack? He was forceful, Georges.

The truth is, I had never screwed anyone. It was very bad, I almost couldn't get it up. Suellen was on the rough side and was impatient; she looked at my dick with that I've-seen-bigger expression. When it was over, I lay in bed, dead tired, and Suellen got up, slipped on her shorts, and left without a word. I thought I would never see her again—and didn't want to. Georges asked no questions; he was discreet. Weeks later, in the middle of a conversation, he asked if I had written the scene. I said yes. The fuck was fucking great.

I may be mistaken, but it was during this time that he

mentioned having begun a new novel. Goddamn, after two decades without a line, Georges Fullar was writing again. I was crazy curious to know everything, but held back. I knew he would shut down at the first sign of intrusion. I changed the subject, we spoke of women and even soccer—I don't know the first thing about soccer. That night we had Japanese food instead of sandwiches from Cervantes (I couldn't take any more ham with pineapple). We drank half a bottle of sake. He started rattling on about rare poisons, he was interested in the topic, doing research, reading books; colorless poisons, tasteless and odorless, you with me? And that same night he spoke for the first time about mecicitronine. He was familiar with all the properties of the compound, all its effects and characteristics. A poison with an acid taste, slightly bitter, but colorless and lethal, that leaves no trace in the body. He was fascinated by it. Mecicitronine dissolves in the bloodstream and the guy has a heart attack. Weird, huh? At the time, I didn't understand why he had such interest. I figured it was for the book.

In subsequent meetings he didn't mention poison, nor did he talk about the book. I also stopped telling him about mine. I can't explain it, but I think knowing that Georges was writing a new novel made me uneasy . . . I kind of went into a tailspin. I was an idiot writing my paltry little book while a genius was crafting a masterpiece two floors below me. All I could think about was his book; all I wanted was to find out about it. Does what I'm saying make sense?

There came a night when I couldn't resist. He was in the kitchen making pasta. I said I was going to pee and snuck into his office. I was looking for a rough draft, a page from the book, a block of notes, anything. Okay, I was being kind of obsessive, but when you read Georges Fullar you'll understand. I *needed* to do it. I saw the typewriter, the mahogany chair, the desk, books about poison, some blank sheets of paper scattered around. No text. I went back to the living room disappointed, a bit suspicious. Was the old man lying to me?

I don't know if he noticed I had gone into the office, but he cut me off for two or three months after that dinner. He started canceling one plan after another, and telling me that the following week he also couldn't hang out, and didn't even make up excuses. He could have said he was writing or that he wanted to be by himself, whatever. I found it highly offensive of him to just disappear like that.

This period was hell for me. My parents were separating and those weekly meetings with Georges were like my therapy. Besides which, as I already said, I was no longer able to work on my own book. I reread it and found it to be a piece of crap. I became depressed, and that's no laughing matter. Then one day, a Wednesday, he called me on the building's intercom and invited me down to his apartment. He never called me on Wednesdays because he liked watching soccer on TV. I found it strange, but I went.

When I opened the door, it was another Georges. He had aged ten years in those months. Exhausted, without any strength. We made small talk, but his sense of humor was gone. He didn't use profanity anymore. I asked what was happening and he said he had come to a crucial part of his book, a part in which . . . in which the character killed a woman. With poison. "And I've never killed anyone," he said, anguished. "I don't know what the feeling is like."

I said that he could imagine it, that he was creative and brilliant enough to describe the feelings of committing a murder, but he wasn't listening, he didn't want to listen. He kept repeating that he had tried to write but felt drained. Shit.

"Suellen," he said finally. "Would you help me kill Suellen?"

I thought he was joking. But he kept those hard eyes on me and asked again. He took a small vial from his pocket. Mecicitronine. "Boy, I need your help," he said. And he did. He was on his last legs, Georges.

I never thought about killing anybody, you know? But at the time the idea didn't seem so absurd. I took the vial of poison from his hand. It was a white powder that looked harmless, like talcum powder. I envisioned Suellen with the expression she wore when we had sex, and I thought it would be amusing to see her whore's eyes lifeless, her cocksucking throat clogged with mucus and vomit.

I agreed. I wanted to know where and when, and he told me he had an appointment with her that night. I'd rather not go into detail.

Suellen arrived and was disappointed when she saw me. She went straight to Georges and kissed him, to show she wanted nothing to do with me. He took my hand, slipping me the vial, and told me to go to the kitchen and make a caipirinha for her. I closed my hand around the vial. Suellen was a true whore; she immediately sat on Georges's lap.

In the kitchen I mixed ice, lime, sugar, cachaça, and some of the mecicitronine. I handed Suellen the caipirinha. She drank it while talking about a series on Brazilian TV about prostitutes. Georges watched her very attentively, saw when she lost control of her speech, lost control of her body—in a word, died. We took the corpse out through the back door, placed Suellen in the trunk of my car, and left her on a bench in Lido Square. By then it was late at night.

In the days that followed, nothing appeared in the newspapers. Lots of people are murdered in Rio de Janeiro. And a whore who suffered a heart attack isn't news. Georges told me

I could call him if I had a problem, if I felt any remorse or guilt. To tell the truth, I felt fine. I didn't like Suellen. And there was still Georges's book to consider. One day he called me to say he had finally written the passage in question. "God-damn good," he said. He was excited, Georges. Obviously I was proud of having helped, of being part of it, you know?

Our meetings went back to being like they had been be-fore. Sandwiches, wine, good conversation. Suellen never came up. Georges received lots of books from people and gave me almost all of them as gifts. He recommended some, but without explaining why I should read this one or that. He just handed them over and I accepted them. We didn't talk anymore about our own books, as I already said. Actually, he didn't speak about his and I ended up abandoning mine at the first of the year. It made no sense to go on. I knew I would only be able to write after reading Georges's new novel, un-derstand? It was like some invisible barrier, the grandeur of his creation.

One day, he called me to his apartment. He opened the door with a smile I had never seen. He was in ecstasy, Georges. He told me to sit down and handed me a brown package. "The finished manuscript," he said. It was light but weighed heavy in my hands. You can imagine, I was very nervous. I started to open the package to look at some of the pages but he took it away and said it wasn't for me to read. He just wanted to celebrate. I was really pissed. I insisted he at least let me see the title. But Georges was seductive and knew how to please. He said I was listed in the acknowledgments and changed the subject. We opened a bottle of wine and ordered sandwiches. No matter how much I talked about other things, all I wanted was to read the book. And there came a moment when I looked at him in the rocking chair and thought that I really wanted to be like him, that I wanted to publish a book as good as his. I would never be able to. We have to be aware of our limits. There is such a thing as talent, you know?

One idea leads to another. Before I realized it, I had returned to my apartment with the excuse of taking some medication and now I had the vial of mecicitronine in my hand. I went back downstairs in time to open the bottle of wine with him and pay for the sandwich delivery from Cervantes. By now you've got the picture: Georges didn't die of a heart attack; I killed him. I put the poison in his sandwich and he didn't notice the bitter taste because of the pineapple. You can call it insanity, obsession, anything you like, but I needed to read that book. More than that, I needed to publish that book under my name and be successful, a fucking winner.

Georges was old, tired of life. I feel I did him a favor. And myself as well. Georges ate that last sandwich with gusto. He choked, hiccupped, died. In the rocking chair. The glass shattered on the floor. I saved the package from the pool of red wine and didn't even wait for him to stop moaning. I took out the manuscript: *The Story of Georges Fullar.*

Chapter One: His name. My name. An elderly writer meets a younger one, full of dreams and ambition. The older writer is tired of life, thinks about suicide, but the youth's vitality does him good.

Chapter Two: The two converse and become friends. The veteran decides to test the limits of the younger man: he sees if he is capable of killing a woman. And of course the two do kill the woman. This happens in Chapter Five and is beautiful, poetic, tense. Their friendship grows, but the old man stays interested in the ethical boundaries of his junior. The old man tells him that he has finished the book but denies him access to the text. The youth can't resist and kills the old man.

Kills from envy, from pity, to steal the work. People don't need a motive for killing. He kills him with a knife, not with poison in a sandwich from Cervantes. Georges was wrong about that; I was smarter. At the end comes the letter. The letter in which the old man explains to the youth that he knew he would be murdered, that he knew the other couldn't contain his curiosity, and that the younger man must do with the book what he considers appropriate now.

Do you realize what a stroke of genius this is? Metalanguage at its best. Well written, well structured, I'm never going to accomplish anything like that. I thought about it for days. I saw them take away Georges's body. I even went to the funeral—there was hardly anyone there. Dead of a heart attack, said the newspapers. I wanted to publish his book under my name, but I can't. I need to tell everything so people will know what really happened. It's our story. He wrote our story. The truth is all there. You can arrest me, Detective Aquino. And release what I just told you to the press, to the world. I'm not doing it for myself; I'm not doing it for Georges either. I'm doing it for mystery writing. It's one helluva book, and it needs to be read. Hopefully, that way the Brazilian crime novel can finally emerge from the shit.

THE WOODSMAN

BY LUIS FERNANDO VERISSIMO

Bangu

The dead man called late afternoon the "hour of long shadows." That was the title of the manuscript I found in the apartment where he and the blond woman had been murdered. *The Hour of Long Shadows.* Poems, handwritten, in a pile on top of the living room table. One of the few things in the apartment not splattered with blood.

It didn't surprise me that the guy wrote poetry. There are poets in Bangu too, why not? But everything about the dead man denied poetry. Everything about him was antipoetic, from his physical appearance to his biography, which Detective Friedrich gave me. Beginning with his name, Tadeu. But there it was, the manuscript, poems written in ballpoint pen. *The Hour of Long Shadows* and his signature, in a neat pile waiting to be found. But Detective Friedrich hadn't noticed the pile. Police never notice poetry. I do. I even write some. I write my verses but don't show them to anyone. They're private musings. But that doesn't matter. We're not here to talk about the fleeting soul of a police reporter but about a double murder.

The two corpses lay on the sofa. The blonde in a nightgown. Beautiful. Even covered in blood she was still beautiful. He only had on underwear. Both had been stabbed to death. Deep cuts made—I don't know why it immediately occurred to me—with a butcher knife. Or knives. So much carnage, both at the same time, it could only have been done by more than one butcher.

My editor, Mosquito, had asked me to take a look at that slaughter in Bangu. "It might lead somewhere." My editor's name is Mesquita, but he's small and thin and is always buzzing in our ears, which is how he got the nickname Mosquito, but he doesn't know. "It may lead somewhere" is Mosquito's way of saying that the story may yield more than just another killing in a Rio suburb. Something extra behind the bloodshed to serve up to our readers.

"Look for Detective Friedrich," Mosquito had instructed me. "He owes me a couple of favors."

Detective Friedrich was a large, fat German with the expression of someone who had seen everything in life and had no wish to see it all again. He only said "Ha" when I told him I brought greetings from Mosquito. But he let me into the apartment before the bodies were removed and told me everything he knew about the victims. The dead man's antipoetic name, the identity of the blonde, everything. The neighbors had said a lot, but Friedrich already knew the couple. He told me that the blonde, Cristina, never left the house by herself, only in the company of the man. The rest of the time she stayed locked up in the apartment. That was why the detective knew them. One day when the man wasn't there, there was a fire in the kitchen. Friedrich had helped the firemen break down the door and rescue the woman. Afterward he had recommended that the man not leave the door locked like that, but the guy ignored him. He said nothing, just grunted. Maybe his species lacked the power of speech.

Friedrich invited me to have a beer at a bar near the scene of the crime. I asked if I could take the poetry manuscript with me and he consented with a gesture of indifference. At the bar he told me that after the fire he had begun an investigation. On his own.

"What led you to investigate that man?"

"Not the man, the woman."

"Beautiful, huh?"

"And you saw her covered in blood. Imagine what she was like without the blood. Cristina . . ." The detective spoke the woman's name reverently, as if summoning her to sit there with us. Her or her hologram. I could be mistaken, maybe fat Friedrich also had the soul of a poet. Bangu might be a hotbed of secret poets for all I knew . . .

"I discovered everything about the two of them. He already had a criminal record. Petty stuff. He was a nobody. Even his crimes were mediocre. She was the mistress of Nogueira, owner of a chain of butcher shops in the South Zone. Very rich. She lived in an apartment Nogueira had bought for her, in Laranjeiras. That was where they had their trysts. Everybody knew about the mistress in Laranjeiras, including Dona Santa, Nogueira's wife, and their two sons. In the family, the code name for her was *Laranjeira*."

"How did you discover all this?"

"It's impressive how much people open up when they see a badge."

"And?"

"And one day Nogueira has a major stroke and is at death's door. And the suspicion emerges that the old man had made a will leaving everything, including the butcher shops, or a large part of his fortune, to Laranjeira."

"So?"

"So right now it's all conjecture. It's my hypothesis. Which might be wrong, but I think it's correct." Friedrich took a dramatic pause, ordered another beer, and continued: "Here's the hypothesis: this story is like *Snow White*."

"*Snow White?!*"

"Remember the story? The evil queen is jealous of Snow White's beauty. She asks the magic mirror who's the fairest in the land, and the mirror, with the frankness that characterizes all mirrors, says, *It's not you, it's Snow White*. The evil queen then hires someone to kill Snow White. A woodsman."

"A nobody."

"Right. The woodsman is supposed to take Snow White to the forest, kill her, and bring her heart to the queen, as proof that he killed her. The woodsman takes Snow White to the forest, and what happens? He falls in love with her. He's dazzled by her beauty. He decides that instead of killing her he's going to let her go. Or, in the case of our woodsman, stay with her. Get it? The woodsman is a minor character in the story of Snow White. A mere detail, a supporting actor. But without him and without his decision to spare Snow White there would be no story. The woodsman ends up being the most important character of all. A simple woodsman."

"How does he prove to the queen that he eliminated Snow White?"

"He takes her the heart of some animal or other, as if it were Snow White's. In the case of our Tadeu, he could even buy a heart from one of Nogueira's butcher shops; it'd be an ironic touch. Although Dona Santa, who had helped her husband in the butcher shop in the difficult early days, would inevitably recognize a cow's heart. But our Tadeu doesn't do any of that. He simply disappears with Laranjeira. Or with Snow White. And hides out in Bangu."

"According to your hypothesis, then—"

"The evil queen is Dona Santa, who has nothing saintly

about her. Snow White is Cristina. The woodsman is Tadeu, who brings Cristina to Bangu and keeps her locked in an apartment, certain they'll never be discovered, until they are discovered. And executed, at the order of the evil queen. That will be the line of our investigation. I don't foresee any difficulty in finding the killer. Or killers. Nogueira's sons do whatever their mother orders. They're terrified at the prospect of being left out of the will. And they had access to sharp knives. In short: for this story to match Snow White's, all that's missing are the dwarfs."

"Did old Nogueira die after all?"

"Not yet. He's in a coma. No one knows what's in his will. He may have left everything to Laranjeira. Even the butcher shops."

Several beers later Friedrich was relating what his father told him about Bangu, in the days when a famous textile factory and a soccer team that didn't do badly in the Rio championships were there, where Zizinho, Parada, and even the great Domingos da Guia had played.

"Today people only come to Bangu to disappear," said Friedrich. "Like me, who disappeared here six years ago and was never seen again."

Mosquito had warned me that after a few beers Friedrich would start getting maudlin. I considered asking if he'd been the one who fingered the couple's hideout to Dona Santa. Perhaps as a form of revenge, I don't know. But I thought it best not to say anything.

I went back to the office, carrying the manuscript. Maybe there was something there I could use in my story. Something about impossible loves or the like. Readers like a bit of poetry with their bloodshed. I thought about Tadeu, the nobody, the mere woodsman, who one day finds himself the owner of the most beautiful woman in the world, who owes him her life but whom he must lock inside the house. I imagined how the break-in of the apartment by the butchers must have gone down. Perhaps they arrived in late afternoon, the time of long shadows. Perhaps Tadeu feared the time of long shadows every day, and what they could bring. Later I thought about what I would tell Mosquito.

"You were right, it did lead somewhere. It's basically the story of Snow White. Minus the dwarfs."

ABOUT THE CONTRIBUTORS

Caroline Bittencourt

TONY BELLOTTO is author of the best-selling Bellini mystery novels, which have been released as major feature films and translated widely, establishing him as the preeminent writer of Brazilian detective fiction. He is also a guitarist and songwriter for the famed Brazilian rock band Titãs (The Titans), which has released twenty albums and sold over six million albums. Bellotto also writes for the newspaper *Globo* and hosts a television show.

Fábio Terral

MV BILL (a.k.a. Alex Pereira Barbosa) is a rapper, writer, and activist. In 2005, with his coauthor Celso Athayde, he launched *Cabeça de Porco*. The following year he published a best-selling nonfiction work, *Falcão: meninos do tráfico*, which inspired a documentary. In collaboration with Celso Athayde, he created the NGO Unified Central of Favelas (CUFA). He is host of the programs *Aglomerado* on Brazilian TV and *A voz das periferias* and *O som das ruas* on FM radio in Rio.

Arnaldo Bloch

ARNALDO BLOCH, a journalist and writer, was born in 1965 in Rio, where he still resides. He began his career with the magazine *Manchete* and since 1993 has been a reporter for the newspaper *O Globo*, where he has a weekly column. He published the novels *Amanhã a loucura* and *Talk Show* and a biography of Fernando Sabino for the series Perfis do Rio. In 2008 he launched, through the publisher Companhia das Letras, the family saga *Os irmãos Karamabloch*.

Raquel Godoy

FLÁVIO CARNEIRO was born in Goiânia and lives in Rio. He writes short stories, essays, children's fiction, and novels, in addition to a pair of film scripts. He wrote the Rio de Janeiro Trilogy, comprising the novels *A Confissão*, *O Campeonato*, and *A Ilha*. His stories and essays have been published in the US, Germany, France, Portugal, and Mexico, among other countries. In the crime genre his most recent novel is *O livro roubado*, set in Rio.

Manya Millen

ARTHUR DAPIEVE was born in Rio in 1963. He is a journalist, writer, and professor at the Catholic University (PUC) in Rio. Since 1993 he has authored a weekly column on culture for the daily newspaper *O Globo*. He also worked for the *Jornal do Brasil*, the magazine *Veja Rio*, and the website *NoPonto/NoMínimo*. In addition to books of nonfiction, mostly about music, he has written the novels *De cada amor tu herderás só o cinismo* and *Black Music*.

Marcelo Tabach

MARCELO FERRONI was born in 1974 in São Paulo and lives in Rio with his wife and two children. Since the end of 2006 he has been editor of the Alfaguara imprint of Editora Objetiva. He is author of the novels *Método pratico da guerrilha* (winner of the São Paulo Literature Prize in the New Author category) and *Das paredes, meu amor, os escravos nos contemplam*.

J. Egberto

GUILHERME FIUZA is the author of various books, including *Meu nome não é Johnny* (adapted for the screen), *Bussunda—A vida do casseta*, and *3,000 dias no bunker*. He is coauthor of the miniseries *O brado retumbante* on TV Globo (with Euclydes Marinho, Denise Bandeira, and Nelson Motta), which was nominated for an International Emmy in 2013. He is a columnist for the magazine *Época* and the newspaper *O Globo*.

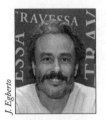

Alexandre Torreão

ALEXANDRE FRAGA DOS SANTOS was born in 1973 in Rio's Tijuca district. He has worked as a federal police agent for eighteen years. He is author of the novels *Oeste—A Guerra do Jogo do Bicho*, *Canibal de Copacabana*, and *Quadros de demônios vão ao confessionário*. He roots for the Vasco soccer team and is the father of José Artur.

Anaik Von Der Weid

LUIZ ALFREDO GARCIA-ROZA is a native of Rio de Janeiro with degrees in philosophy and psychology. A former professor at the State University of Rio de Janeiro (UFRJ), he left academic life after publishing eight books on philosophy and psychoanalysis and soon gained renown as a writer of crime fiction. He is the creator of Inspector Espinosa, protagonist of almost all his stories. His debut novel, *The Silence of the Rain*, won both the Jabuti and the Nestlé Literature prizes.

Charles A. Savage

CLIFFORD E. LANDERS, a preeminent translator from Brazilian Portuguese, has translated novels by Rubem Fonseca, Jorge Amado, João Ubaldo Ribeiro, Patrícia Melo, and Paulo Coelho. He received the Mario Ferreira Award and a prose translation grant from the National Endowment for the Arts in 2004. His *Literary Translation: A Practical Guide* was published by Multilingual Matters Ltd. in 2001. A professor emeritus at New Jersey City University, he now lives in Naples, Florida.

ADRIANA LISBOA, born in 1970 in Rio, is a novelist, poet, and short story writer. She is the author, among other works, of the novels *Symphony in White* (winner of the José Saramago Prize), *Hut of Fallen Persimmons*, *Crow Blue* (an *Independent* book of the year), and *Hanói*; and the poetry collection *Parte da paisagem*. Her books have been translated in seventeen countries. She is part of the board of directors of Denver-based NGO US–Brazil Connect, geared toward education.

Julie Harris

RAPHAEL MONTES was born in 1990 in Rio. A lawyer and writer, he is considered by Scott Turow to be one of today's most promising young contemporary fiction writers. *Roulette*, his first novel, was a finalist for two prestigious Brazilian literary prizes. *Perfect Days*, his second novel, has been phenomenally successful, was translated into numerous languages, and published in the United States by Penguin Random House. *The Village*, his third novel, has earned him comparisons to Stephen King.

Bel Pedrosa

VICTORIA SARAMAGO was born in Rio in 1985, and is an assistant professor of Brazilian literature at the University of Chicago. Her publications include the critical study *O duplo do pai: o filho e a ficção de Cristovão Tezza* and the novel *Renée esfacelada*. Her career as a critic and fiction writer was chronicled in Julia de Simone's documentary *Romance de formação*.

Marcelo Diego

LUIZ EDUARDO SOARES is a writer, anthropologist, and political scientist. With a postdoctorate in political philosophy, he occupied the positions of national Secretary of Public Safety (2003) and coordinator of Safety, Justice, and Citizenship for the State of Rio de Janeiro (1999–2000). He is currently a professor at the State University of Rio de Janeiro (UFRJ). Among his published works are the best sellers *Cabeça de Porco*, with MV Bill and Celso Athayde, and *Elite Squad*.

Gabriel Sayad

LUIS FERNANDO VERISSIMO was born in 1936 in Porto Alegre, Brazil, where he still resides. A columnist for the newspapers *O Globo*, *O Estado de São Paulo*, and *Zero Hora*, among others, he boasts a vast literary oeuvre that includes children's books, humor, comics, and novels, published both in Brazil and abroad. Many of his works have been adapted to cinema, TV, and the theater. His *Diálogos impossíveis* won the Jabuti Prize for Best Book of the Year.

Bruno Veiga